D0758853

MECHANICS' INSTITUTE
MECHANICS'
MERCANTILE LIBRARY

BULLETS

ALSO BY STEVE BREWER

THE BUBBA MABRY SERIES
Lonely Street
Baby Face
Witchy Woman
Shaky Ground
Dirty Pool
Crazy Love

THE DREW GAVIN SERIES
End Run
Cheap Shot

NON-FICTION
Trophy Husband

BULLETS

BY STEVE BREWER

INTRIGUE PRESS | DENVER

Book layout and design by Speck Design, www.speck-design.com

Brewer, Steve.
Bullets / by Steve Brewer.
p. cm.
ISBN 1-890768-50-2
I. Title.
PS3552.R42135B85 2003
813'.54--dc21
2003009250

10 9 8 7 6 5 4 3 2 1

For Kelly, whose sacrifices let me remain "gainfully unemployed."

I

Some people are ridiculously easy to kill. Lily knew Max Vernon was such a man the moment she set eyes on him.

He sat alone at a corner table in a bar at the Tropical Bay Casino and Resort, peering between plastic palmettos at the tourists slamming quarters into clanging slot machines. The bar was done up like Rick's Café American in "Casablanca," palm trees, stucco arches, and lazy ceiling fans, but its sides were open to the crowded casino floor and there was no piano player to drown out the midnight cacophony.

Max Vernon's high forehead glistened, and he smiled to himself like a man quietly celebrating a successful run at the craps table. He was average-sized and in his late forties, and Lily guessed his slicked-back hair would be gray if it weren't dyed an unnatural flat black. His face was lean and weathered, but practically obscured beneath his most distinctive feature—a thick black eyebrow that stretched across his forehead like a caterpillar on steroids. The eyebrow made it easy to match him to the photo she'd been given.

Vernon wore the typical Las Vegas uniform, pointy collar open wide over the lapels of his sharkskin suit, a gold medallion hanging around his neck on a chain. He wore two rings on each hand, and his thick fingers fondled a tumbler of what looked like Scotch.

Yes, Lily thought, this one will be easy.

She took a steadying breath and ambled toward him, her hips swaying. Vernon spotted her halfway across the bar and watched hungrily as she approached. Lily knew she was hard to miss. She'd spent an hour in front of a mirror, preparing. She was six feet tall with the four-inch heels on, with another four inches of curly red hair cresting high over her forehead, then tumbling down to her shoulders. She wore elbow-length black gloves and a flame-red dress that clung to her body like a coat of paint. By the time she reached Vernon's table, his mouth was hanging open.

She stopped at his table and rested her fingertips on the back of an empty chair.

"You expectin' someone?" she asked, making her voice cool and husky, laying on her Southern drawl a little thicker than usual.

"No, ma'am." He smiled broadly and pushed the empty chair out from the table with his foot. "Please join me."

Lily lowered herself into the chair, letting the dress crawl up her long thighs. Vernon licked his lips.

She rummaged around in her black leather shoulder bag, making him wait, then snapped it shut and set it on the floor beside her chair. She crossed her legs, looked him in the eye.

"Buy a lonely lady a drink?"

She smiled for the first time, and he reflected it back for all he was worth. Lily guessed he'd had his teeth capped.

"You betcha." He raised a hand as high as he could reach and snapped his fingers until a pneumatic waitress floated over. The waitress, like all the ones at Tropical Bay, wore a deeply plunging safari jacket over a leotard and thick "nude" stockings. In Vegas, Lily mused, all the waitresses look like they've forgotten their pants. A woman's got to dress like a hooker to compete.

The waitress took her order for a white wine and slinked away, and Max Vernon said, "How can you be lonely in Las Vegas, with all these people around?"

He gestured toward the busy casino floor, but Lily didn't break her lock on his eyes.

"Doesn't matter how many people are around," she said. "Loneliness doesn't go away in a crowd. It's like an itch you can't reach."

"Maybe you just need somebody to scratch your itch."

"Are you good at scratching?"

Vernon shifted in his seat.

"I've never had any complaints," he said. "But maybe you'd like to find out for yourself?"

Lily leaned forward, rested her elbows on the tabletop. Vernon's gaze shot down to her cleavage, but he wrestled it back to her face in time to see her seductive smile.

"You got a room here?" she asked.

"A suite. Right upstairs."

"Let's go there."

He hesitated, glanced over toward the bar.

"Don't you want your wine?"

"I'm not thirsty anymore," she purred. "I'm hungry."

"Shit fire, let's go then."

Vernon got up from the table so fast, Lily thought he might tip it over. She picked up her shoulder bag as he threw a wad of bills on the table, then stepped close to him, threaded an arm through his. Vernon beamed at her. Lily thinking: Jesus, why doesn't this guy shave that eyebrow? Pluck it, something. Makes him look like Cro-Magnon Man.

"Right this way," he said, then led her across the casino floor toward the elevators. The lobby was just beyond those elevators, though the hallway made two turns before the exit appeared. Casinos were designed so the exits were all but invisible. The money boys wanted the suckers to stay on the casino floor, dropping one more quarter in one more slot. Lily spent a lot of time in casinos.

Elevator doors slid open just as she and Vernon arrived, and some goober in a "CAT" hat stepped off, gawking at Lily. Vernon didn't notice; he was too busy grinning at her like a cougar.

They stepped aboard the elevator and the doors closed. Lily pretended to teeter a little on her heels, leaning into him, letting her breasts press against his arm. She didn't think it was possible for his smile to get any wider, but it did. Looked like the corners of his mouth were headed into his ears.

"Guess this is my lucky day," he said. "Big night gambling, then running into you. Who knows what'll happen next?"

She batted her false eyelashes at him. "You ain't seen nothing yet, champ."

He har-harred as the doors slid open and they walked down a long corridor. He fumbled with the card-key, got the door open and gestured her inside. The sitting room was painted a soothing sea blue and the art on the walls depicted half-naked island girls frolicking on a beach. Rattan furniture sat around a coffee table made of a sheet of glass perched on the back of a carved wooden elephant. Lily drifted across the room and peered into the bedroom. The king-sized bed's comforter was splashed with a pattern of palm fronds. Its headboard was teak, vertical slats decorated with carved frogs and lizards. Perfect.

"Nice room," she said. "That's a big bed."

"Just right for two."

She looked at him from underneath the long lashes. "Maybe we should try it out."

"I'm all for it," he said. "Just let me step into the bathroom first. I've had a lot to drink. Need to drain the old radiator."

Lily faked a little giggle, then strolled into the bedroom. "I'll just be waiting in here."

She figured Max Vernon wouldn't take long. He was too eager to see what came next. Drunken jackass, so hot to bed a stranger. Hadn't even asked her name, nothing. She stepped out of her high heels, but kept her gloves on as she dug through her purse and came up with a pair of handcuffs.

When Vernon appeared a minute later, she was standing hip-cocked beside the bed, one hand upraised, the cuffs dangling from a finger.

"Want to have some fun?"

Vernon's smile faltered, but he quickly propped it up. "Well, hell, lady. I'm game if you are."

"Take off your clothes and stretch out on the bed."

Vernon undressed in record time. His arms and face were tanned by desert sun, but his body was pale and skinny and thatched with curly hair. His uncircumcised bright-pink penis made Lily think of an aroused dog, ready to hump somebody's leg.

"You want to turn out the light?" he asked as he crawled onto the bed.

"No, I like to watch. Lie face down."

"Like this?"

"That's right. Now reach your arms up here so I can cuff you to the headboard."

"I never been handcuffed before. You've got the key, right?"

"In my purse. Don't worry. This'll be fun."

"Promise?"

"Trust me. You've never experienced anything like it."

He cackled and reached his arms above his head. Lily bent over him and deftly slipped the cuffs through the headboard slats and clicked them around his wrists. She yanked against them, making sure the slat would hold.

"Good," she said. "Now you just hold still for a second." She turned to the armchair where she'd left her purse.

"Close your eyes," she said over her shoulder. "This part's a surprise."

He chuckled and squeezed his eyes tight.

Lily pulled two four-inch-long pieces of wooden dowel from her purse. They were wrapped together tightly with shiny steel wire. She stepped to the bed and crawled onto it on her knees. She hiked up her dress to her waist and straddled his lower back. His skin felt hot against the inside of her thighs.

"Lift your head up a little."

He raised his chin from the bed, arching his back. Lily quickly unwrapped the wire until it was a taut twenty-six inches attached to the two handles. She slipped the wire over his head, down to his throat.

"Hey," he said, and she yanked the handles and tightened the garrote around his neck.

Max Vernon gasped as the wire cut into his flesh and cut off his air. He bucked beneath her, twisting against the handcuffs, trying to get free. Lily didn't watch his face redden or his eyes bulge as she tightened the wire. She'd seen it all before. Instead, she watched the muscles in her arms standing out from the effort. A minute, and he stopped moving underneath her. A minute more, and she rolled off him and got to her feet.

The sheets were dappled with blood that oozed from the thin cut around his neck. His eyes were open wide under the thick brow and his purplish tongue hung out of his mouth.

Lily went to the armchair and got her purse and her shoes. Then to the bathroom, where she peeled off the red dress, but kept on the long black gloves. She quickly examined her naked body in the mirror, saw none of the blood had gotten on her. She dumped the contents of the shoulder bag on the counter beside the sink: Dark sunglasses, a short blond wig, T-shirt, a pair of jeans rolled up around a pair of black sneakers. She removed the red wig and dressed in the spare clothes. She pulled the blond wig over her short, dark hair and looked in the mirror as she adjusted it on her head. The change in hair color and style altered her whole look, made her tanned skin look darker. She peeled off the false eyelashes and blinked a few times. Tossed the fakes into her purse. She stuffed the heels and the red dress in there, too, then put on the sunglasses.

Lily came out of the bathroom and squatted beside Max Vernon's clothes long enough to find his fat wallet and put it in her purse. She hurried across the sitting room, opened the suite's door and checked the long corridor. Nobody.

She stripped off the long gloves and stuffed them in her handbag, then stepped out into the hall, listening for the door to click shut behind her. She strode to a fire exit and pushed through the door with her hip. Went down two flights of stairs before letting herself back into a corridor, then walked to the elevator.

Down to the ground floor and straight through the lobby to a line of cabs waiting outside Tropical Bay's front door. Lily climbed into the back seat of the first one in line.

The driver was a fat black man who turned to smile at her.

"The airport," she said. "I'm in a hurry."

2

The dealer was a Vegas veteran, a squat, warty old warhorse whose name tag said "Agnes." She claimed to have dealt cards to Bugsy Siegel, Frank Sinatra, and Joey Bishop in her youth, but she'd slipped down the ladder over the years and now worked at Lucky's Back Door, a dim card room off Desert Inn Road, so far outside the tourist zone that it barely stayed afloat. Agnes wore her hair spun into a lacquered beehive tinted a pale pink. To Joe Riley, the hairdo looked like a wad of cotton candy stuck on the head of a toad.

Joe watched Agnes' liver-spotted hands as she deftly distributed the cards. Two down to each player, five in the middle of the table. Texas Hold'em, the brand of poker they like best in Vegas. Joe preferred Omaha, had played it earlier in the evening at one of the big resort casinos, but he'd stumbled onto this no-limit game at Lucky's three hours ago and it had treated him fine so far. He was up more than two-thousand dollars on the night, enough to keep him in motel rooms and fast food for weeks.

Two grim snowbirds who'd barely held their own in the game decided to call it a night and left together. Joe knew he should follow them. It was past 2 a.m., and these late sessions didn't come as easily as they once did. He turned forty a month earlier, toasted the arrival of middle age drunk and alone in a motel room in Nowhere, Nebraska. He already had a dusting of gray through his black hair, and every time he looked in the mirror, he found a new wrinkle. Twenty years of all-night poker and steady carousing are hard on a man. What's that they say? It's not the years, it's the frigging *mileage*.

He stifled a yawn and looked around the green felt. Only three players remained, and Agnes seemed ready to close the table. The other two players were idiots who were nearly cleaned out. Why give them a chance at a lucky comeback?

Joe worried a little about the quiet black guy, Mookie. His shaved head sat on a thick neck, and he was broad-shouldered and barrel-chested. His forearms looked like chocolate anacondas resting against the edge of the table. But Mookie had been throwing back tumblers of Crown Royal for the better part of four hours. Joe figured he'd need help to get out of his chair.

His talkative partner was a white guy with a big brown pompadour, so big Joe wondered how his scrawny neck could hold up so much hair. He wore a white Saturday Night Fever suit and six gold chains around his sun-leathered neck. Chunky fake Rolex. Pinky ring. And he cracked his gum when he chewed. Asshole like that, Joe wouldn't mind taking all his money, especially if it would get him to shut up.

"Vegas used to be Sin City," Monsieur Pompadour was saying. "Now it's a fuckin' amusement park. Little kids running around, roller coasters, shit like that. Pisses me off. Vegas was the only place left where it was cool to be an adult. Gamble, get drunk, get laid, that's what Vegas was all about. Now, they've screwed it up with this 'wholesome family entertainment.'"

Mookie grunted, which seemed to encourage his buddy.

"I've lived here twenty years, and it just keeps getting worse. The traffic, the fuckin' tourists in their Bermuda shorts and their cameras. Buncha amateurs, pouring money into the casinos. The real gamblers have to come to dumps like this to get away from them."

The guy was driving Joe crazy. "We making speeches here or we playing cards?"

"Hey, it's a free country, last time I looked. Doesn't seem to be distracting you. You're winning."

"And I want to keep it that way. I want a travelogue, I'll go watch the Discovery Channel."

"All right, boys," Agnes said. "This ain't the kitchen game. Let's play poker."

The skinny guy reached for his cards. "I want Vegas back the way it used to be, that's all I'm sayin'. Back when Frank and Dino and Sammy were around. When the town had some class."

The loudmouth didn't look old enough to remember the Rat Pack, but Joe didn't pursue it. He was too busy keeping a straight face. He'd lifted the corners of his two hole cards and found the ace of spades and the ace of diamonds. Two bullets.

"Waitin' on you, Delbert," Mookie said. His voice was deep and thick, sounded like it was coming through a wall.

Delbert bet fifty bucks and Joe raised him fifty more. Mookie studied Joe for a moment from beneath furrowed brows, then called the bet. Delbert matched the raise and the dealer flopped over three cards. A six, a four, a nine. Delbert bet fifty again, one eyebrow cocked at Joe, waiting. Joe raised another fifty, but went no higher. He wanted to keep them playing.

They called the raise, and Agnes turned over a jack of spades. Joe studied the cards on the table. Nothing there for building a straight or a flush. No pairs toward a full house. His pocket rockets could take it all.

Delbert bet fifty this time, and Joe saw the bet and raised fifty. The two guys across the table exchanged glances, gave each other little eyebrow moves that said, "I don't know what he's got, either."

Neither got out, though, and Agnes flopped the last card. The ace of hearts. Joe felt heat grow within him. Three aces. No way for these two losers to match his hand.

He glanced across the table, measuring how much each man had left in his dwindling stacks of chips. Delbert had more than his friend, who only had four hundred dollars. Joe picked three hundred-dollar chips off his stacks and tossed them into the center of the table.

"Shit, man," Mookie mumbled. Then he shrugged his big shoulders and threw chips into the pile.

Delbert's face flushed and his narrow eyes flitted between Joe and Mookie. Joe knew he'd call the bet. Delbert was the kind of guy always feels the world owes him something, that his big chance is right around the corner. He'd never recognize the bad beat, not until it was too late.

Delbert pushed three hundred-dollar chips to the center of the felt. He flipped over his cards. Two sixes, which, matched with the one on the table, gave him three of a kind. Good cards, but not good enough.

Mookie said, "Beats my two pair," and tossed his cards aside. He and Delbert kept their eyes on Joe, who allowed himself a smile as he turned over his cards.

"Three bullets," he said. "Bang. Bang. Bang."

Delbert scowled. Mookie muttered and shifted in his chair.

Agnes pushed the pot to Joe, who tried to take their minds off their losses while he stacked his chips.

"You know so much about Vegas," he said to Delbert, "maybe you've seen a friend of mine around here. I've been looking for her."

Delbert said nothing for a long time, busy glaring and cracking his gum. Finally he said, "What's her name?"

"I think she's living out here under a different name," Joe said. "Let me show you a picture."

He pulled the battered photograph from the inside pocket of his summer-weight gray suit and handed it over, wondering how many sets of hands had handled it the past few months.

Delbert held the photo up close to his pointy nose. Joe knew what he was seeing; he'd looked at that photo a million times himself. A tall, sleek woman, shown from the waist up. A pile of red hair that Joe was certain was a wig. Dark sunglasses that hid her eyes.

"Can't tell much about her from this," Delbert said. "This the only picture you've got?"

"Yeah."

Delbert handed the photo to his partner. Mookie gave it a bleary glance and tossed the photograph back to Joe.

"No?" Joe slipped the photo back into his pocket. "I'll keep showing it around. Maybe I'll turn her up."

He stood and began gathering his chips onto a tray.

"The fuck you think you're going?" Delbert said.

"Calling it a night."

"Why don't you sit down and give us a chance to win back our money?"

Joe didn't look at him. "Your buddy's tapped. Let's quit while you've still got cab fare."

Delbert stood up so quickly, his chair fell over backward. "Don't worry about me, motherfucker. Just sit down and give me a chance."

Joe gave Delbert an unblinking stare, waiting for the man to wilt, as he knew he would.

Agnes croaked, "Sit down, son. It's late. We don't want any trouble in here."

Mookie hadn't moved, but Joe didn't like the way he was looking at him, measuring the distance across the table. Joe picked up the last of his chips and stepped back.

"That's right," he said. "We don't want any trouble. Luck was with me tonight. No hard feelings."

Delbert glanced to Mookie, waiting for his friend to back his play. But Mookie sat still as a stump.

"All right," Delbert said, raising his hands in surrender. "If that's the way it is. Take our money and go home."

Joe walked across the cardroom to the cashier's cage. He heard Delbert grumbling, but he didn't look back toward the poker tables. The cashier looked asleep on her feet, but she counted the chips and handed Joe nearly three grand in cash. He tipped her and turned away from the window to find Delbert coming toward him, skinny chest thrust out, strutting like a bantam rooster under his cockscomb of hair.

"Hey, man," he said. "About that picture you showed us. I might see her around somewhere. Where can I reach you if I do?"

Yeah, Joe thought, I'm giving you bozos my address.

"I'll be around," he said. "Maybe we'll play some more poker together."

Delbert smiled tightly. "I'd like that."

Joe stepped out into the night and lit a Camel. Nearly three o'clock in the morning, and still stiflingly hot outside. Las Vegas in July. Jesus.

He took a deep drag on the cigarette, then started hiking up the empty sidewalk toward where he'd left his old Chevy on a side street. He wouldn't have to worry about parking fees for a while, long as those dopes' money filled his pockets.

Lucky's Back Door was at the edge of the dusty barrens that surrounded the Strip, what Joe thought of as No Man's Land. A few flat-roofed stores and boarded-up buildings littered either side of the street, but they were shut up tight for the night.

He hadn't gone a block when he heard footsteps behind him. One man striding along, his feet heavy on the concrete, the other hustling to keep up. Joe glanced over his shoulder, but he knew what he'd see. Mookie and Delbert, coming after him, wanting their money.

Joe turned a corner past a steel-shuttered pawn shop. The Chevy was just ahead, a block away, but he might not make it before the pair caught up to him. He stopped and pressed his back against the pawn shop wall, listening.

When the hurrying footsteps were practically on top of him, he wheeled around the corner, swinging his left fist with the full force of his two-hundred pounds. It connected precisely on Delbert's pointed nose, which went pop-squish.

Delbert screamed and stumbled backward, his hands coming up to his face as blood exploded from his nostrils.

Mookie's eyes were wide and his arms hung loose at his sides. Joe took a step toward him and brought his foot up sharply, smooth as a field-goal kicker. The top of his foot caught Mookie between the legs and lifted him up on his toes. Mookie gasped. He clutched at his crotch and fell to the sidewalk.

Joe turned back to Delbert, who still reeled around, his hands over his face, thick blood seeping through his fingers.

"You want more?"

Delbert shook his head, made a sound like a wounded

puppy. He bent forward from the waist, letting the blood drip to the sidewalk rather than on his white suit.

Mookie moaned and curled into a ball on the sidewalk. Joe guessed he'd be pissing blood for a few days. And Delbert would need a nose job to put everything back where it belonged.

"You guys need to learn to lose gracefully," Joe said. "Lot healthier that way."

3

Lily sat at a Double Diamond slot machine at the Isleta Gaming Palace south of Albuquerque, mesmerized by the whirring dials as she used the side of her fist to press the button that made them spin. She'd put ten dollars of Max Vernon's money into the machine, winning just enough the past two hours to keep playing.

She needed to stop. She needed to call Sal. Get some food. Get ready for her flight. But she kept pressing that button.

Lily had visited several of New Mexico's Indian casinos in the past, and Isleta ranked on a par with the others. The mud-colored building looked new, but its interior already showed the wear-and-tear of steady foot traffic. The carpet was worn and some of the slot machines were out of order. Still, Lily felt comfortable here. The slots were the same makes as the ones in Vegas, but this uncrowded casino had little of the artifice and stupidity of the Las Vegas Strip.

After a restless night in a motel near the Albuquerque airport, she'd dressed early Friday morning and called a cab to take her to the nearest casino. She'd had a few hours to kill before her next flight, and the hypnotism of the slot machines was just what she needed to take her mind off the latest killing.

At least she wasn't wearing a hot, itchy wig. Lily's natural hair was short as a man's, better for swimming that way, better for pulling on wigs or hats when she needed a disguise. The blond wig had served her well when she went through airport security the night before, using a fake identification, but she was glad to be rid of it.

The night flight to Albuquerque had been nearly empty, which suited Lily fine. The fewer people who saw her in disguise, the better. She was flying home this morning under her own identity, so she'd dropped the wigs and the red dress in a trash bin outside the motel. Nothing to tie her to Vegas now. She could relax. But she felt tense and weary and her eyes were scratchy.

She hit the button again, watched the dials spin. She'd be home in a few more hours. Clean clothes and something to eat and some laps in the pool would make her feel renewed.

But first she needed to call Sal. She hit another button that cashed out her quarters, the coins clanking into a metal tray. She gathered them into a plastic cup, went to the lobby and fed some of the quarters into a pay phone. She dialed Sal's number and heard a secretary answer, "Venturi and Associates."

"This is Lily. Let me speak to Sal."

She listened to Muzak—sounded like the Mantovani Strings playing the Beatles' "Yesterday"—while she waited for Sal to pick up the phone. Lily thinking: As much money as Sal Venturi makes, he ought to have better music for his clients. Tightwad.

"Lily!" Sal always shouted her name when he came on the phone, as if they were long-lost friends. "How'd everything go?"

"Perfectly. Transfer my money now."

"Sure, Lily. The usual wire transfer? The usual place?"

"Any problem with that?"

"None whatsoever. I deposited the client's cash yesterday."

Yesterday. Lily thought of the song on the Muzak. How yesterday she'd been in a different city under a different name, putting an end to the life of some schmuck named Max Vernon. Unlike in the song, none of it felt "so far away."

"Listen, Lily, where are you? We need to talk about another job."

She glanced around the casino lobby. A wide-bodied Native American man in a security guard uniform eyed her from across the way.

"Not now, Sal. I've got to catch a plane."

"You have your cell phone with you?"

"It's at home. I'll be there in a few hours. Call me then if you want. But I'm not interested in another job right away."

"But this one's easy, Lily. A cakewalk."

She pictured fat Sal at his crumb-strewn desk, the sweat glinting on his bald head, his glasses halfway down his nose. Smarmy little rat would say anything to hook her into another job. Whining, wheedling. Lily couldn't face it right now. She sighed. Problem with her line of work was she didn't always deal with the finest people.

"I'm on a pay phone. Call me later."

She hung up before he could protest. She went back into the casino, had her quarters changed into paper money, went outside. She didn't want to think about another job. Lately, none of them sounded like cakewalks to her.

She'd thought a lot about retiring in recent months. She had enough money salted away to support her for a few years. She could go to college, get some training, make something of herself. It's never too late to start over.

But no regular career paid as much for as little work as killing people. And Lily was good at her job—careful, methodical, a mechanic. She never left a trace. She'd been a contract hitter for a decade without ever being arrested. Never suspected, never so much as questioned. She did her job, then got the hell out of town, covering her tracks, always flying to out-of-the-way destinations before returning home. Maybe, she thought, I've just been lucky. Nobody's luck holds out forever.

She tried to picture herself working a 9-to-5 job, like coaching swimming or working at an art museum. Maybe she could even work security at a casino like that big Indian cop. But she had none of the credentials required for anything more than an entry-level job. Hell, she didn't even have a résumé. Wasn't like she could tell a potential employer what she'd *really* done for a living since high school.

She'd have to fake an entire life. New documents, invented employers, false addresses. She could do it; she knew several forgers who could create a whole new identity for a price. But then where would she be? Always looking over her shoulder, waiting to be found out. Just so she could spend all day saying, "Would you like fries with that?"

She shook her head as a Yellow Cab pulled up to the curb.

"Don't think," she muttered under her breath. "Go home. Get some rest."

4

Joe Riley woke up late Friday morning to a beam of sunlight that lasered through a slit between the curtains and hit him in the eyes. He creaked out of bed and went to the bathroom to wash his face and brush his teeth.

He started coffee in the little percolator supplied by the Pink Elephant Motor Lodge. The coffeemaker wheezed and gurgled. Going to take a while.

Joe pulled on some pants and lit a Camel. His left hand ached and the knuckles were puffy. He made a fist and flexed it several times, trying to loosen it up. Even when you win a fight, you end up losing. Sore hands.

He went to the motel room's large front window, opened the drapes and squinted against the glaring desert sunshine. The Pink Elephant's namesake pachyderm—a life-sized concrete monstrosity—glowed on its perch beside the shoulder of the Strip.

The Pink Elephant was an old motel, once on the sandy outskirts of the city. Now, Tropical Bay towered across the street, filling the view to the west with Asian architecture and weary palm trees. To the north, the Strip carried on its round-the-clock freak show of light and noise—the giant black pyramid of Luxor, the fake skyline of New York, New York, the Eiffel Tower replica at Paris, the giant bronze lion in front of the MGM Grand, the distant spire of Stratosphere.

The hell am I doing here? Joe thought. Vegas was the last place he should spend time. Too many temptations. But the trail led here, and he'd followed it too far to turn back now.

He hunted up a clean shirt, then noticed the little red light blinking on the telephone on the nightstand. He punched "0" and listened to it ring.

"Front desk. This is Mona."

"Hi, Mona. Joe Riley in room 102. You've been holding my calls. Got a message for me?"

"Hold on."

Joe looked around while he waited. Fake oak paneling, pressed-wood furniture, and a carpet the color of phlegm. He'd spent a lot of time in similar rooms the past few months, enough for a lifetime.

Mona came back on the line and told Joe he had a message to call Sam Kilian.

"Thanks," he said and started to hang up.

"You want the number?"

"I've got Sam's number."

He cradled the receiver and snuffed out his cigarette in a tinfoil ash tray on the nightstand. I'll call Sam in a minute, he thought, but first I need coffee.

He was on his third cup of hot, bitter swill by the time he finally raised Sam at the precinct house back in Chicago.

"Is this Sam Kilian, famed crime fighter?"

"That's me. How you doing, Joe?"

"Okay. Didn't get much sleep last night, but I'll survive."

An uneasy pause.

"You gambling, Joe?"

"A little poker."

Sam grunted his disapproval. He and Joe had spent many a night gambling together back in Chicago, back when they were partners. But Sam discovered Gambler's Anonymous a couple of years ago, and he'd brandished the stiff morality of the convert ever since.

"Just enough to win some spending money," Joe said. "It's expensive, moving around all the time."

He looked around the crummy room. Mr. High Roller.

"I'm worried about you, Joe. You shouldn't be in Vegas."

"Believe me, it's not my choice. Hotter than hell here. But it's the only lead I've got. Give me something better to go on, and I'm out of here."

Joe pictured Sam at his messy desk, his big feet propped up, red hair curling above his freckled face. Sam went around with a smile all the time, like he knew something you didn't. Used to spook the hell out of perps during interrogations.

"Wish I could," Sam said. "That homicide you wanted me to track down, the one in Scranton, Pennsylvania?"

"Yeah?"

"No good. Guy's wife paid somebody to kill him, but they've already caught the dude who did it."

"Damn. Sure looked like it could be her handiwork."

"You can't believe everything you read in the newspapers. This one's strictly local."

"Too bad."

"I caught a fresh one this morning you'd enjoy, though. A male torso, found in a Dumpster on Lower Wacker Drive. Scared the hell out of the wino who found it."

"Just a torso?"

"That's right. No face, no fingerprints, nothing. Just the trunk."

"Shit, that'll be tough. Unless you can find the rest of the parts."

"Believe me, I'm looking. For now, all we know is hair color and a general idea of his size, back when he had legs and all."

"White guy?"

"Think he might be Irish."

"How come?"

"He's hung like a horse."

Sam laughed loudly and too long. Something about the laugh reminded Joe of the summer before, a barbecue at Sam's house. Sam and his wife, Ellen, had invited Joe over, trying to make him feel better after his divorce became final. Sam had been braying at some joke at the time, squinting against the smoke from the grill, wearing a stupid apron emblazoned, "Kiss the Cook." He'd been surrounded by Ellen and their three freckled kids, and Joe remembered thinking he'd never seen Sam happier.

Sam Kilian, respectable middle-class citizen, family man, homicide detective. All the things Joe should have at this stage of his life, all the things he'd lost.

"So what do you do now?" Sam asked. "Just hang around Vegas, showing her picture around?"

"That's what I've been doing. Big zero so far."

"Why don't you give it up? Come back here. Garcia's okay as a partner, but he's no Joe Riley."

"You already know the answer, Sam. Not until I catch her and pin Bennie's murder on her. That's the only thing that's going to make it all right again."

"You're chasing a ghost. You've got nothing to go on."

"I've got the photo."

"Right. In which she's wearing a disguise."

"Hey, it's gotten me this far. I found that casino worker up in Detroit, said a woman who matched the photo spent hours playing the slot machines. Then last week that airline clerk in Memphis recognized her, said she'd gotten on a plane for Vegas."

"Doesn't mean she's still there."

"Gotta start somewhere. I'm here. I'm looking for her."

"But it's been what, six months? You've been all over the country, chasing her, and you're no closer than you were."

"I've got to clear my name."

"Hell, by the time you get back here, nobody will *remember* your name. It's all history. Let it go."

Joe sighed. "We've had this conversation before. Nothing's changed but my location."

"Yeah, but Vegas . . . "

"Don't sweat it, Sam. Everything's under control."

Sam let his silence speak of his doubts.

"Thanks for checking out that tip in Scranton," Joe said. "I appreciate it."

"Sure. You still scanning the newspapers, hunting for homicides that look like her work?"

"Every day."

"Call me when you get another lead. I'll help you check it out."

Joe hung up and lit another cigarette. His hands worked automatically. His brain was far away, thinking about Bennie Burrows, the loan shark who'd been snuffed back in Chicago.

Should've never dealt with the little shit, he thought. That was my first mistake. Try to buy my way out of trouble with Bennie's money, and look where it lands me. Trapped in a seedy motel room, middle of the fucking desert, air outside hotter than the surface of the sun. Meanwhile, *she* could be anywhere, doing anything, killing somebody else.

And Joe couldn't do a damned thing to stop her.

5

Las Vegas Police detectives Susan Pine and Harold Campbell leaned against opposite walls as they rode the elevator up to the penthouse executive suite at Tropical Bay. Susan already had learned to keep her distance from her new partner. Harold always reeked of cigarettes, and an undertone of something else lingered on his breath as well. Tooth decay, internal rot, something. Susan could barely stand to share the elevator with him.

"I don't like this," she said. "Too much like being summoned by the top man. He wanted to see us, he could've come down to the crime scene."

Harold shrugged his narrow shoulders. He was a man of few words, another thing that annoyed Susan. When the brass promoted her to Homicide a week earlier and paired her with an older detective, she thought she'd learn from him, pick up the secrets of investigating murders. But Harold was dead weight, following Susan around, letting her ask the questions and search for clues. Harold was only a few months from the forced retirement age of sixty-five, and he acted like opening his mouth might jeopardize his pension. With breath like his, maybe he was right.

Susan chewed her fingernails. She was nervous about leaving the crime scene, even for a few minutes. It was her first homicide, and she wanted to watch over every detail as the lab techs worked Max Vernon's suite. She probably should've stayed there and sent Harold on this errand alone.

"You ever met this guy Staley?" she asked.

Harold shook his head. The harsh lights of the elevator glinted on his wavy Brylcreemed hair and threw deep shadows around the pouches under his eyes. Susan could see white whiskers on his chin.

"Seen him on TV," he said. "He's made quite a splash."

"Too much of a big shot to come downstairs, see where somebody's been murdered?"

Harold shrugged again. His hand went to his shirt pocket, fondled his cigarette pack. Susan thinking: He tries to light one of those things in here and I'll shoot him where he stands.

The elevator glided to a stop, and the doors opened. Susan and Harold stepped into a huge room, half the size of a basketball court, decorated with rattan furniture and bronze sculptures and potted palms. The plush carpet was the color of money and real zebra and tiger skins adorned one paneled wall. The place looked like a cross between a corporate office and the Jungle Room. Two walls were solid glass, looking out at nothing but blue sky.

Mel Loomis, Tropical Bay's chief of security, stood next to the elevator doors, solid and still. Susan wondered if he'd been waiting there since he told them they'd have to come upstairs to view the videotape from the security camera outside Vernon's room.

"Good," Loomis said. "You're here."

Anger still came off him like heat waves. Susan had noted downstairs that he seemed to take the murder personally—

nobody got killed in *his* hotel. She could tell it still was eating at him by the tightness of his jaw, the deepened creases in his broad face.

And what a face it was. Susan had almost sputtered with laughter when she first met him. The man looked exactly like Curly Howard, that fat guy from The Three Stooges, the one who'd always been her little brother's favorite when they were growing up in Barstow, spending all their time in front of a TV while their mother worked two jobs. Loomis even wore his hair cut nearly to his scalp, same as Curly. Didn't he *know* he resembled a Stooge? Did he play to the resemblance on purpose? And why the hell would he do that?

"Mr. Staley's ready for you," Loomis said, and she and Harold followed the big man to the far corner of the room, where Ken Staley himself sat at a slab-of-glass desk, talking on the phone.

Susan recognized Staley's silver hair and tanned, square-jawed face from newspaper photos. Rich bastard was a regular fixture in the Las Vegas Sun-Journal, always photographed at charity events and society balls. The three-thousand-room Tropical Bay had opened nearly a year ago with much fanfare. Since then, Staley had been as omnipresent as Big Brother.

Staley hung up and gestured Susan and Harold into two armchairs in front of his desk. He wore a slinky maroon silk shirt and more jewelry than Susan thought appropriate on a man. Loomis remained standing next to Staley's desk, practically at attention, the creases on his navy blue suit sharp enough to cut somebody.

Susan introduced herself and Harold, who sat silently, concentrating on plucking at a loose thread on the front of his houndstooth blazer. Susan felt like pinching him.

"Thank you for coming up to see me," Staley said. "I know you're busy."

"That's right," Susan said. "We're only here because we want that videotape."

Staley gave them a hundred-watt smile and said, "I've just been watching it myself. Here, I've got it cued up."

He plucked a black remote control from his desktop and aimed it at a TV that sat on a cart off to his right, ten feet away. The TV came to life, showing a slightly fuzzy view of a long hallway.

A man and woman appeared on the screen, their backs to the camera, and walked down the hall. Susan leaned forward as the couple reached a door and the man fumbled with his card key.

The man she recognized, though it was a little eerie to see Max Vernon up and walking around. The woman looked sleazy, maybe a hooker. Lot of makeup, big hair, a red dress two sizes too small. She'd be tall even without the high heels that made her three inches taller than Vernon. Susan was short and thin as a rail, barely big enough to pass the police department's physical requirements. Tall, sexy women with knockout bodies made her feel like spitting.

"She's big enough," Loomis said. "Takes a lotta strength to cut into somebody's neck like that."

Susan thought he was right, but she said nothing. She stared at the screen, trying to soak up every second the woman was caught on tape.

The redhead smiled at Vernon as she went into the room. The way her head was turned, it was if she were smiling directly at the camera. Vernon followed her inside and the door shut.

"Nothing else happens for a while," Staley said.

He pressed the fast-forward button on the remote. The hallway wavered and seconds flew past on a digital counter in the lower right corner. The hall remained empty until a heavyset man in a blue suit hurried into the picture and down the hall, walking like Charlie Chaplin.

"That's one of my guys," Loomis said. "Right outside and never heard a thing. Idiot."

Staley chuckled, but kept his eyes on the screen and his thumb on the button. "You fire him yet?"

"No. I want him here. Make his life miserable."

Susan tried to imagine how the security chief would do that, but what came to mind was the constant razz she took from the macho jerks in the squadroom.

"Here we go," Staley said, as the picture leaped and resumed normal speed. "Exactly nine minutes later."

On the screen, the door opened and a blond head poked out and looked up and down the hallway. Then a woman stepped from the doorway, wearing sunglasses, jeans and a T-shirt, and strode off to a fire exit.

"She looks different," Harold said. "Shorter. Different clothes. Sure it's the same woman?"

"It's her," Susan said. "She just changed clothes, put on a wig."

"How can you be sure?"

"Look at her purse. It's the same. Black shoulder bag."

Harold squinted at the screen.

Staley piped up. "Could be a different woman with the same purse."

She shook her head, and clutched her own purse in her lap. "Would you let some other man carry your wallet around?"

Staley flashed a matinee-idol smile. "Point well-taken."

Susan turned to Loomis, who still stood stonily near Staley's desk. "Where did she go next?"

"We're not sure. Stairwell camera's on the fritz. I've got my people looking through tape from other cameras. See if we can pick her up."

"I need to know how she got out of the hotel."

"Lady, there's lots we need to know. But I've got cameras in every corridor. I've got more than fifty cameras watching the casino floor. That's a lot of tape. We'll find her, but it'll take a while."

"When you do find her, I'll need those tapes, too," she said.

Staley swiveled his chair to face Susan. "Why's it so important how she left?"

She wasn't sure how much to say. If she made Staley unhappy, she'd hear about it from the chief. She'd learned during her nine years on the force that the casinos run everything in Las Vegas. They *are* everything in Las Vegas. Without them, Vegas would be a wide spot in the road, a desolate outpost instead of the Playground of the World.

"This looks to me like a professional hit," she said. "The woman was prepared. She brought the garrote, the handcuffs, the change of clothes. She seemed to know exactly what she was doing. I figure she had an escape route planned, too."

"She might still be in the hotel," Loomis said.

Susan figured he'd like that. Give him a chance to catch the killer himself. If that happened, the police wouldn't even be called. Casino owners had a history of handing out their own harsh justice.

"No, she's gone," Susan said. "Look at how well she planned it. She was miles away from here before the body was cold."

"What about you, Detective Campbell?" Staley said. "This look like the work of a professional to you?"

Harold hesitated, looked like he was weighing each word. "Could be. But I've never heard of a professional killer who's a *woman*."

Susan gave him a sharp look, but Harold didn't turn to face her. His expression relaxed into its typical rumpled, dreamy look. Probably fantasizing about retirement again, she thought bitterly.

An intercom buzzed on Staley's desk. He thumbed a button and said, "Yes?"

"Mr. Staley, there are two gentlemen here demanding to see you."

"Who are they?"

"They're, um, both named Mr. Vernon."

He pressed the button and said, "Send them up."

Staley looked over to Loomis. "Shit. The Vernon twins. They're not going to be happy about Max."

Before Loomis could answer, Susan said, "These are the brothers of the deceased?"

"Hi and Norm Vernon. You know them?"

Susan shook her head. "I've heard of—"

"They've been around Vegas since the beginning." Staley had an irritating habit of talking over people, in love with his own voice. "Born and raised here. Live all by themselves out in the desert. They own half the goddamned city and think they can push around the other half."

Susan got to her feet and brushed at the wrinkles on her skirt. "They won't push me around."

Staley smiled. "You know, Mel, I think she's right."

Loomis said nothing, and he didn't return the smile.

Susan glanced at Harold, who remained seated, looked like he could drift off into a nap. Christ.

Then the elevator door opened and two cowboys hustled

into the office. Both wore Western-cut suits and wide-brimmed brown Stetsons. Susan saw that Max Vernon's eyebrow was a genetic trait. Both his brothers had the single brow, too, though theirs had gone gray and bushy. Each sported a thick mustache, too, so they appeared to have two stripes of gray hair dividing their faces into thirds. They were identical in every way, except one of them wore thick, black-rimmed eyeglasses.

"Goddammit, Ken," said the one with the glasses, "how the hell does something like this happen in your hotel?"

"Calm down, Hi. There was nothing we could do about it. Looks like Max picked up a woman in the bar and took her up to his room. She killed him there. Nobody heard a thing."

"A *woman*?" the other Vernon shouted. "A *woman* killed our little brother?"

"Looks that way, Norm." Staley picked up the remote again and hit the rewind button. "You know how Max was. Go after anything in a skirt. Looks like he picked the wrong bimbo this time."

The Vernons muttered and cursed. The one with the glasses, Hi, had a tremble in his jutting lower lip, looked like he might start crying. Susan shifted uncomfortably. Worst part of Homicide is dealing with the mourners, being the one to bring the bad news, seeing grief all the damned time.

Staley hit a button just in time to freeze Max Vernon and the woman outside the hotel room door.

"There you go," he said. "Max took her inside. Little while later, she comes out, wearing a wig and a different set of clothes. A maid found Max this morning. He was naked, handcuffed to the bed. A wire was twisted around his neck."

"Lord love a duck," Hi said, a quaver in his voice. "How did Max let himself get in such a position?"

"He was a moron, that's how," Norm said. "Staley's right. 'Anything in a skirt.' Finally found one who'd rear up and kill him."

"Excuse me," Susan said. "I'm Susan Pine and this is Detective Campbell. LVPD. We're handling this case."

She showed them her badge, but Hi was too busy looking her up and down to notice.

"*You're* leading the investigation?"

"You got a problem with that?"

Hi hesitated, then said, "No, ma'am, I don't. Long as you catch the woman who killed Max."

His voice caught in his throat and his eyes glinted behind the thick glasses.

"We'll catch her," Susan said, "but it's not going to be easy."

"Goddamned Max," Norm said. "I've told him a hundred times—"

"Wasn't your brother married?"

"So?"

Susan let that one go.

"We'll need to question his wife," she said. "And we'll need to interview both of you as well. But right now, we need to get back to the crime scene."

Hi nodded and took a deep, shuddering breath. He handed her a business card from his pocket. It read, "Vernon Air Conditioning," and had an address on the west side of town and several telephone numbers.

"Air conditioning?"

"That's one of our businesses," Hi said. "The main one. Our daddy was the man who brought air-conditioning to these parts. Made living out here possible."

"You can be reached at these numbers?"

"Leave a message," Hi said. "They always know where to find us."

She nodded and went to the TV. She pushed the "eject" button and took out the videotape.

"I'll need those other tapes as soon as you manage to find the killer on them," she said to Loomis, who glowered at her.

Susan tucked the tape into her purse and strode off toward the elevator. She stopped and looked back over her shoulder. Her partner still sat in his chair, blinking at the assembled men as if he'd awakened in a strange place.

"Come *on*, Harold."

6

Joe Riley was eating a midday breakfast of bacon and eggs at a diner near the Pink Elephant Motor Lodge when he spotted the brief story in the afternoon edition of the Las Vegas Sun-Journal.

"Holy shit!"

His waitress—a fiftyish woman who'd fallen face-first into a vat of rouge—scuttled over to his table and said, "Is everything all right, sir?"

"Fine, fine." He read the article's few paragraphs again, more carefully this time, and what he found made his pulse race.

LOCAL MAN SLAIN AT NEW CASINO

A well-known Clark County man was found slain this morning in a suite at the new Tropical Bay Casino and Resort.

Police identified the man as Max Vernon, who is involved in several businesses in the Las Vegas area, including The Cactus Ranch casino.

Vernon, 48, was apparently strangled with a wire after his wrists were handcuffed to a bed in his room. Police officials declined to release further details.

Sources said police were looking for a tall woman who was seen accompanying Vernon.

Joe was holding his breath, and he let it out in a huff. Jesus Christ. This Max Vernon was killed the same way Bennie Burrows was murdered two years ago in Chicago. The garrote, the handcuffs, the hotel room bed. And police are looking for a tall woman.

It had to be her.

Joe leaped up and threw some money on the table. Then he was out the door of the diner, the newspaper tucked under his arm, trotting toward the domed towers of Tropical Bay.

He'd gone a block before the heat fully hit him and he had to slow to a walk. Hot wind snatched the breath from his mouth. He gasped his way to the corner, then waited for a light to change so he could cross the car-crowded expanse of Las Vegas Boulevard.

While he waited, Joe looked over the article again, wondering who Max Vernon was and whether his "businesses" disguised something shady. Bennie Burrows had owned legitimate Chicago businesses—a video rental place, a bakery, a used-car lot—as fronts for his loan shark racket. Joe knew all about Bennie's illegal banking; he'd been into him for thirteen grand when Bennie went to the Big Vault in the Sky.

The light changed and Joe hustled across the wide street. Tropical Bay was designed for arriving vehicles, not pedestrians, and no sidewalks led from the street to the entrance. He had to dodge carloads of gawking tourists as he hurried up the tree-lined driveway.

Air conditioning in the lobby greeted him like an old friend, and he gulped the cool air as he approached the front desk.

Joe no longer carried a badge, but he still had business cards that identified him as a homicide detective for the

Chicago Police Department. That was good enough for the desk clerk, who told him the crime scene was on the fourteenth floor.

Joe felt right at home when he stepped off the elevator on fourteen. Yellow "Crime Scene" tape sealed off a room, and three uniformed cops loitered in the hall, looking bored.

"I need to speak to whoever's in charge of the investigation."

A tanned cop with bulging biceps squinted at him. "And who the hell would you be?"

"Joe Riley. I used to be a homicide detective in Chicago. I've got some information about this death."

"*Used* to be?" The cop wasn't budging. The brotherhood in blue doesn't always extend the hand of fellowship to cops from out of town. And, former officers? They're no longer in the fraternity.

"I'm retired," Joe said, then he stared at the cop, waiting for him to make some crack about how Joe was too young. But the cop just shrugged his muscular shoulders and said, "I'll tell her you're here."

As the cop stepped over the knee-high yellow tape, Joe said to the other cops, "'*Her*?'"

They snickered, but said nothing.

A few seconds later, a slight, frazzled woman wearing a knee-length skirt and a wilted blouse stepped over the tape and introduced herself as Detective Susan Pine. Joe noted that the uniforms edged away from her, like she was a bomb ready to go off.

After he identified himself, she said, "What do you want?"

"I want to look at the scene. I think this murder is exactly like one I investigated in Chicago."

She raised her hand to her mouth, started to chew a fingernail, then seemed to think better of it.

"No way I'm letting you into this crime scene," she said. "That's impossible."

"But if I could see the vic—"

"He's already gone. Coroner took him away an hour ago. We're still dusting for prints and all, but there's nothing to see."

Joe was silent for a moment. "This case in Chicago, she didn't leave a trace there, either."

"What case are you talking about?"

"A loan shark named Bennie Burrows, killed about two years ago by a woman. Strangled him with a wire, handcuffed him to the bed first."

The detective studied him.

"You're still working Homicide in Chicago? What are you doing in Vegas?"

Joe bit his lower lip. He needed to tread carefully here. "I'm not on the force anymore. Took early retirement after fifteen years. But I thought I could help."

Pine was shaking her head before he could finish. Her dark hair swung against her neck.

"If you're retired, you've got no standing," she said.

"I just thought you could use the information."

She looked him over again, didn't seem to like what she found. I probably don't look my best, Joe thought. My clothes are sweaty and rumpled and my hair's windblown and I'm too excited. She probably thinks I'm some kind of nut.

"Listen," he said, "did anyone get a look at the killer?"

She shook her head.

Joe pointed to a video camera high in a corner of the hallway. "What about the security video? Did you get her on tape?"

Pine said nothing, but Joe could see something click in her eyes. He fished the worn photograph from his shirt pocket.

"Could this be her?"

The detective took one look at the photo, and Joe knew he'd hit pay dirt. Her dark eyebrows arched and her face flushed.

"Where did you get this picture?" she asked.

"Bennie took it. He was a shutterbug. Photography was his hobby, only thing that made him even slightly human. This was the last picture he took before he was killed. We figure Bennie snapped her picture—like a souvenir—right before she handcuffed him to the bed. The killer busted his camera, but the techs were able to salvage the film. "

Pine said nothing, stared some more at the photograph.

"That's her, isn't it? The same one."

"Could be. This one started out with red hair, too."

"I think it's a wig."

She nodded. "The woman who did this had red hair when she went into the room, but she was a blonde when she left."

"I'll bet you haven't found the slightest trace evidence from the scene. No prints, nothing, right?"

"Plenty of prints," she grumbled. "It's a *hotel* room. How will we ever tell if any of them are hers?"

"You won't find hers. This woman's a mechanic. She doesn't make mistakes. And I'll bet she's already blown town. Have you checked the airport?"

"For what? We don't even know what we have here."

"It's gotta be the same woman."

Pine took a last look at the photograph, then handed it back to him. Joe put it in his pocket, relieved that she hadn't thought to confiscate it. It was his only copy.

"In Chicago," he said, "she hit Bennie, then went straight to O'Hare. We lost her there, of course. O'Hare's a big place. But maybe that's her pattern."

Pine glanced over her shoulder into the room like she wanted to get back in there.

"We're not done here yet."

"You're wasting your time. She doesn't leave a trace. She's a fuckin' ghost."

The detective's dark brows knitted.

"Don't tell me how to run my investigation. I'm going strictly by the book on this one. And I don't remember the book saying anything about letting out-of-town cops get involved. Especially ones that are *retired*."

"Okay, don't take my word for it. I'll give you a phone number. Ask for a homicide cop named Sam Kilian. He used to be my partner. He worked Bennie's death with me. See if everything I've said isn't true."

"Even if it's true, how does that help me?"

"Maybe if you and Sam put your heads together—"

She shook him off. "I don't have time for this. If I get a chance, I'll call your buddy in Chicago. But I'm not promising anything."

"You'll check the airport?"

"When I get a chance. I don't have much in the way of manpower."

He glanced toward the trio of uniformed cops who still hung around in the corridor. She saw him looking and blushed.

Joe could see this was going nowhere. How would he have reacted, back when he was working cases in Chicago, if some asshole from out of town started offering theories? He would've figured the guy for a head case and ignored him, just as Pine was doing. At least she was being polite about it.

He took a matchbook from his pocket. The paper cover said "Pink Elephant Motor Lodge" on the front and listed the address and phone number on the back.

"This is where I'm staying," he said, handing her the matchbook. "If you change your mind, if you want my help, call me."

She glanced at the matches. "You going there now? I could reach you there later this afternoon?"

"Leave a message," he said. "I've got somewhere I've got to go."

He turned toward the elevators as she said, "Where's that?"

"To the airport."

7

Ken Staley stood at his office's tall windows, looking out over the Strip, when the elevator doors opened and he heard his wife screech his name. For a second, he felt like diving through the window. A thirty-story plunge might be preferable to listening to Patti again.

"My God, Ken," she shrieked, "have you seen the afternoon paper? They've already got a story about this murder. What are you going to do about it?"

He steeled himself and turned to face her. She'd made her way across the big office and stood on the far side of his desk, hands on hips, her face clenched with anger.

Patti was thirty-eight—nearly twenty years younger than Ken—but her surgery-tightened face showed no sign of the approach of middle age. She still stood tall and straight, her hair was an expensive shade of blond, and her makeup was impeccable. But her lipsticked mouth was curled in disgust and her eyes looked wild and mean.

"Well, my dear, what would you expect me to do about it?" he said, as mildly as possible. He couldn't speak sharply when she was in this mood. He'd never hear the fucking end of it.

"Call the editor," she snapped. "We can't take this kind of publicity. Not now. Not if you're going to turn this dump into a money-maker."

This dump? His beautiful hotel, with its gardens, its five swimming pools, its tasteful décor, cost more than 200 million dollars to build. He'd personally overseen every detail of the design and construction and decoration of Tropical Bay since Day One. It meant everything to him. His hands tried to curl into fists. He put them in his pants pockets so she wouldn't see.

"I think it's too late to kill the story," he said. "Didn't you say it was already in the paper?"

Patti's jaw clenched and she blew a gust of air up toward her blond bangs. "Jesus, do I have to explain everything to you? There'll be a bigger story in the morning edition tomorrow. This is all they had time to do because they were up against their deadline. Believe me, I know something about the media and how it works ..."

She talked on, but Ken had seized on something, her knowledge of the "media." Patti had spent about ten minutes in TV news fifteen years ago, one of the many jobs she'd held before she found her ultimate calling as his socialite wife. She knew shit about the media or anything else, but she believed her brief internship at a tiny TV station in California made her an expert. She was always mouthing off about the local talking heads and how crappy they were. Like she could do any better. Like her shrill voice wouldn't cause television owners throughout Nevada to change the fucking channel before the paint peeled off their walls.

"Are you even *listening* to me?"

Ken snapped back. "Sorry, my dear, I've got a lot on my mind."

She rolled her eyes and opened her big purse and began to dig around in it, talking all the while.

"You think your average tourist wants to come to a resort where people get *killed*? Maybe we wouldn't worry if we were the only hotel in town, but just look out that window. They've got choices, Ken, lots of choices. Why would they pick Tropical Bay? Because we've got a reputation for *murdered* guests? I don't think so."

He sighed. She was right. Bad publicity could be deadly. Not to mention what the murder would do to his own personal reputation among the elite of Las Vegas casino owners. The fact somebody had dared to commit murder at Tropical Bay showed disrespect.

Patti finally found what she was looking for in her purse—a long, thin cigarette. She clamped it between her red lips, torched it with a gold Dunhill lighter and blew smoke toward the ceiling. He'd asked her a million times not to smoke in his office; he hated the smell it left behind. But he said nothing about it now.

"What are you going to do?" she demanded.

Ken took his hands out of his pockets and dropped into his leather swivel chair. She squinted against her smoke, waiting.

"I'm going to take care of it," he said.

"And how are you going to do that?"

"The Vegas way. Believe me, you don't want to know any more than that."

"Bullshit. I want to know everything. Show me you're not fucking this up. I've got a lot riding here, too, you know. We've got every penny sunk into this white elephant—"

Patti was interrupted by the elevator doors opening. Mel Loomis rumbled into the room. As he crossed the office, Loomis glanced at Patti and frowned, but then he locked eyes with Ken, who had to rein in the impulse to have Loomis pitch her through the nearest window.

"Mel, just the man I want to see," he said. "I've got a job for you."

Loomis stood at attention next to Patti, who ignored him. Ken knew she didn't think much of Loomis, probably had to bite her tongue to keep from blaming him and his security staff for the murder. But something about Loomis' menacing bulk made her keep her mouth shut.

"We can't rely on the cops to find the woman who killed Max Vernon," Ken said. "You saw how that detective was today. She doesn't know her ass from a slot machine. I want you to find the killer."

"Yes, sir."

"Handle this personally, Mel. You've got lots of sources in this town. Find her and make her disappear. We don't need the publicity of a trial."

Loomis' mouth stretched thin. "Be my pleasure."

He turned toward the elevators, purpose in his stride.

"Keep me posted," Ken called after him.

He turned to Patti. She'd taken the cigarette from her mouth and she was smiling, as if, goddammit, she couldn't help herself, she was impressed.

Ken beamed at her. "See, my dear. It's all being taken care of. Mel's just the man for the job."

Patti looked over her shoulder to make sure the elevator doors had closed behind Loomis, then said, "I hope to hell you're right."

8

Delbert Nash spent six impatient hours in the emergency room of University Medical Center, waiting, waiting, the morning slipping away as the injured and infirm paraded past him. The fat-ass nurses wouldn't give him a painkiller until after he'd been examined by a doctor, but people kept arriving with more severe emergencies, and Delbert kept getting pushed back in line. Finally, around noon, he got to see a doctor for a grand total of three minutes. Young Turk, all rumpled, like maybe he hadn't slept in days, took one look at Delbert and pronounced his nose broken.

"Hell, I *know* that much!" Delbert shouted. "I knew that when I got here. Question is, what can you *do* about it?"

The doctor wrote on his clipboard, ignoring the outburst, probably heard such shit all the time. Delbert tried to steady himself, tried to speak calmly.

"I mean, Doc, can it be fixed?"

The doctor squinted at him, then looked back at the clipboard and wrote some more. Delbert wanted to yank the goddamned clipboard out of his hands and bang him over the head with it, get his undivided attention.

"Not here," the doctor said finally. "We can patch you up, hold things in place, but I'm guessing you'll need a plastic surgeon if you want to look the way you did before."

Delbert cursed and fumed, but the doctor was unfazed.

Ten minutes, two hundred dollars and one puny painkiller later, he exited the hospital to find the black limousine waiting for him. Delbert thinking: Good old Mookie. The waiting limo's the first thing that's gone right all day.

Out of habit, Mookie got out of the long car and walked around to open the rear passenger door. Delbert noticed that Mookie was walking funny, kind of bow-legged. He guessed Mookie's balls were swollen to the size of grapefruits.

Mookie's eyes widened when he got a good look at Delbert, who wore a clear plastic mask that covered the top half of his face. Delbert saw himself reflected in the limo's black windows: Beneath the plastic mask, his nose looked like a flattened purple sausage.

"Don't say a fuckin' word," he warned.

Mookie shook his head and went back around the car. Delbert slumped onto the limo's padded leather seat and reached up to gingerly adjust the plastic mask. Goddamned thing had elastic straps that went around the back of his head, messed up his hair. Not that it mattered. Until his face healed, he'd look like a *victim*, no matter how sleek his pompadour.

The car rocked as Mookie climbed behind the wheel. He wore his chauffeur's uniform, though he hadn't bothered with the hat, and he looked big and menacing in the black suit. Mookie made a good running buddy. He let Delbert do the thinking, and his bulk often came in handy—the presence of a large black man has a calming effect on people. Plus, Delbert got free use of the limo whenever Mookie wasn't busy with a client. In Vegas, you get picked up in a limo, people assume you're a high roller.

By God, Delbert thought, I *am* a high roller, a man who

deserves some respect. Vegas is my town. The son of a bitch who ruined my face was an out-of-towner, a fucking tourist. Delbert sneered at such chumps, the way carnival workers look down on the "sheep" who waste their money on rides and games and cotton candy.

Had to admit, the guy threw a mean punch. Of course, he'd blindsided Delbert. Maybe he wouldn't have been so tough without the element of surprise. If Delbert could've sicced Mookie on that guy, he'd be the one coming out of a fucking hospital.

"Where to, Delbert? You wanta go home?"

Delbert and Mookie shared a tiny rental house in downtown Vegas, within walking distance of the Fremont Street casinos, convenient when the limo wasn't available. The place was a dump, no question, and Delbert spent as little time there as possible, but he was tempted to go home now. Lie down, try to ignore the throbbing in his face. But he'd had eight hours to think about the guy who'd ruined his nose, and he was too worked up to rest.

"Head for the Strip. We've got things to do."

Mookie started the limo and let it glide from its parking space. "What kinda things?"

"We're gonna find the bastard who roughed us up last night and give him a taste of his own medicine. We're gonna get our money back."

Mookie absorbed this news while slowing for a red light. "But we don't know his name or where he's staying or nothing. How we gonna find him?"

"We'll find him."

Mookie glanced at Delbert in the rear-view mirror.

"All right," he said. "Let's go get him. But we need to work fast. I've got a client at four o'clock."

Delbert checked his watch. "That only gives us about three hours. Step on it, will you?"

"I don't even know where I'm going, Delbert."

"We'll start at Lucky's. Maybe somebody there knows him."

The light changed and Mookie swung the big car onto Las Vegas Boulevard, headed south.

"Hey, Delbert?"

"Yeah?"

"Shouldn't we get something to eat first? I'm hungry."

"You're always fuckin' hungry."

"I was waiting a long time outside the hospital. I never got breakfast or lunch 'cause I was afraid I'd miss you."

"You can go another hour or two without lunch."

"I don't know. If we're gonna hurt this guy, I need to eat. Keep my strength up."

Delbert sighed.

9

Hi Vernon cradled the phone and stood up from his ornate desk. He looked out the triple-paned window to where a great expanse of mottled desert led to bare brown mountains and clear blue sky. Probably a hundred-and-six degrees out there, he figured. Don't know how people stand it.

Here in the isolated two-story house Hi shared with his brother Norm, it was a perfect sixty-eight degrees, day and night, winter or summer. The Vernons had access to the finest air-conditioning systems money could buy—at wholesale prices—and the brick house was as well-insulated as a refrigerator. The Vernon boys understood the value of climate control.

Hi snagged the pointed toe of his cowboy boot on the leg of his desk, nearly went tumbling across the room. He caught himself and straightened up and smoothed his jacket before walking on, thinking, I've got to be more careful. Shit like that keeps happening to me. I could break a hip.

Hi thought a lot lately about being a senior citizen; his and Norm's sixtieth birthday was coming up in a few weeks. Most folks didn't consider sixty to be aged anymore, but it felt that way to Hi. Every creak and groan and mystery pain reminded him he was getting old.

Certainly too old for the shit Norm was cooking up. Norm, that hothead, was in the next room, a study identical to the one where Hi had been making his phone calls. The matching dens, with their mahogany desks and built-in bookshelves, were among the few luxuries they'd allowed themselves when they built this place thirty miles south of Vegas, on the site of the original Vernon homestead. A few sagging sheds and a ramshackle barn still stood around the place, and the big house itself was plain inside and out, about as much atmosphere as a deer camp. A place for men. Hi couldn't even remember the last time they'd had a female visitor. It had been months, at least. Another sign the Vernon twins were getting old.

Norm sat at his desk. He'd removed his suit jacket and rolled up his sleeves, but he still wore his hat pushed back on his head, the angle of the brim mimicking his upswept eyebrow. The desktop was covered in guns and swabs and ramrods and tins of oil. Hi couldn't imagine the guns needed cleaning—Norm always kept them in perfect shape—but one couldn't argue with preparedness. They'd be doing some shooting soon, no two ways about it.

Hi recognized his old Remington pump-action shotgun among the weaponry. Norm's Winchester rifle was there, too, along with three revolvers and a mean-looking black Glock.

Norm looked like he was about finished with the guns, and Hi thought: I'll need to find something else for him to do pretty damned quick. Norm had too much energy, all pumped up over Max's murder. Both of them were mourning Max, but Norm's grief manifested itself as white-hot anger. Hi needed to find a way to channel that rage into something productive until they were ready.

Norm's temper had always been the one thing that separated them. Hi didn't get hot and bothered when things went wrong. Norm would rant and rave and stomp around, and he needed cool Hi to show him how to use his anger. But when it came to nut-cutting time, Hi would prefer his twin beside him over any man in the world. Or any six men, for that matter.

Norm looked up from the revolver he was cleaning and said, "You got news?"

"Made some calls. Nobody knows of a contract being put out on Max, but everybody has a theory about who might've ordered it. And they've all got the same theory."

Norm squinted at him. "Teddy Valentine?"

"The one and only. Apparently, everybody in this town knows Marla's been screwing Teddy on the side. Everybody but us, anyway."

"If I'd known it, Teddy Valentine would already be a fading memory."

Hi pushed his glasses up, thinking.

"Max must've known. I mean, everybody at The Cactus Ranch knows about it, and Max practically lived at that goddamned little casino. You think he just didn't give a shit that his wife was banging his floor manager?"

Norm set the gun on the desktop and leaned back in his swivel chair.

"You know Max. He was probably too busy screwing every waitress in the place to pay any attention to Marla."

"Got him killed," Hi said.

"I told him a million times he needed to learn to keep his dick in his pants, but he wouldn't listen."

"You warned him about Marla, too."

"I sure as hell did." Norm's face flushed. Hi could see he was getting worked up. "That little chippy, half his age. She was a *showgirl*, for shit's sake. I've never seen one of 'em who wouldn't open her legs for any passing playboy."

Hi could remember plenty of showgirls who didn't sleep around. Some of them were even married. But Norm was on a roll. No sense arguing over trivialities.

"And that fuckin' Teddy Valentine. Knew he was trouble the first time I ever saw him. In his slick suits and his gold chains and all that fuckin' hair. Thinks he's a tough guy 'cause he's Eye-talian. Like every wop in the world is some kinda Mafia big shot. Who's he tryin' to kid?"

Norm had Valentine pegged. The man tried to act like a gangster. Not bad for business at The Cactus Ranch. A little aroma of organized crime makes the suckers behave themselves. But Hi had checked Teddy out himself, and he was no gangster. Just a street punk who'd gone Vegas.

Norm picked up the revolver and examined its open cylinder. The chrome pistol gleamed in the desert light pouring through the windows. He started sliding fat bullets into the chambers.

"Guess we oughta go have a little talk with Teddy," Hi said.

Norm grinned at him. "We gonna go see the grieving widow, too?"

"Let's talk to Teddy first. Maybe he did this on his own. Maybe she didn't know anything about it."

"We can ask Teddy," Norm said, still grinning. Wasn't much mirth there. It was an animal reaction, a fearsome showing of teeth.

"Think he'll talk? Maybe he'll get all noble and refuse to rat her out."

Norm snapped the revolver's cylinder shut. His eyes gleamed.

"He'll talk."

10

Lily was cranky and tired of traveling, but she still changed cabs twice between Phoenix's Sky Harbor airport and her place in Scottsdale. She felt certain no one had tailed her from Vegas, but she believed in taking every precaution.

She paid the last cabbie outside the condo complex where she'd lived the past two years. The buildings were white with red tile roofs, arranged in a square around a large swimming pool. It was the pool, and its surrounding gardens and palm trees, that sold Lily on the condo in the first place. She swam laps every day when she was home, which wasn't nearly often enough.

The air in her place was hot and stale, with an undertone of something else, maybe something rotting in the trash. She turned on the A/C, then went straight to her bedroom to change into a black tank swimsuit. She stepped into sandals, grabbed a towel, and headed for the pool, the heat buffeting her as she walked between flowerbeds to the calm blue water.

The pool area was empty, which suited Lily fine. She often swam in the middle of the day, when most tenants were at work and the rest were hunkered indoors, avoiding the heat. She preferred the solitude.

She tossed her towel onto a chaise lounge and kicked off

her sandals. The concrete was blistering underfoot, and she plunged into the cool water before she was burned.

The water felt fresh and clean and caressing. She let her momentum carry her forward through its depths until she was nearly out of air, then kicked to the surface and started swimming, her arms slicing through the water.

Swimming was what she needed to release the tension she'd carried around since Vegas. Jobs like that one always strung her out—picking up the mark in a public place, killing him in a hotel room. Always the worry that something could go wrong, no matter how carefully she'd planned every move. Only when she was back here, in the swimming pool's soothing embrace, could she relax.

She turned fluidly at each end of the pool. Her breathing was so regular—stroke, stroke, stroke, breath—it was like meditation.

Lily had discovered the Zen of swimming when she was a gangly girl, growing up in the South. The family home, where her mother's people lived, was near Camden, Alabama, in an area of rural woodland carved by creeks and dotted with ponds. Swimming holes were everywhere you looked. Lily's mama always called her "the water baby" because of how much she loved to swim.

Her family relocated every year or two, looking for work or fleeing creditors, her daddy too drunk and too mean to stay on one job for long. Whenever they landed in a new town, the first thing Lily did was check out the nearest body of water. Sometimes, she'd have to walk a mile or two, just to reach some snake-infested bayou where no one else dared go for a dip. But Lily always found water.

Everyplace she'd inhabited in the past ten years had, as its main feature, a large pool. Sometimes the apartments themselves had been dumps, but as long as the pool was long, clean, and cold, Lily was happy.

She paused at the shallow end, standing and breathing deeply, letting oxygen flood her muscles. She blinked the water from her eyes and looked around the quiet condos. Mostly, working couples lived in them, regular folks with jobs, families, and money troubles, with brief moments of happiness. Lily barely knew her neighbors, and avoided contact with them. If somebody asked, she said she was in sales and traveled a lot.

She liked this place, the pool, the year-round flowers. But she didn't know how much longer she'd live here. She'd probably stayed too long already. A permanent address was a hazard.

She could make money on the condo. Scottsdale was trendy, and real estate prices kept climbing. Her profit, and the cash she had stashed in five different banks around the Southwest, was enough to buy her a whole new life somewhere. But she wasn't sure she was ready to move again. Not yet.

She kicked off the wall of the pool and resumed swimming laps.

Max Vernon's face, with that ridiculous eyebrow, came unbidden to her mind. He'd been an oily sort, a womanizer, and she felt no remorse over killing him. Most of her targets were sleazeballs, the type that would make her mama say, "That man needs killing," but Lily didn't have to persuade herself they were bad men. She just did her job. Let other people worry about ethics and evil and heaven and hell and who deserved death. She was an assassin, and assassins didn't ask such questions.

She tried to change her line of thinking, but other targets floated up in her memory. Faces and body types and locations. Bullets and hot blood and cold steel. The surprise in the eyes of a dying man.

None more surprised than Johnny Hendricks, her mentor. Johnny, an old Mississippi dandy with a weakness for Panama hats and ice-cream-white suits, had taught her well. How to kill. How to keep from leaving evidence behind. How to make a clean getaway.

But one day Johnny made a mistake. Drunk, he'd tried to get too familiar with Lily, had pawed at her, backed her into a corner. And Lily slipped a knife into his stomach and slit him up to the sternum.

She remembered Johnny's eyes, two pools of blue, as he fell backward, clutching at the wound, trying to hold in his own guts. He'd bled to death before Lily could even catch her breath.

Christ, that was eight years ago, nearly nine. And she'd been on her own ever since, killing and running and killing again.

Lily stopped swimming and gripped the side of the pool. This was no good. The swimming wasn't doing its job, wasn't washing the thoughts from her brain.

She climbed out and toweled off and shuffled back to her condo, looking forward to something to eat and a long nap. She changed into a bathrobe and ran the towel over her short, dark hair. In Arizona's arid climate, her hair dried in minutes.

Lily went to the kitchen in search of food, and it didn't take long to see she was out of luck. The refrigerator held nothing but a few condiments and a jug of water and some leftover Chinese takeout that had grown fuzzy green mold. She tossed out the soggy container and rummaged through the cabinets. But unless she was in the mood for corn flakes without milk, she'd need to go somewhere to eat.

She groaned. She didn't feel like driving to a grocery or a café. She wanted a nap, but if she didn't eat first, her growling stomach would keep her awake.

The phone rang. Lily cursed. Another interruption, something else standing between her and her soft bed.

"Lily! It's Sal. Made it home okay, huh?"

"What do you want?"

"Wanted to talk to you about another job opportunity."

"Not now, Sal. I'm beat."

"It's now or never. This one's a rush job. You don't take it, I'll have to give it to someone else."

She opened her mouth to tell him to do just that, but then she remembered her earlier thoughts—money and moving and a new life. Maybe one more job would get her started in that direction.

"How much?"

"Thirty grand, less my commission."

Whew. Her share would come to twenty-four-thousand tax-free dollars. She could live a year on that.

She flopped into a chair and hung her long legs over the arm. "Let's hear it."

"Like I told you before, this one's a cakewalk."

"Don't sell it to me. Just tell me the facts."

"All right. Guy in Albuquerque wants to take out his business partner. The partner's a regular citizen, no idea what's coming."

Lily smiled at the irony. Albuquerque. She'd just been there. If she'd let Sal tell her about this in their earlier conversation, she might not have come home at all.

"Why does the partner want him dead?"

"The mark's got a new girlfriend, a gold-digger. The mark's not doing his job anymore, too busy being in love. The partner's afraid they'll get married and he'll end up splitting his company with the bimbo. He wants to leave it all to his snot-nosed kids."

"What kind of company?"

"They sell carpet. What the hell difference does it make?"

"Just asking."

Lily paused, waiting for what she knew would come next.

"So," he said, "you interested or not?"

"Give me the details."

"All right! I knew I could count on you. The mark's name is Martin Holguin. Everybody calls him Marty. He works during the day at Albuquerque Carpet Barn. West side of town somewhere. He lives on the east side, though, by those mountains they got there."

Sal rattled off an address. Lily plucked a pen and pad off a side table and wrote it down.

"What's the girlfriend's name?"

"I don't know. You need it?"

"Would I ask if I didn't need it?"

"Sorry. I'll get it for you. Anything else?"

"How soon?"

"Sooner the better. The partner's getting worried because Marty's talking marriage."

She said nothing, thinking about some poor schmuck, ready to walk down the aisle.

"What's the matter, Lily? Something wrong?"

"I'm tired."

"But you'll take the job?"

"Might as well. Nothing to eat around here anyway."

"What?"

"Forget it. I'll take the contract. Call you later."

She hung up before he could say anything else. Sal annoyed her more than usual lately. Another sign she should get out of the business. *Everything* annoyed her.

Lily slumped off to her bedroom and started packing a bag. The client wants the hit done right away, she might as well accommodate him. Get it done, get back home, take some time off. She needed some down time so she could decide what to do with her life.

She got an idea. She'd *drive* to Albuquerque. It was only six or seven hours. She'd take her little Miata. Put the top down and zoom across the desert. Give her time to think. And she wouldn't have to fool with airport security or rental cars or fake ID. Just take a nice sunny drive in her convertible, pop this guy in Albuquerque, then cruise back home. Might even be pleasant.

The thought of getting behind the wheel of the sporty car raised her spirits. She'd pick up some fast food and hit the open road.

"Look out, Marty Holguin," she said under her breath. "I'm coming for you."

II

Delbert knew the card dealer would tell him what he wanted to know. Old broad tried to play it cool, but she kept sneaking looks at Mookie, who stood silently, a big black wall keeping her cornered at Lucky's Back Door. Her eyes nested in a pile of pouches and bags and wrinkles, but Delbert could see fear in them.

"Come on, Agnes," he said. "The guy was at your table when we got here last night. He must've said something, his name, something like that, when he sat down."

Agnes shook her head slightly and chewed on her lower lip. Delbert could barely stand to look at her fat old face, much less at her pile of pink hair, but he held his stare on her, knowing she'd cave.

"Look what he did to my face, Agnes," Delbert said. "This guy's dangerous. You don't want to protect a guy like that."

She glanced over at Mookie again. Mookie didn't twitch, standing there with his arms crossed across his thick chest. Delbert had to admit his partner looked menacing, if you didn't know what was going on behind those baleful eyes. Mookie probably was thinking about food or what cartoons he'd watch on TV later, but Agnes didn't know that.

She sighed and looked at the floor. "He said his name was Joe."

"Any last name?"

She shook her pink head. "No, he didn't say where he was from, either. All I know is, he said he was 'retired.'"

Mookie snorted and Delbert shot him a look.

"You've heard that before, right, Agnes? These fuckin' gamblers, that's what they always say, they're 'retired.'"

Agnes said nothing, kept studying the floor. Delbert knew she was breaking every code of the Las Vegas casinos: You don't talk about the customers. You stay away from trouble.

"Last chance, Agnes. You got anything else?"

She shook her head, but Delbert figured she was holding something back. Otherwise, why wouldn't she look him in the eye?

"I find out you knew something else about this Joe and you didn't tell us, you're gonna find Mookie waiting for you some night when you leave work. You get my meaning?"

Agnes raised her head and looked at Delbert, then at Mookie. Delbert saw a spark of rebellion in her eyes, like she was about to tell them to go to hell. But fear took over again, and she coughed up exactly what they needed to know.

"He was a smoker. I noticed the book of matches he was using. They were from that motel down at the end of the Strip, the Pink Elephant."

Delbert began to smile, but his rising cheeks pressed against the plastic facemask and pain rocketed through his shattered nose. He blinked back tears and said hoarsely, "Good girl, Agnes. We'll go check that out."

He took a cardboard coaster from a table, turned it over and wrote a phone number on the back. "You see this Joe in here again, you call me right away. Got it?"

Agnes nodded as he handed her the coaster. She kept her eyes downcast, ashamed.

Mookie and Delbert sauntered out to the curb, where they'd left the limo parked by a hydrant. Delbert slid into the back seat while Mookie walked around to the driver's side.

Mookie swiveled in the seat. "Where to, Delbert?"

"Where the hell do you think?"

"I dunno."

"Weren't you listening just now? To what that old broad said?"

Mookie's eyes looked blank.

"The Pink Elephant, that old dump across from Tropical Bay."

"Oh. Right."

Delbert muttered curses as Mookie steered the car south. Fucking Mookie hadn't even been listening while he played his role at Lucky's.

"What we gonna do when we get there?" Mookie asked.

"Talk to the desk clerk, find out which room our boy Joe Something is in."

"Yeah? And then?"

"We'll go knock on his door."

Mookie chuckled. Big lug was finally getting it.

Delbert leaned back in the seat and adjusted his facemask. Fucking nose was killing him. Use the pain, he told himself, let it remind you of what that bastard did to you.

"Sumbitch won't know what hit him," he growled, making Mookie's laugh rumble some more.

Five stoplights later, Mookie swung the limo into The Pink Elephant's asphalt parking lot and stopped in front of the motel office. He got out and came around to open the back door. Delbert thinking: This is good. Folks inside see the limo, see my chauffeur opening my door, they'll know I'm not somebody to dick around with.

He got out of the car and pushed through the office's glass door. A bell tinkled above his head and the desk clerk—a tall, thin woman with caramel-colored skin and a tidy Afro—looked up at the sound. She wore a name badge that said "Mona Carter."

"Hiya, Mona, how you doing?" he said brightly.

She eyed him suspiciously. Up close, she looked older than he'd first guessed. In her thirties, old enough to have seen a lot of shit in this town.

"I know you?" she said warily.

"My name's Delbert Nash. And this here's my friend George Washington Moore."

Mookie stepped up to the counter that separated them from the clerk, and said, "My friends call me Mookie."

He smiled shyly. Shit, Delbert thought, I need Mookie to scare the crap out of this woman, not flirt with her.

"We're looking for a guy who's staying here," he said. "Name of Joe. You know him?"

Mona took a step backward, putting some distance between them, shaking her head.

"I think you do," Delbert said. "Mookie, convince her to help us out."

A gate stood open at one end of the counter. Mookie was through it and right up against the woman in a flash. Her hands automatically came up to protect her face and Mookie grabbed her by both wrists.

"Tell the man what he needs to know, sister," Mookie said. "Go better for you that way."

"I don't know the guests' names," she said. "I mean, some guy named Joe? Hell, probably half of 'em signed in as 'Joe.'"

"You'd remember this guy," Delbert said. "A little older than me—thirty-nine, forty, something like that. About six feet tall, big through the shoulders. Short black hair with a little gray in it. Looks kinda like that actor, what's-his-name. Clooney."

Recognition dawned in Mona's face, but she said, "Doesn't sound familiar."

Mookie started squeezing her arms, bending them down. Her eyes went round from the pain.

"Don't hurt me," she said. "I've got kids at home."

"Like we give a shit," Delbert snapped. "You better tell me now, you want to see those young'uns again."

Mona's mouth opened wide as Mookie squeezed harder.

"Okay, okay. I think I know who you mean. Sounds like the guy in 102."

"Let her go, Mookie."

Mookie dropped her arms and stepped back. Mona rubbed at her wrists. Her dark eyes had filled with tears.

"Now," Delbert said, "would Joe be in room 102 right this minute?"

"I don't know. I haven't seen him today."

"You got a key to that room?"

"Yeah, but—"

"No buts, lady. Hand over the key, or go another round with Mookie."

She blinked back tears and pulled a drawer open underneath the counter and fished around until she had the right key. She held it up and Mookie plucked it from her hand.

Delbert smiled. It made his face hurt.

"See, Mona? Everything's fine, long as you cooperate with us."

She went stony, staring at Delbert.

"Now, we're gonna go down to room 102 and take a look

around. You're gonna do nothing, got it? You're not calling the cops. You're not warning this guy Joe. You see him before we do, don't say a fuckin' word about any of this. You understand?"

She nodded.

"We want to surprise old Joe," Delbert said. "Ruin our surprise and I'll send Mookie back for another conversation with you."

Delbert turned on his heel and went out the door, Mookie right behind him. They walked briskly down a shaded sidewalk toward Room 102.

"Too bad we had to rough her up," Mookie grumbled. "She's a sweet-looking mama."

"Keep your mind on business."

Delbert knocked on Joe's door and waited a few seconds. Hearing nothing from inside, he used the key to unlock the door. He gestured Mookie to go in first, just in case.

The room was empty. Couple of shirts hung in the closet and the usual toiletries littered the bathroom, but no Joe.

"Look around," Delbert said. "See if there's anything here that'll tell us about this guy."

He stood watch at the door while Mookie went over the place, opening drawers and looking under the bed. Mookie grunted that he'd found something and Delbert found him squatting in the closet, holding a black duffel bag with an ID tag attached to the handle.

"Good work, Mook. What's it say?"

"'Joe Riley.' That must be his name, huh? And there's an address in Chicago."

"We know people in Chicago, don't we? Maybe we can find out a little more about this Joe Riley while we wait for him to come back."

Mookie looked around the room. "We gonna wait here?"

"Let's wait in the limo. We'll park across the way, watch the room, see when he comes back."

Mookie's big face crumpled. He had something on his mind.

"Maybe we should get some lunch first, huh, Delbert?"

"Just go get the limo."

12

Joe Riley showed the tattered photograph to a dozen people at McCarran International Airport without a lick of luck. He was losing hope when he finally caught a break.

A bright-eyed redhead at the America West Airlines counter was more than willing to help. She'd worked the night before, she said, and had just arrived at work to pull a shift for a co-worker who'd gone out of town. The clerk's badge said "Alice." She was in her mid-thirties, and she had jutting cheekbones and a pointy chin. One look at her freckled hands showed why she was so cooperative—no wedding ring. Joe tried his most winning smile as he showed her his business card.

"I'm trying to locate a woman who might've flown out of here last night," he said. "Here's her photo, but she probably looked a lot different. I think she was wearing a short blond wig."

He handed Alice the photo and was surprised when she said immediately, "I remember her."

"You do?"

"Sure. She *was* wearing a blond wig. I wondered about that at the time. You know, maybe she'd had chemotherapy or something, so she didn't have any hair. She was pretty and all, but—"

"You could tell it was a wig?"

"Oh, yeah." She smiled slyly. "Women notice."

"Do you remember her name?"

Alice shook her head. "Lotta people came through here last night. But I remember her face and that wig."

"What about where she was going? Any ideas?"

"I know exactly where she was going. I worked the gate."

"Yeah? And?"

"She was flying to Albuquerque."

Joe's heart pounded. He gingerly took the photo from Alice's grasp and put it back in his pocket. Then he said, "Can you get me on the next flight to Albuquerque?"

She winked at him. "You bet."

Alice punched away at her computer keyboard, then looked up at him. "It's leaving in two hours."

"Perfect."

"You need a round-trip ticket?"

"No. I don't know where I'm going next. I'll be back here eventually, though. My clothes are at my motel."

Joe handed over his MasterCard, hoping there was enough room on the card to cover the expensive same-day ticket. The card was close to maxed out.

Alice efficiently ran the card and printed the ticket. She put it in a paper folder and wrote a phone number on the outside of the envelope.

"Why don't you call me when you get back to town?" she said. "Let me know if you found who you were looking for."

Joe smiled as he took the ticket.

"I'll do that."

13

Sal Venturi's afternoon snack consisted of a mocha cappuccino and two Hostess Twinkies. He leaned over his desk as he bit into the moist cake, trying not to get crumbs all over his lap.

Sal was a man of large appetites. Cigars, bourbon, fine food, and tons of sugar, all making Sal a happy man; a fat man, too. He'd given up wearing belts years ago, and his suspenders were stretched tight as banjo strings.

His secretary, Velma, would say out the side of her mouth, "You're a regular health nut, Sal." That Velma, what a card. Sal could take a hint, though. He made sure she was busy every afternoon before he dug into the cache of sweets he kept in the bottom drawer of his desk. Who needed grief from a fucking secretary?

His intercom buzzed, and Sal swallowed mightily before he pushed the button to respond. "What?"

"Man here to see you," Velma said. "A Mr. Loomis."

Sal hesitated. He didn't know any Loomis. He glanced at his desk calendar. No Loomis. Why didn't Velma tell this guy to take a hike? She knew better. Nobody sees Sal Venturi without an appointment.

He pushed the intercom button, ready to tell her to make this Loomis an appointment for next week or something.

But his office door swung open and a big man in a blue suit sauntered inside like he belonged there. The man looked to be in his mid-forties, about Sal's age. He had a thick neck and a torso like a barrel. Wore his hair cut so close, Sal could see pink scalp peeking through. His features were all centered too closely in his round face. He looked familiar, but Sal was sure he hadn't met him before.

"Hey!" Sal shouted. "What do you mean, busting in here?"

The man's expression didn't change. He walked up to Sal's desk, staring at him with cold gray eyes. Killers had eyes like that; Sal had seen plenty of them over the years. He set down his Twinkie and slid open the middle drawer of his desk. He slipped a fat hand into the drawer, groping for the flat pistol he kept in there.

Loomis came around the desk so quickly it was as if he just appeared next to him. He slammed the drawer shut on Sal's hand.

"Ow! Shit! The fuck you doing?"

Loomis held against the drawer, preventing Sal from pulling his hand free.

"Need to talk to you."

"So fucking talk already," Sal squealed, "but get off my hand. You're breaking it."

Loomis leaned toward him until his mouth was near Sal's ear. "I don't get some cooperation, that hand's gonna be the least of your problems."

Tears sprang to Sal's eyes. Felt like his hand was in a meat grinder.

"Give me a chance here," he pleaded. "Whatever you want. Just let go of that drawer."

Loomis let the pressure off the drawer and Sal pulled his hand free and clutched it to his chest.

"Son of a bitch!" he shouted. "What was that for?"

The big man pushed Sal, who rolled backward in his chair, away from the desk. Loomis opened the drawer and removed the little pistol. He casually pointed it Sal's way.

"This what you were hunting for? This little peashooter?"

"What do you expect? Somebody comes barging into my office. I've got a right to protect myself."

Loomis hitched up his leg and rested a thick haunch on the corner of Sal's desk. "Kind of clients you deal with, you probably need protection."

Sal let go of his injured hand long enough to push up his wire-rimmed glasses. Who the fuck was this guy?

"I don't know what you mean," he said, trying for indignant. "I'm an attorney—"

Loomis leaned forward and slapped Sal on top of the head with the pistol. It happened so suddenly and hurt so much, it felt like he'd been struck by lightning.

"I know all about you," Loomis said. "You're a lawyer, all right, but you don't spend much time in courtrooms. Your real business is lining up hitters."

"'Hitters?' I don't know—"

Whap! Again on top of the head. Sal rubbed a hand over the spot, expecting blood, but found only perspiration.

"I been asking around," Loomis said. "I hear you've got a woman on your string."

Sal licked his lips. He didn't want to tell this big oaf anything, but he didn't want any more pain, either. Sal couldn't stand being hurt. He always knew, if somebody came around, sweating him like this, he'd tell all. Nothing noble about Sal Venturi.

"I know a woman who kills people. Is that what you want to hear?"

Loomis smiled. His rubbery lips stretched without showing any teeth.

"That's better. This woman, she did a job last night at Tropical Bay."

"I don't know anything about—"

Loomis slashed sideways with the gun this time, caught Sal on the temple. His head bounced around on his neck and he couldn't see for a moment. The blurry vision cleared and he found Loomis leaning toward him. Shit. Would've been better to pass out. At least he could've bought some time. Where the hell was Velma? Sal prayed she was calling the cops.

"Yeah. Shit. Yeah, okay? She had a contract on a guy. He was staying at that hotel."

The big man stood, making Sal cower, but Loomis walked around to the opposite side of the desk.

"Pick up that pen and write down her name and address."

Sal felt himself blanch. He gives him Lily's name, and she'd be back to Vegas in a hurry. As scared as he was of this guy, Lily worried him more.

"I couldn't do that," he said. "My work is strictly confidential—"

Loomis snapped the slide on the pistol and pointed it at Sal.

"You depressed or something?"

"What do you mean?"

"I mean, you must be depressed, if you're planning to commit suicide with this little gun."

"I'm not—" Sal sucked in his breath. He'd hand over Lily, or he wouldn't live to finish his Twinkie.

"I don't know if I can write," he gasped. "I think you broke my hand."

"Do your best. I'll make it out."

Sal's left hand shook as he picked up the pen and awkwardly printed "Lily Marsden" and her Scottsdale address on a page of Venturi and Associates stationery. He tore out the paper and handed it over. Loomis glanced at it, stuffed it in his shirt pocket.

"Good boy. You just bought yourself another chance at a long life."

Loomis turned away. As he reached the door, he set the pistol on top of a glass-fronted bookcase.

"Hang on a second," Sal said. "Who the fuck *are* you?"

Loomis paused. He shrugged his broad shoulders, like it didn't matter, and said, "Mel Loomis. I work for Ken Staley at Tropical Bay. Mr. Staley is not a man you want to fuck around with."

"But I didn't—"

"Shut up. You let your hitter knock off somebody in our hotel. That's bad for business."

"You mean you're tracking her down because—"

"Didn't I say shut up?"

Sal snapped his mouth shut so quickly, his teeth clacked together.

"Max Vernon was a piece of shit," Loomis said, "and I don't care that you had him killed. But you made a mistake letting it happen at the hotel."

Sal opened his mouth to object, but Loomis cocked an eyebrow and Sal remembered to shut up.

"I don't give a damn who ordered the hit," Loomis said. "That's not my problem. I'm supposed to take care of the hitter. That's all. But Max's brothers, now that's a different story. I wouldn't be surprised if they're on their way here right now. They're pissed off, son. I was you, I'd find a new line of work in a hurry."

Loomis showed himself out.

Sal sat perfectly still for a minute, thinking. Loomis was right. If some goon like him could figure out Sal's connection to the killing, then it shouldn't be hard for the Vernon brothers, who had their fingers in every pie in town.

"Shit," Sal said aloud. He thought again about Lily and what she'd do when she learned he'd ratted her out to Loomis. "Double shit."

He used his good hand to dial Lily's number. It rang four times, then an anonymous, electronic-sounding voice told him to leave a message. Sal hesitated. What the hell would he say? He hung up the phone and pushed the intercom buzzer.

"Velma, get your ass in here."

She opened the door and leaned against the jamb, cracking her gum.

"Yeah?"

"You just let anybody come waltzing in my office?"

"What was I supposed to do? Chase him off? Big, mean-looking guy like that?"

Sal opened his mouth to yell at her, but swallowed it. He couldn't afford to piss her off. He still needed her.

"I think the son of a bitch broke my hand. You want to drive me to the hospital?"

Velma shrugged and cracked her gum. "Sure. Right now?"

"No, next fucking week. I'll just sit here with my broken hand until you feel like giving me a ride."

"Don't get your shorts in a wad. I'll get my keys."

Sal gingerly poked at his scraped, swelling hand, wondering if the fine bones underneath that layer of fat were shattered. He looked around his desktop and spotted the remains of the Twinkie. He started to reach for it, but changed his mind.

For once in his life, Sal Venturi had lost his appetite.

14

Hi Vernon shook his head as he watched his brother load gear into a burlap bag. He wondered what Norm had planned. All his life, Hi had heard stories about twins who could finish each other's sentences, who could read each other's minds. But near as he could tell, that was a bunch of happy horseshit. He'd been around Norm every day for nearly sixty years and, most of the time, he didn't have the slightest clue what his brother was thinking.

"What we need all that stuff for, Norm?"

"You'll see."

"All right, be mysterious, dammit. Can you at least tell me if you're about ready?"

"Hell, yeah. Let's go."

Norm held the sack out away from his body as he walked, as if it were full of rattlesnakes rather than tools, gloves, and a tight coil of barbed wire. He had a big hogleg revolver hanging out of his coat pocket. Hi wore a shoulder holster to hold the ugly black Glock, and its bulk made his suit coat bulge. He yanked at his lapels, trying to straighten things out, then followed Norm into the sandy yard.

"Let's take your car," Norm said. "I've got too much on my mind to drive."

Hi unlocked his twenty-year-old Lincoln Continental

and flipped a switch to unlock the passenger-side door for Norm. He knew Norm thought he was crazy, keeping his car locked when there was nobody around for miles, but Hi loved this car. Big, black, squared-off land barge. Not like the Lincolns they make nowadays, all curvy and sleek, look like something a Japanese factory would squirt out. Hi's car felt *substantial*.

He cranked up the engine and they roared away, up the two-mile-long driveway that connected to the nearest highway, a spiral of tan dust rooster-tailing behind them. Then, ba-boom, up onto the blacktop, the Lincoln quickly leveling out at eighty miles per hour, headed for Vegas.

Once they reached the city limits, Norm shouted over the roaring air conditioner, "Where you reckon he'll be?"

"This time of day? Home, I guess. He doesn't go to work until eight or something."

"What if he's not there?"

"We'll find him."

"Then we go find Marla?"

"Hell, she'll be at home, won't she? Playing the grieving widow?"

Norm's teeth showed beneath his big mustache. "Might have to make it a double funeral. Her and Max together."

"Maybe she'll decide she can't go on living without him."

Norm snorted, said, "There's your turn."

"I see it, dammit."

Teddy Valentine lived in Spanish Hills, a suburb that had sprung up from the desert on the southwest side of Vegas. The developers had yellow billboards all over town, advertising their "Extraordinary Custom Homes." Teddy's might've been "custom," but Hi didn't see much extraordinary about it. Looked like every other rambling stucco house in every other subdivision around Las Vegas—Spanish tile roof, a patch of vivid lawn the size of a welcome mat, rock gardens full of cactus and yucca.

It was mid-afternoon, and most people were still at work. The wind-whipped streets were devoid of life, not even dogs or children (which Hi lumped into the same category) running around. No sense in subterfuge, he figured, as he steered the Lincoln right into Teddy Valentine's driveway, parking it next to a sleek, red Corvette.

"Look at that fuckin' car," Norm said. "Man drives a flashy car like that, his pecker must be about one inch long."

"Does appear he's compensating for something," Hi said. "Reckon we'll find out what he's made of here shortly."

They strolled to the front door, Norm holding the burlap bag out away from his body. Hi noticed shiny barbs poking through the loose fabric. They caught the sunlight like deadly glitter.

Norm rang the doorbell and they waited a while, then he rang it again. Finally, the front door was snatched open and there stood Teddy Valentine, wearing a white bathrobe with The Cactus Ranch logo on the breast. His thick black hair was mussed and his unshaven face looked blue where the stubble stood. His eyes sparked when he saw them and he glanced over his shoulder with something like panic. He caught himself and pulled his face together and said, "The big boss men. How's it going?"

Norm pushed his way into the living room before Teddy could consider closing the door. Hi followed, his hand inside his jacket on the butt of the Glock. He didn't think Teddy would try anything, but the Italian was young and tall and well-built. Hi drifted toward a wall and leaned against it, keeping his hand on his gun and his eyes on Teddy.

"You look like you just got outta bed," Norm said.

Teddy seemed to have noticed the burlap bag for the first time. He tried to look Norm in the face while he talked, but his eyes kept straying nervously to that dangling bag.

"I wasn't feeling so hot. Think I'm getting a cold or something. I'll be all right in time for work."

Hi heard a distant footfall. Someone else was in the house. He stepped away from the wall and glanced at Norm. He'd heard it, too. Hi nodded at him and unholstered the Glock. Norm pulled the revolver from his pocket and pointed it at Teddy's chest. Teddy's jaw dropped. Hi eased toward a hallway that split off to his right.

"Hey, fellas," Teddy said, "what's with the guns?"

"You don't know?" Norm said. "Max sent us."

Hi wanted to turn around, see Teddy's reaction to that, but he crept forward, searching for the source of the noise. He checked a couple of empty rooms, found his way to Teddy's bedroom. The king-sized bed had scarlet silk sheets, thrown back and rumpled. The walls were red brocade with fake gold trim around the edges.

"Kee-rist," Hi said aloud. "This fucker thinks he's Liberace."

A strip of light showed under a door. Hi slipped up to it, pistol at the ready, twisted the knob and threw open the door.

A yelp of surprise. A tall, leggy woman stood in a small bathroom, her back against the tile wall, squeezed in tight between toilet and tub. She wore a short black nightgown with spaghetti straps and her hair was a tangled pile of blond wire.

Hi lowered the Glock and smiled at her.

"Howdy, Marla."

15

Mel Loomis loved the corporate life. Soon as he got the information he needed from that weasel Sal Venturi, he was on his company-provided cellular phone with Ken Staley, telling him he needed to fly to Phoenix. By the time Loomis drove to the airport, Staley had Tropical Bay's private jet warmed up and ready for the runway. A short hop to Phoenix, where a car was waiting. No little piece-of-shit foreign job, either; a Cadillac, comfortable, new, and formidable. As requested, the car had a loaded .45-caliber pistol in the glove compartment.

Loomis had worked a lot of jobs over the years—night watchman, bartender, bouncer, security for a number of firms and small casinos. But working for a big-money corporation was the sweetest. Throw enough dollars at a problem, you get immediate results.

Loomis steered the Cadillac up to the address in Scottsdale. The place was a condominium complex, done up in red tile and white stucco and palm trees. Reminded him of places he'd visited in the Mediterranean, years ago, when he did a stint in the Navy. But Scottsdale didn't have the rolling hills and sea breezes of the Riviera. It was as flat and hot as a skillet.

He tucked the .45 into his belt as he got out of the Caddy. He didn't think he'd need the gun, not yet. He planned to just look around, get a feel for the place, see if the woman was even home. But it paid to be careful. This Lily Marsden was a contract killer. Most likely, she had a few guns lying around the house.

Loomis found her unit and checked to make sure no one was around before he stepped through some greenery to peek in a window. He could see into her bare kitchen. No sounds coming from inside, nobody moving around. He made his way around to the back, by the pool, and found sliding glass doors. He checked the lock, found it would be a snap. He got out his pocketknife.

A few minutes later, Loomis was inside Lily's condo. The place was spartan and stuffy. The few houseplants were wilted from thirst. Lots of clothes in the bedroom closet, but Lily Marsden clearly wasn't home much. He wondered where she was right now.

He used his cell phone to dial a number in Vegas.

"Venturi and Associates."

"Is Sal there?"

"May I say who's calling?"

"I'm the guy who visited earlier today. Put him on the phone. Now."

"Yes, sir."

Loomis paced around the condo's living room while he waited.

"Hello?" Venturi's voice sounded squeaky.

"I'm at that address you gave me. The woman's not here."

"I can't help that! How am I supposed to know whether she's home? I'm not her mother."

Loomis let silence build over the phone line. He didn't need to sweat Venturi. Fat bastard was too scared to stay quiet long.

"You know where I just came from? The fucking emergency room. Had to have my hand bandaged up. X-rays say it's not broken, but it's all black and blue. And I may have a concussion!"

Loomis smiled to himself. The attorney tried hard to act indignant, but fear kept that chipmunk squeak in his voice.

"Did the doctor give you a prognosis?"

Venturi hesitated. "What do you mean?"

"Like, you're not gonna live long unless you tell me what I need to know."

Venturi said nothing for a minute. Loomis waited patiently, letting the silence do its work.

"She may be on a job," Venturi said finally. "I gave her a contract earlier, before you showed up here. I didn't think she would've already left."

"Where?"

"Albuquerque."

"She just got back from Vegas, doing a job, and now she's already gone off to Albuquerque?"

"It was a rush job."

"Fuck, what are you guys, Federal Express? You deliver overnight?"

Venturi didn't answer.

"Where's she staying?"

"I don't know. She never gives me any details. She just calls me when the job is done and I send her the money. I'm never directly involved because—"

"Shut up." Loomis thought for a moment. "Who's the target?"

"Now, look, I can't just give out—"

"Tell me now, or I'll be back in Vegas in an hour. And you'll be dead ten minutes later."

No pause this time.

"Guy name of Marty Holguin. He sells rugs."

"You're shittin' me."

"It's a long story. Anyway, he lives at Seventy-three Vista Grande Lane, up in the foothills."

Loomis memorized the address. He could call the plane, have it ready to go when he got to the airport. Be in Albuquerque in a couple of hours.

"Are we done now?" Venturi squeaked. "I don't want to be involved in this any further—"

Loomis pushed a button and—beep!—cut him off.

16

Hi Vernon kept his pistol trained on his sister-in-law while Norm worked over Teddy Valentine. She sat on a couch in the living room, her tanned knees together, her feet splayed, her hands covering her mouth. Tears ran from her eyes, leaving snail-tracks of black mascara. Teddy grunted and wept and gasped, but Hi didn't turn to see. This was Norm's show. Might as well let him enjoy it.

Besides, Hi had seen plenty already. He'd watched, fascinated, while Norm trussed a naked Teddy to a wooden chair from the dining room. Norm wore heavy canvas gloves he'd brought in the burlap bag, and he'd used a pair of oversized pliers to twist the barbed wire tight around Teddy's wrists. Norm wrapped the wire around his ankles, too, tying them to the legs of the chair. The barbs bit into the flesh and blood dribbled onto the white carpet.

Teddy had been gagged to hold down on the howling while Norm was trussing him up, but now he spewed expletives and threats and pleas through clenched teeth while Norm used pliers on him.

Hi glanced over his shoulder. Norm bent over Teddy, talking quietly into his face. Norm had removed his Stetson and sweat sparkled on his forehead above his bushy eyebrow. His eyes were hard. Norm always looked that way when his mean streak got out of control. When they were boys, Hi knew such a look meant to go hide somewhere until Norm got a chance to cool down.

"I'm gonna ask you again," Norm said tightly. "Did you or did you not order a hit on Max?"

Teddy's face was so wet with sweat and tears, it looked like someone had thrown a bucket of water over him.

"I *told* you," he whimpered, "I don't know what you're talking about."

Norm used both gloved hands to grab Teddy's left nipple with the pliers. He twisted, and Teddy arched his back against the pain. He shut his eyes tight and wailed through clenched teeth.

Norm relaxed his grip on the pliers and leaned into Teddy's face.

"It's like this, Teddy. I am gonna kill you today. If nothing else, I'd kill you for having Marla over here, screwing her before we've even put Max in the ground. But how you die? That's up to you. Tell me what I want to know and I'll make it a quick bullet to the head. But you keep pretending you don't know anything, and this will last 'til morning."

Teddy blinked open his eyes. His lower lip trembled.

Marla sobbed loudly and buried her face in her hands. Her blond mane spilled forward. Hi thinking: Marla figures she's going to die, too. Maybe she's not as dumb as I always thought.

Norm hadn't broken his eye-lock with Teddy. He said, "Shut that bitch up, Hi."

Hi took a step toward Marla, his gun pointed at her head. She looked up and quickly stifled her weeping.

"That's better," Norm said. "Now what's it gonna be, Teddy?"

Teddy took a shuddering breath and tried to look brave. "Let her go and I'll talk."

Norm straightened up. "Oh, that's what's bothering you? You think we'd hurt Marla?"

"She didn't know anything about it," Teddy said. "She didn't do anything."

"Bullshit."

Teddy's lower jaw jutted out. The boy still had some fight left in him. Marla lifted her face from her hands and hope blossomed in her teary eyes.

"Let her go or I tell you nothing."

Norm whipped the revolver from his waistband and wheeled. Boom! Marla slammed backward into the sofa. Blood spurted out of a ragged red hole in her forehead.

Hi wrinkled his nose as gunsmoke wafted toward the ceiling.

"There now," Norm said to Teddy. "You don't have to worry about her no more."

"I, I, I—"

"You seem to be developing a stutter there, Teddy," Hi said. "Maybe Norm needs to use those pliers on your tongue."

"All right, all right! It was Marla's idea! She was in love with me. Told me we could get Max out of the picture, and she'd inherit The Cactus Ranch. Then we could get married and shit. She had it all worked out. I just made some phone calls—"

"Who'd you call, Teddy?" Norm's voice was low and menacing. He tucked the revolver into his waistband and picked up the pliers again.

"Lawyer here in town, Sal Venturi. He makes people disappear, you know?"

"He sent some woman to kill Max?"

"Yeah. I mean, I guess so. I didn't know it was no bitch who'd do the job. Makes sense, though, if you knew Max—"

Norm clamped the pliers on Teddy's nipple and gave them a savage twist.

"Aiyeeee!" Teddy writhed in the chair, which made the barbed wire cut tighter into his skin.

"Don't talk bad about Max," Norm said. "That would be speaking ill of the dead."

Once Norm removed the pliers, Hi asked, "How much did you pay, Teddy?"

Teddy gulped air before he could answer. "Twenty-five grand. Including Venturi's commission."

"Where'd you get the money, Teddy? You got twenty-five grand just lying around the house?"

"I took it. From Max's office."

"You stole the money?" Norm said. "You had Max killed with his own money?"

"It was Marla's idea!"

"Fuck that."

Norm bashed Teddy across the face with the big pliers. Blood showered across the room, dappled the carpet. Norm hit him twice more, laying open the skin to the bone. Teddy's head bobbed around on his neck. Out cold.

Norm raised his arm to hit him again, but Hi said, "Norm!" and his brother stopped and turned toward him.

"We need to finish," Hi said. "Somebody might've heard that shot."

"I'm not done with him."

"Sure you are."

Hi raised the Glock and shot Teddy in the face. The back of his head exploded onto the wall beyond.

Norm stared at Teddy for a moment, then turned back to Hi.

"Shit. I wasn't done."

"Let's go, Norm."

"You old horse's ass. You never let me have any fun."

17

Joe listened to the phone ring six times in Sam Kilian's Chicago home before Sam groggily answered.

"Sam, it's Joe."

"Joe? Jesus, what time is it?"

"It's like one a.m. No, it's two your time."

"Christ, I've only been asleep an hour. The kids were up half the night, puking their darling little guts out. I think they've got the flu."

"You're awake now. Listen, I've got news."

Joe glanced around the Albuquerque airport. A handful of passengers lounged around a waiting area and a few janitors were sweeping up. All the cafes and newsstands were locked up tight. A couple of armed security guards eyed him, but they were a long way off. No one was within earshot. He waited for Sam to ask what he had. He wanted to make sure Sam was fully awake before he sprang it on him.

"I've got her, Sam."

"You what?"

"I've found our girl. Or, as good as. I've got a name. I've got an address."

"Holy shit!"

"Quiet. You'll wake the whole family."

"How'd you do it?" Sam whispered.

"Legwork, buddy. Just like I've always told you."

He quickly recounted the murder in Vegas, the similar m.o., and the flirty airline clerk who recognized the photo.

"She got me on a plane to Albuquerque right away. I got here and showed the picture all over and nothing, right? Nobody's seen our girl. But I remembered she likes to gamble. So I asked somebody and it turns out there's a big-ass Indian casino just south of the airport. I go over there and show her photo some more and there's this security guard, and he's seen her, but she had short dark hair."

"Knew that was a fuckin' wig," Sam said.

"That's what I told him. And not only did this guy remember her, he says no way was the dark hair a wig. Her hair was nearly as short as mine."

"So now you know what she looks like."

"Not only that, but the guard knows where she went. She arrived by cab, and he knows the driver, another Indian guy who's always cruising the casino. One thing leads to another, I find her motel, and I get a positive ID on her. Lily Marsden. Scottsdale, Arizona."

"Might be a fake."

"Maybe. But she flew to Phoenix from here under that name. I think she was going home."

There was a pause, then Sam said, "You going after her?"

"I'm booked on a redeye, takes off in about five hours."

"What are you going to do when you get there? You're not a cop anymore, Joe."

"I know that." Joe didn't want an ethics lecture. "I'll see what the situation is when I get there. Get her under surveillance. Call the locals and let them have the bust."

"Don't go playing hero, man. That won't solve anything. You need to see that woman in a courtroom."

"I know, I know. But it's her, Sam. I'm sure of it. I'm so close I can taste it."

Another pause.

"That's great, buddy. Go get her."

"Sam? I need a favor. Run her through the computers first thing in the morning, will you? See if you turn anything up?"

An electronic voice came over the line and demanded that Joe deposit another dollar-thirty-five into the pay phone to keep talking.

Sam talked over it, saying, "Will do."

"Gotta go. I'll call you later."

"Joe? Be carefu—"

The electronic voice started again, and Joe hung up. He walked to the waiting area, looking for a place to stretch out, but he knew he was too wired to sleep.

18

Detective Susan Pine yawned so wide, it felt like her jaw would come unhinged. One hell of a long day. Started bright and early with her first murder case, Max Vernon, strangled over at Tropical Bay. Now, ten hours later—Friday evening, when she should be having dinner, going on a date, having a *life*—she's in a blood-spattered living room, with a couple of corpses to keep her company. Was this life in Homicide? Was this her future?

At least she had a future. More than she could say for Teddy Valentine and Marla Vernon. Valentine still sat naked in the straight-backed chair, bloody barbed wire around his wrists and ankles, a ragged hole between his eyebrows. Marla was rocked back on the sofa, her legs askew, a bullet through her head, too.

"Sick bastards," she muttered. "Jesus."

"What's that, Detective?" one of the evidence techs asked.

"Nothing. Keep busy. I want to get this scene wrapped up and go home."

The tech turned back to his work, squatting on the floor, placing a little flag next to a brass shell casing. Cameras flashed.

Susan stood in the center of the room, her hands on her

hips, and turned slowly, her eyes taking in every detail. The only place she let her gaze slip was the spot on the wall where Teddy Valentine's blood and brains had created a masterpiece of abstract expressionism. She'd seen enough of that already.

She estimated the evidence techs needed another hour to finish up. The coroner could bag the bodies and get them out of here. Then Susan and Harold would go back to the squadroom, start working up their reports. Way things were going, she wouldn't get home until midnight.

Where the hell was Harold anyway?

"Anybody seen Detective Campbell?"

The same tech looked up at her. "Think he went outside for a cigarette."

"Figures."

Susan marched to the front door and poked her head out, looking around for Harold. A couple of uniforms held the reporters and TV cameramen at bay out at the curb. The reporters eyeballed her, but they didn't recognize her as a homicide detective and didn't shout questions. Just as well. In the mood she was in, Susan might start shooting at them.

She sniffed the air, following the scent of smoke around the corner of the house, where Harold stood in the dark, the tip of his coffin nail glowing orange.

"Hey," he said. "Everything okay?"

"No, everything's not okay. We've got two victims in there and I don't have the slightest idea who killed them."

"Sure you do."

"What?" Susan maneuvered to the side, trying to get upwind of the cigarette smoke and Harold's rank breath.

"You've got all kinds of ideas," he said. "So do I. The problem's not coming up with possible killers. It's narrowing down the list."

Susan paused. Since they were made partners, this was the first thing Harold had said that made a lick of sense. Maybe she could learn something from him after all.

"How do we do that?"

Harold fumbled in his pocket, came up with another cigarette, lit it with the butt of the first, and tossed the glowing butt into the neighbor's yard.

"Ain't gonna be easy," he said. "Probably a lot of people wanted Valentine dead."

"You knew this guy?"

"Seen him around. He was a prick."

"And Marla? Did you know her, too?"

"No. But she's in her nightgown at Teddy's house. Looks to me like they were doing a little daytime celebrating."

"Celebrating what? Her husband's death?"

"Sure." Harold took another drag on his cigarette. The glow illuminated his ravaged face. His eyes looked weary.

"Think Teddy and Marla had Max Vernon killed?"

Harold shrugged, huffed out smoke. "Too late to ask them now."

"I tried to reach Marla earlier. Ask her about Max. Nobody was home."

"She was over here, busy being dead."

Susan said nothing for a minute, trying to piece it all together.

"So Teddy and Marla have a thing going. They figure they can bump Max and get him out of the way."

"That's what I'm thinking," he said.

"That wasn't Marla on the videotape."

"No, she's even taller than the woman who killed Max. Besides, why would Max hook up with his own wife at Tropical Bay?"

"A romantic evening?"

"Doesn't sound like Max. Way we keep hearing it, Max was a hound. He picked up some skirt and she killed him."

"Okay. So you think Teddy and Marla hired that woman. They knew he'd take the bait—"

"Maybe Max just picked up the wrong skirt. Maybe they had nothing to do with it."

"Then why do they get dead the next day?"

Harold sucked the cigarette down to the filter and tossed it onto the neighbor's smooth lawn, where the other one still smoldered.

"You trying to burn down the neighborhood?"

"Can't leave butts over here. Contaminates the crime scene."

"So you contaminate the neighbor's yard instead?'

"Screw 'em."

Harold coughed and spat on the ground. Susan didn't mention that phlegm was a contaminant, too. She was thinking about Marla and Teddy. They were small-timers, running around behind Max Vernon's back. Could they have located a contract killer?

"See, it doesn't matter whether they hired the hitter," Harold said, reading her mind. "They're dead. We can't charge them with conspiracy to commit murder. The question now is, who killed them?"

"And why," she said.

"Right."

"Max's brothers?"

"Could be. They were pretty pissed. Say they came over here, found Teddy and Marla messing around. Might be a motive right there."

"But what's with the torture? Looks like somebody took his time killing Teddy."

"Get him to talk. Tell them about the contract."

"So they could do what? Go gunning for the hitter?"

Harold shrugged again.

"Maybe it's got nothing to do with the brothers," she said. "Maybe somebody's got a grudge against The Cactus Ranch. The owner, his wife, the floor manager, all killed."

Harold shuffled his feet in the dark. He'd had his nicotine dose, looked like he was ready to go back inside.

"Could be."

"Maybe we ought to look at that guy I told you about. The one at Tropical Bay, said he was cop. He seemed way too interested in Max's death."

Harold slipped around some shrubbery that crouched darkly against the side of the house, Susan on his heels.

"And then there's Ken Staley," she said. "He and that guy Loomis were plenty unhappy that Max was killed at Tropical Bay. Staley's already called the chief, trying to get it hushed up."

Harold hunched his shoulders as a couple of the TV cameramen turned on their cameras and threw bright white light at them across the front lawn. He jerked a thumb at the corralled reporters, said, "Too late for that now."

Susan wanted to talk some more, do more speculating with Harold. The old guy finally was showing some signs of life. But Harold ducked through the doorway and into the bloody living room.

He looked around at the busy evidence techs and sighed.

"Are we about done here?" he said loudly. "Think you could finish before my retirement comes up? I'd rather not spend my golden years in this dump."

19

It took Joe an hour Saturday morning to find Lily Marsden's address in Scottsdale. He roared up and down residential streets in a rental car until he finally located the right street, a quiet cul-de-sac lined with scrawny palm trees. As he pulled up to the condo complex, he got a sinking feeling. A patrol car was parked outside Lily Marsden's open door. A uniformed cop wearing rubber gloves was going inside.

Shit. Somebody beat him to the punch. He wanted to get to her first, look her in the eye when he accused her of Bennie Burrows' murder. But clearly the local cops were all over her.

Joe parked and strolled up to the door. No crime scene tape up anywhere. No sign of any detectives. Just a couple of young uniformed cops inside, "rookie" stamped all over them, looking around the place like they had no idea what they were doing. Maybe he could bluff his way inside.

Joe knocked on the doorframe and the two cops turned toward him.

"What's going on?"

The taller of the two cops said, "You a neighbor?"

"No, I'm a cop. Well, a retired cop. Homicide outta Chicago. I'm looking for the woman who lives here."

The tall cop relaxed and smiled, looked happy to have somebody with some experience on the scene.

"Burglary call," he said. "Manager noticed those glass doors over there had been jimmied."

Joe glanced around the living room. Sony television, a VCR and a stereo occupied a bookshelf against one wall.

"Looks like they left the goods," he said. "Anything missing?"

The tall cop shrugged. "Who can tell? The owner's not here and the manager doesn't know where to find her. We were just gonna lock the place up and file a report."

"Mind if I look around first?"

The cop's eyes narrowed. "Who'd you say you were again?"

"Name's Joe Riley. I've been tracking this woman, Lily Marsden. This is her place, right?"

"That's what the manager said. Why you looking for her?"

"I think she's a killer."

Both of the Junior G-men gaped at him. "No shit?"

"None at all. I think she killed a guy I knew in Chicago. Another guy in Las Vegas on Thursday night. Maybe more."

"Get outta here."

"I'm serious. I just want to look around, get a feel for her. Only take a minute."

The cops swapped a look. The tall one said, "Help yourself." Apparently, the short cop never spoke.

Joe walked through the condo, taking his time, opening drawers and looking under furniture. He found a pistol taped under a dresser drawer, another stashed on a closet shelf. He left both where they were.

"Think we ought to bag those guns?" the tall cop asked.

"I don't know of any shootings. The two guys I think she killed, she strangled them with wire."

"Jeez."

Joe went to the kitchen, the pups right on his heels. Joe thinking: They act like they're on a freaking field trip. Wonder what they're supposed to be doing right now? Who's out there protecting the public of Greater Scottsdale?

He reached for the refrigerator door and the tall cop said, "Nothing much in there. Don't think this lady's home much."

Joe cocked an eyebrow at him. "You looked in the fridge?"

The short cop blushed, and Joe guessed he'd been hunting up a snack. The youngsters were right, though. Hardly anything in the refrigerator. Dying houseplants. Dust on the furniture. The place hadn't been occupied lately.

Joe returned to the living room, gave it one last look. His gaze settled on a phone on an end table.

"Mind if I use the phone?" he asked.

"Sure. Go ahead."

Joe dialed *69 and listened to the beeps for the last number that called this line. It rang a couple of times, then a woman said, "Venturi and Associates."

He hadn't expected to be lucky enough to get an answer. "Hi there. Who's this?"

"This is the Venturi and Associates law firm. Velma speaking."

She had a flat tone to her voice, like she'd been bored with her job for a long time. Sounded like she was chewing gum, too, cracking it into the phone. Joe hated that habit.

"Hello, Velma," he said. "I'm trying to locate your office and I don't have the address."

"Okay, sugar. Ready? It's fourteen-forty-seven Tropicana Boulevard. You know where that is?"

"In Vegas, right?"

Velma laughed. "Right, in Vegas, west of the Strip. That's a good one. 'In Vegas.'"

Joe chuckled merrily along, thinking, here I go, back to Las Vegas.

"Do you have an appointment with someone here?" she asked.

"No, I'm looking for Lily Marsden. Does she work there?"

Velma's voice went stiff and cold. "I'm sorry, but I don't know anyone by that name."

"I thought maybe she was connected to your firm."

"We don't have anyone by that name. We're a small firm. I know everyone here."

"Maybe my information's wrong. Sorry to bother you."

Velma hung up without saying good-bye.

20

Hi Vernon never slept better in his life. He woke up late Saturday morning, feeling cool and relaxed against his cotton sheets, sun pouring in the window and birds chirping outside.

He got up, pissed, brushed his teeth, and combed his hair and thick mustache. He put on a bathrobe and went downstairs to the kitchen to see if Norm was up yet, and whether he'd made coffee.

Norm was waiting in the kitchen, showered and dressed already, an empty plate pushed aside and the morning newspaper propped against his coffee mug.

"Look who finally rolled out of bed," Norm said. "Thought you was gonna sleep all day."

"Up yours. Old men get to sleep in on Saturdays."

"I thought we plumb wore you out yesterday," Norm said, his mustache bristling. "All that activity too much for you."

"You did all the hard work. I was just along for the ride."

Hi poured some coffee from the speckled enamel pot that sat on the gas stove. Cowboy coffee. Strong enough to remove rust and unclog drains. He took a healthy sip, then said, "What are you doing up so early? Have trouble sleeping?"

"Little bit."

"Worried about yesterday?"

"Hell, no. I was thinking about today. We need to go see Sal Venturi, find that woman."

Hi took another sip before he said anything.

"I don't know, Norm. Gonna be a lot of heat after yesterday's work. And Teddy and Marla *were* responsible for it. Maybe we've done enough."

Norm gave him a stony stare. "I don't reckon Max would've seen it that way."

"No, but—"

Hi stopped and cocked an ear. He could hear a car. A ways off yet, but headed their direction. He stepped over to a window and looked out to the west. A plume of dust rose from the long driveway.

"We got company," Hi said. "I'd better put on some pants."

He was tucking in his shirttail by the time the doorbell rang. He gave his face one last glance in the mirror, smoothed down his tumbleweed of an eyebrow, then went over to a window that overlooked the front yard. A white Chevy Caprice was parked there, looked like an unmarked cop car. He could hear Norm answering the door. Shit.

Hi reached the parlor to find Norm talking to the two detectives he'd seen the day before at Ken Staley's office. The young woman wore a plain brown suit and a purse slung over her shoulder. The other cop, an older man with wavy gray hair and a face like a bloodhound, waited by the door, letting his partner do the talking.

"Hello, what do we have here?" Hi said as he reached the bottom of the stairs.

The woman showed Hi her badge and introduced herself as Detective Susan Pine. Hi didn't catch her partner's name, but he said to the woman, "I remember you. We met yesterday. How's the investigation coming?"

"We're making progress," she said, "but there have been two more murders."

Hi glanced at Norm, couldn't tell whether his brother had let on yet that he knew about Teddy and Marla being dead. Was it in that newspaper Norm had been reading in the kitchen? Hi hesitated, but he needn't have worried. Norm picked up his cue.

"You better brace yourself, Hi. This lady here says Marla's been killed."

Hi made a show of acting surprised. He didn't know how well his expressions communicated, especially to women. His face was hidden behind the eyebrow and mustache and thick glasses. It was a disguise that served him well in business, but women often didn't seem to know what he was thinking.

"Oh, my God," he said. "What happened?"

"Somebody shot her," Norm said. "Shot Teddy Valentine, too."

"Teddy? That guy from The Cactus Ranch?"

"That's the one," Norm said. "Night floor manager."

"My Lord!" Hi was playing it up now, and he wondered whether he was coming on too strong. But the little lady detective seemed convinced. The skin around her dark eyes crinkled in sympathy.

"I'm sorry to bring you this bad news," she said. "But I felt we should talk to you first thing this morning."

"Does Marla's family know?" Nice touch, Hi.

"They were informed last night, but it was pretty late. We thought we'd rather come out this morning, tell you two face-to-face."

"We appreciate that," Norm said. "I just can't believe Marla's gone. She was so young and full of life."

"I've always worried about that girl," Hi said. "She was a showgirl, you know. When she was younger. Always had a taste for the night life."

"Lot younger than Max, too," Norm said. "That often spells trouble."

Detective Pine gave Hi the hard eye now, like maybe she suspected they were putting her on. She might have more on the ball than it appeared at first glance. Skinny and squirrelly, the kind of high-strung woman Hi always tried to avoid. But her voice was low and her gaze was direct. Better watch myself around her, Hi thought, and I sure as hell better keep an eye on Norm.

"Well, thank you for driving all the way out here," he said. "I guess we oughta call the funeral home, see if we can help with the arrangements."

The detective said nothing.

"This sure is a shock."

She kept staring at him. Hi felt a little flop in his stomach, and he wondered what she really wanted. If it was just to give them the news, she could've done it over the phone. Her partner leaned silently against the wall, studying his fingernails.

"I hate to ask," the woman said, "but where did you two go yesterday after Staley's office?"

Hi felt Norm looking at him.

"We went to the funeral home," Hi said. "Started making the arrangements for Max, then we came back here."

"Made a lot of phone calls," Norm added. "Business stuff. Max was an important part of our operations. He'll be hard to replace."

Susan Pine showed no sign of hearing Norm. She kept her stare on Hi.

"What about later in the afternoon?" she said. "Around four o'clock, something like that?"

"We were right here," Hi said. "Why do you ask?"

The detective's cheeks flushed, but she bulled ahead.

"You two could be considered suspects in these deaths. You were naturally upset about your brother's murder. And Mrs. Vernon and this Teddy Valentine seemed to be having some sort of affair."

"Really?" Hi said. "I'll be damned. I didn't know anything about that. D'you, Norm?"

"No. I sure would've been upset if I'd known they were messing around behind Max's back."

Susan Pine flushed some more.

"We're not a hundred percent sure that's what was going on, but she was at Valentine's house in a nightgown when she was shot."

"Son of a bitch," Hi said. "Excuse my French, but that sure seems fishy."

The detective gave him that level stare some more, but Hi didn't volunteer anything else.

"Anybody who could vouch for your whereabouts?" she asked.

Hi pretended to think it over. "No, I don't imagine there is. Norm and I were the only ones here. As you can see, we don't have any neighbors close by."

Susan Pine rifled through her purse as he talked. She pulled out a little notebook and a pen and wrote something down. Hi didn't like the looks of that.

"See here, young lady," he said. "Are you planning to arrest us or something? 'Cause I'm thinking you wouldn't want to make a mistake like that. We know a lot of people in Vegas."

"So I've heard," she said dryly. She didn't look up, just wrote some more.

"You know, Las Vegas wouldn't even exist if it weren't for us Vernons," Hi said. "Our daddy's the one who air-conditioned the first casinos and houses around here. Before that, Las Vegas wasn't nothing but a place to water your cows."

"Hmm-mm." Her mind clearly was elsewhere. Hi wished to hell he knew what she was thinking, but he'd never been much good at reading women. They were complicated.

She flipped over a page in the notebook. "Do you own a nine-millimeter pistol?"

Hi glanced over at Norm, who was staring at the detective with steely eyes. Uh-oh. Hi sure as hell hoped Norm wasn't planning to make some kind of move.

"We've got all kinds of guns," he said. "Have to have 'em, living way out here in the boondocks."

"Any of them been fired recently?"

"Don't think so. Norm, you been shooting any coyotes lately?"

"Nope."

Susan Pine looked from one brother to the other.

"Mind if I examine these guns?"

Norm's face flushed. "What the hell—"

"Easy, Norm," Hi said. "No sense getting your back up. This lady's just doing her job."

"So you'll show me the guns?"

Hi grinned at her. "I don't think so. You want to come sniffing around our house, you're gonna have to get a warrant."

"You got something to hide?"

"Nope. But them's the rules. You want to bird-dog us, you're gonna have to go through the proper channels. And you can bet we'll have a lawyer there to greet you."

The detective studied him a minute, then closed the notebook and put it back in her purse.

"All right," she said. "We'll play it your way."

She turned and nodded at her partner, who opened the door for her. A gust of hot wind swirled into the room.

"Ma'am?" Hi said. "I hope you're not planning on wasting a lot of time chasing after Norm and me. That's not gonna do you any good. You'd be better off hunting whoever killed our baby brother."

She gave him a curt nod and stalked out into the heat, her silent partner right behind her. The door closed.

Hi waited a few beats before he turned to Norm. His brother was grinning widely, his mustache stretched from ear to ear.

"See there?" Norm said. "They got nothing on us. Not a damned thing to worry about."

"I don't know. I didn't like that woman's looks. She's one of them nervous types who'll worry a problem to death."

"Don't give her another thought," Norm said. "We got bigger fish to fry. I want to go talk to Sal Venturi."

Hi started to object, but Norm had that look in his eyes.

"Hell. Can I at least have some breakfast first?"

21

Ken Staley sat at his kitchen table, staring through the patio doors at the emerald-green golf course that rolled past the rear of his palatial home. The maid had already cleared away his breakfast dishes, and he was having one last cup of coffee before heading to Tropical Bay. He closed his eyes and pictured himself perched in his top-floor office, like a tick on a dog's ear, sucking money out of the casino and hotel rooms below.

Nice imagery, he thought, seeing myself as a bloodsucker. Maybe I need to work on my self-esteem.

"Have you *seen* this?" Patti's voice came from behind him. Good Lord. He immediately regretted dawdling over this last cup. He could've made his escape.

He turned toward the doorway. Patti stood there, thrusting a newspaper toward him as if it were a spear. She wore a terry-cloth robe and she had a white towel wrapped around her head like a turban. Her face was covered in a pale green goo, all except her eyes, which were surrounded by pools of pale skin.

"The hell is that on your face?"

"Cucumber masque," she said tightly. Looked like she was afraid to move her lips and crack the green gunk. "It prevents wrinkles."

"I thought we had Dr. Scott to tend to your wrinkles." He knew he was taking a chance. Patti liked to pretend she'd never had a face lift or a boob job or a liposuction. Like a woman her age could naturally look like a fucking Barbie doll.

"Up yours," Patti said through stiff lips. "Have you seen the paper?"

She walked over and forced the Sun-Journal into his hands. It was folded open to an inside page. He'd seen the headline earlier: "Police Search for Clues in Murder at Posh New Resort." He should've left for the office the minute he saw the newspaper, gotten the hell out before Patti read it.

"I thought you were getting the editor to play it down," she said.

"I tried. He said he'd see what he could do to bury the fact it happened at Tropical Bay."

"It's right there in the goddamned headline."

"I'll call him again. I talked to the chief of police, too. Asked him to keep it quiet. But, Christ, Patti, it's a murder. There's no hiding it."

"If your security goons were any good, they would've just put the body in a Dumpster behind Luxor or Bellagio. Let *them* eat the bad publicity."

"I'll mention that to them," Ken said. "Next time there's a murder, act like it's Watergate. Hide everything. Pretend nothing happened. See how the cops like that."

Patti glared at him through the holes in her green mask.

"Be better than this kind of publicity," she said. "I called Arlene over at the booking office and, guess what? Three tours canceled already, took their business elsewhere."

"Bus tours," Ken sniffed. "Old geezers who play the nickel slots. Who needs 'em? The real gamblers won't let a little murder keep them away."

"You know what our occupancy rate is? Fifty-eight percent. That's what Arlene said. We need every warm body we can get."

Ken stood up from the table. Patti wasn't telling him anything he didn't already know. He'd talked to his people in reservations, booking and the casino while he was eating breakfast, his cell phone going the whole time.

"I did my best, hon," he said, "but Max Vernon apparently was a big deal in this town. Owned one of those old casinos."

"So what was he doing spending the night at *our* hotel?"

Ken thinking, when did Tropical Bay become "*our*" hotel? Patti had been kicking and screaming about costs since he broke ground. Driving him frigging crazy.

"We comped him a suite," he muttered. "He said he wanted to check out the 'new kid on the Strip.' But I think he was just using it as an excuse for a night of partying."

"We *comped* him a suite? And then he does us the favor of getting killed in it? Jesus Christ, what kind of sideshow are you running here? Are you *trying* to ruin us?"

"That's the way the game is played, Patti. He'd do the same for me if I wanted to spend the night at his place."

"Like you'd want to stay in one of those old pig pens. You're acting like Mr. Big Shot Las Vegas, one of the boys, and now we've got a murder on our hands. Meanwhile, we're hemorrhaging money. What about our investors, Ken? They're not going to be happy."

"I'm taking care of it," he said. "I've got—"

His cell phone chirruped on the table. Patti's mouth was open to screech some more, but he held up a finger and snatched up the phone with the other hand.

"Hello?"

"Hey, boss. It's Loomis."

"Mel!" he said loudly. He gave Patti a bright smile. "Just the man I need. Where are you?"

After Loomis mumbled an answer, Ken said loudly, for Patti's benefit, "Albuquerque! What are you doing there?"

Ken listened a while, nodding and smiling at Patti. She crossed her arms over her chest and glowered at him.

"So you're hot on her trail, huh?" He listened a moment, then cupped the receiver and said, "Loomis has tracked the killer to Albuquerque."

"I gathered," Patti said flatly.

He frowned and turned back to the phone.

"How soon can you take care of the problem?"

"Day, maybe two," Loomis said. "She'll tail the target first. I'll be doing the same. I'll pick her up somewhere along the way."

"Right," Ken said. He waggled his eyebrows at Patti. "And you'll do it quietly. No muss, no fuss, no reporters. Right?"

"Be my pleasure."

"Call me when it's done," Ken said, then he punched a button to disconnect. He tried his smile on Patti again.

"See? Everything's being handled. The Vegas way."

22

Joe Riley was surprised Venturi and Associates was open on a Saturday. It looked like a small-scale operation, run out of an old house that squatted between parking lots along Tropicana Boulevard. Lot of old houses close to the Strip had been converted into offices for people who fed off the trouble generated by gambling and drinking—lawyers, bail bondsmen, storefront preachers.

He wondered if Venturi had a sideline. Lily Marsden might need a lawyer, some guy who's connected, who could get information for her, maybe even arrange jobs. Joe remembered a guy back in Chicago, years ago, who'd kept up a front as a legit bail bondsman for years before the cops finally figured out his bounty hunters were killers-for-hire. It was a big scandal at the time.

The secretary told Joe to wait on a sofa in the reception area, then made a point of ignoring his repeated yawns. He hadn't had much sleep in a couple of nights. The office was quiet, and he would've drifted off there on the couch if it hadn't been for the secretary cracking her gum at her desk. She was filing her nails, too. Joe tried to find some music in the swish-swish, crack-crack, but all he got was irritation.

An hour crawled past. He wanted to push his way past the Gum Cracker into Sal Venturi's inner sanctum, shove

Venturi up against a wall and pound him with questions. But he wouldn't get anywhere like that, except maybe jail. A lawyer is like an unexploded grenade. You keep your distance.

No, what he needed was to get friendly with Venturi, make it clear he wasn't trying to nail him for any crime. He just wanted information, enough to give him a bead on Lily Marsden.

The front door banged and Joe's eyes popped open. Two old cowboys with huge mustaches burst into the waiting room. An image flashed in Joe's mind: that old cartoon character, loudass Yosemite Sam, times two. The old-timers walked right past Joe and the secretary, who was so taken by surprise her mouth hung open. Joe could see the white wad of gum clinging to her tongue.

The cowboys pushed through the door into Sal Venturi's office and slammed it behind them. They were already out of sight by the time the secretary managed, "Hey!"

She turned, blinking, to Joe, who said, "So *that's* how you get in to see Mr. Venturi."

The secretary's face flushed. "Think I should call the cops?"

Joe shook his head as he got up from the couch.

"I used to be a cop. Let me make sure everything's okay in there."

He crossed the reception area and pressed his ear against the flimsy door. Joe could hear pretty well, particularly when one of the old coots shouted, "You'll tell us right now, motherfucker, or you won't see tomorrow."

Joe was facing the secretary and she arched her eyebrows in question. He gave her the "okay" sign with his fingers and made a shushing face. He wanted to hear it all.

Venturi stammered and stuttered and backtracked, but he finally said, "Okay, okay. I know the woman you mean. Her name's Lily."

"Lily what?"

"Marsden."

"Local girl?"

"No, she lives in Scottsdale. Down by Phoenix."

Joe heard nothing for a few seconds, then one of the cowboys said, "Turns out you're lying, we'll come back here and fill you fulla more holes than a fishnet."

Movement inside, boots shuffling on hardwood floors.

"Hold on a second," Venturi said. "She's not home. I think she's already gone on another job."

More foot shuffling, then a little yelp from Venturi.

"Shit, what did you do that for?"

"You want another one? No? Then tell us the whole fuckin' story. I'm tired of getting it out of you in dribs and drabs."

"All right, already. She's gone to hit a guy in Albuquerque. Marty Holguin, owns a carpet company."

A sharp smack came from inside the office, and Venturi moaned.

"You better be telling the truth, son. I haven't decided yet whether killing you would do the world any good. But if it turns out you're lying, I'll be back here so fast, you'll think you been struck by the wrath of God."

The two cowboys talked among themselves for a minute, but in low tones Joe couldn't make out. Then one of them said, "Maybe *you'd* better go get her. Bring her back here."

"How am I supposed to make her come back here?" Venturi shouted, panic in his voice.

"I don't give a rat's ass how you do it," the cowboy said. "Lie to her. Hell, you're a lawyer. You'll think of something."

The other cowboy's voice was calm and low. Sounded like he said, "You've got until Monday."

Joe heard nothing else, then the doorknob turned. He pressed back against the wall and held his breath. The office door swung open toward him, so he was behind it as the two cowboys emerged. He got just a glimpse of them in the gap between the door and the wall. They both looked mean as hell and the one without glasses was red in the face. Joe guessed he'd worked himself up, working over Venturi.

The cowboys stalked to the front of the office and out the door without giving the secretary a second look.

Joe came around the open door and peered into Venturi's office. A fat man sat behind a desk, one of his hands wrapped in a gauze bandage. He was bald, and his bulging forehead made his head resemble a shiny bean. His glasses sat crooked on his face and his eyes looked glassy.

Joe turned to the secretary, found her still sitting agape at her desk. He smiled at her. "I don't need to see Mr. Venturi after all. I got what I came for."

He hurried toward the front door, thinking Venturi would snap out of it in a minute, probably call the cops.

"Who *were* those guys?" the secretary said behind him.

"Beats me. Butch and Sundance?"

As he went out the door, he heard her say, "*Who?*"

23

Joe swung his aged Chevrolet into the parking lot of the Pink Elephant Motor Lodge. He needed to get to the airport as quickly as possible, find yet another flight to New Mexico, but he wanted to check out of the motel first. He wasn't sure he had room on his credit card to cover another flight; he might have to use his poker winnings. He sure as hell couldn't afford to keep paying for a motel room he wasn't using.

He let himself into the dim room and started throwing his shirts and shaving kit into his duffel bag. Someone knocked on the door.

Joe muttered a curse at the interruption, then hurried across the room and threw open the door.

A huge black man in a black suit filled the doorway. Joe didn't recognize him at first, but then he saw a little white dude past Man Mountain's shoulder. The white guy was wearing a red suit trimmed with white piping, looked like something one of Santa's elves would wear, and he had a plastic mask over his face, pressing against two blackened eyes and a smashed nose.

"Shit," Joe said. It was the two card sharks from Lucky's Back Door. Delbert and what's-his-name, Mookie. How the hell had they tracked him to the Pink Elephant? And why now, when he was in a hurry?

All this flitted through his head before he even noticed the pistol in Mookie's fist. Mookie waved it at him, gesturing for him to back into the room.

"I don't think so," Joe said, and he snatched at the gun hand, getting a good grip on the big man's wrist. Joe yanked the arm halfway into the room and slammed the heavy door on it.

Mookie howled, but he kept hold of the pistol. Joe squeezed tight to his wrist, holding the arm in place, then slammed the door on Mookie's forearm. Mookie cursed and pulled, but Joe wouldn't let go. The fourth time he slammed the door, the pistol fell to the floor.

He released Mookie's wrist and opened the door. Mookie's face was twisted in pain, but he saw Joe standing there, within easy reach. He lunged forward. Joe slammed the door shut. Bam, against Mookie's face.

Joe snatched open the door again. Mookie had both hands up over his nose and his eyes were squinched shut.

Joe kicked up swiftly, caught Mookie between the legs. Mookie's eyes bulged, looked like two teacups in his dark face.

As Mookie crumpled to the ground, Delbert came into full view. He apparently had forgotten the small, flat pistol that dangled from his hand.

Their eyes met, and Joe said, "Hey, I know you. Phantom of the Opera, right?"

Delbert bared his pointy teeth and whipped the pistol up.

Joe slammed the door and jumped to one side. The door was pretty solid—he'd made good use of it so far—but it sure as hell wasn't bulletproof.

Nothing.

He slipped over to the curtained window and peeked out. Delbert was bent over Mookie, his lips flapping. Delbert looked around the parking lot to see if anyone was watching. As he turned his attention back to the downed man, Joe stepped to the door and flung it open.

Delbert's gun wasn't even pointing his way. He was still bent-over, checking on his buddy. Joe clipped him behind the ear with a short, hard right. It hurt his fist, but it hurt Delbert more. The pompadour bounced around on top of his skinny neck and he fell flat on Mookie's chest. The black man was still clutching his balls and couldn't catch Delbert. Their faces smacked together, though it was clear Delbert didn't feel it. He was already unconscious.

Joe grinned. He'd feel it later for sure. That nose already was all over Delbert's face. It'll be swollen out to his ears by the time he wakes up.

Mookie squirmed, but he couldn't get out from under Delbert without releasing the grip on his tortured testicles, and they seemed to need the most attention at the moment.

Joe picked up the two pistols and stuffed them in his duffel bag as he stepped around the card players.

"You boys have a nice day."

He trotted to the office at the end of the block of motel rooms and jangled through the glass door. A rail-thin black woman watched suspiciously as he came up to the counter. She peered past his shoulder as he approached, and he wondered if she'd heard the commotion outside.

When she looked at him again, Joe saw relief in her eyes. Had this woman known Delbert and Mookie were after him? Had she alerted them that he'd returned to his room? Maybe, but she didn't look unhappy to see he was still walking around. Screw it, who cares? All that mattered now was reaching the airport, and that meant getting out of here before the card players came around.

Joe said, "I'm checking out."

24

Marty Holguin was the kind of guy who jingles his change in his pocket, like he's constantly reminding himself he's got dough. Lily didn't mind it. She could hear him coming a block away.

She heard him now, jingling out into the parking lot of the Albuquerque Carpet Barn, headed for the sleek black Mercedes she'd seen him drive earlier. She waited at the far corner of the lot in her Miata, the engine purring.

She'd already learned a lot about Martin Holguin. Guy had a nice house up in the foothills of the Sandia Mountains with a killer night view of a wide valley filled with Albuquerque's streetlights, looked like a bowlful of gems. Nice car, too, and he wore wide-shouldered suits, could be Armani. He was dark and lean and handsome with a salesman's thousand-watt smile.

Lily compared him to the men she'd known growing up in rural burgs in the South. Snaggle-toothed slobs in overalls. Leathery old men who smoked around the clock and drank hard on Saturdays. Rednecks in their baseball caps and Budweiser T-shirts and hopped-up cars. Not one of the men she'd ever met growing up could clean up as well as Martin Holguin. Nor would it have occurred to them to try.

She wondered briefly if she'd have turned out differently

if she'd ever met a man like Holguin when she was young and impressionable. Would it have made any difference if she'd known there were men like that in the world, ones full of possibilities?

Holguin got behind the wheel of the Mercedes and pulled away. Lily tucked her car in behind his, letting the space between them ebb and flow, as she followed him east on I-40 toward the mountains. She didn't worry about Holguin spotting the tail. He had no reason to be looking for one. He didn't know his partner was planning his removal. He'd never see her coming.

She wasn't crazy about the set-up, though. Holguin's house had an expensive alarm system, which ruled out waiting for him there. Lily could've figured a way around the alarm, but she didn't want to invest the time. She certainly didn't want to bring in an expert to help with the job. She wanted this finished, quickly and quietly, so she could go home to her swimming pool.

She followed Holguin's car off the interstate onto a broad four-lane called Tramway Boulevard. Holguin's car shot through northbound traffic, changing lanes and cutting between cars, making it difficult to keep up. Lily didn't worry. She knew he was going home. She'd overheard him earlier, while she wandered among the carpet rolls at his busy store. Holguin told a clerk about his coming Saturday night with his sweetie. The big date was some black-tie benefit for the symphony orchestra. He'd bitched about how he'd have to drive all the way home to change into his tuxedo, then halfway across town to his girlfriend's condo, and then all the way downtown, where the event was being held at something called the KiMo Theater. The employee looked bored while Holguin told him the whole schedule for the night ahead. Lily had felt like taking notes.

The Mercedes turned east onto a street that slithered up and over the rolling foothills of the Sandia Mountains, to where his home perched high above its neighbors. Lily let the distance between them grow, but she reached his driveway in time to see him hustle into the house. She drove to a wide spot in the winding road and did a quick turnaround so she'd be facing the right direction to follow him back into town.

She was tempted to pull into his semi-circular driveway right now. Ring the doorbell, pop him with the .25-caliber pistol she kept in the glove compartment. Get it done.

But a hit in broad daylight was a little daring, even up here, away from the other houses, surrounded by pygmy evergreens and wild chamisa. She wasn't sure how far the sound of the little gun would carry in these hills. Only the one narrow, winding street in and out of the neighborhood. If somebody hears the shots and calls 911, the cops could get lucky and catch her as she sped back down the hillside.

She looked to the west, where a few scattered clouds burned orange as the sun sank toward the horizon.

Perhaps she should wait until night, when she had the cover of darkness and the neighbors were all snug in their beds, more likely to ignore the sound of distant gunshots. But she wasn't sure she wanted to hit him at the house at all.

A crowded theater was no good, and Lily didn't like the arrangement at the girlfriend's place, either. She'd checked it out earlier, and found that the condo faced the inner courtyard of a U-shaped set of buildings. Lily wouldn't shoot him there. Plus, she'd probably have to shoot the girlfriend, too, and that seemed an unnecessary complication.

She turned it over and over in her mind, thinking of places where she might get Holguin alone. She kept coming back to the twisting road up to his house. She'd been giving him plenty of space, but she could stay pretty close to his car if she needed to; the rolling hills and dwarf forest should keep him from noticing her back there in the dark. She could pull up into his semi-circular driveway, pop him as he's getting out of his car, swing right back out into the street. She'd be on her way to the concealing traffic of Tramway Boulevard before Holguin hit the ground.

That sounded best. For the moment, at least. She'd trail him some more, see if a better opportunity presented itself. But one thing was certain: Martin Holguin wasn't long for this Earth.

She heard a car coming and scrunched down in the seat, raising her hand as if shielding her eyes from the low sun. A gray sedan glided past. Big guy behind the wheel didn't give her a glance.

She straightened up in time to spot Holguin through some trees as he came out the door of his house and punched the buttons to set the alarm system. He looked good in his black tuxedo, tall and debonair.

Lily thinking: Maybe they'll bury him in it.

25

Mel Loomis goosed the accelerator and the gray rental car spurted forward, topping one small hill and then another. Once he was sure the woman couldn't spot him in her mirrors, he pulled into the empty driveway of a big mud-colored house and turned around.

This was going better than he could've hoped. He'd been in Albuquerque less than two hours when he spotted the white Miata trailing Martin Holguin from his carpet store. The top was up on the little convertible, and Mel couldn't get a look at the driver until he passed her outside Holguin's house. She had short dark hair and she looked different from either of the disguises he'd seen on the video, but he was sure he had the right woman. Who else would be following a fucking rug merchant?

Loomis thought about snuffing her right where she sat. She didn't know he was coming. He could pull up beside her, roll down the window, act like he's trying to ask for directions or something. Pow, it's over.

But he was curious. This woman, this professional, how would she do the job on Holguin? He wondered about her methods, how she approaches the kill, how she makes her escape so cleanly. Loomis would've never admitted it to anyone, but he felt he might learn something from her.

He was tempted to wait, let her hit Holguin first, just so he could watch her in action. Maybe even shoot her right after she's done with him, while she's distracted, making her getaway. That would be rich. Lily Marsden makes another successful hit, but then ... look out behind you!

Loomis snorted. He was spending too much time alone in cars. Daydreaming. Going fucking bonkers. Pretty soon, he'd be spinning in place and barking. Like Curly Howard.

He pushed that thought from his mind. Not now. The whole Stooge thing could keep him occupied for hours, glancing at the resemblance in mirrors, brooding and muttering. He didn't need the distraction. This Lily Marsden was a pro. You don't survive long in her business unless you're very good at killing. He needed to be on his toes.

Loomis' big stomach grumbled. He hadn't eaten in hours. He thought about the corporate jet back at the airport, where they'd have a meal waiting for him once this job was done. He hoped it was Mexican food from one of the local restaurants. Make the most of his visit to god-forsaken Albuquerque.

The mountains above him took on a rosy glow from the setting sun. Details on their flanks rose in relief—strewn boulders and midget trees and big slabs of rock standing on end. Damned pretty. Loomis liked mountains. They were big and solid and silent. Like him. These looked like they were embarrassed about something, flushing red.

He let the car creep forward. He wanted to top the next hill, make sure the Miata was still there. Then it would be a contest between his curiosity and his growling stomach. See which one wins out. Marty Holguin's life hung in that balance.

Loomis tapped the brakes as his car topped the rise. Holguin's black Mercedes jounced out of the driveway and took off, back toward the city. The Miata let him disappear around a curve, then followed after the black car.

Loomis gunned the accelerator and the rented Buick leapt forward. He smiled, thinking: Here we go.

26

Mookie found Delbert waiting by the limo when he got out of the hospital emergency room Saturday evening.

Delbert looked even worse than before. His nose was essentially missing-in-action. Just a flattened mass of purple and blue flesh where his nose was supposed to be. His mouth hung open so he could get some air. The bruises around his slitted eyes were wider now, complete circles, and puffy, pushing against the plastic mask. He looked like a half-awake raccoon.

"The fuck you been?" Delbert said. "I been standing out here two hours. Had to pay off a security guard to stay in the no-parking zone."

"How much?"

"Twenty bucks. What difference does it make? What took so long?"

"My arm's broke."

Mookie held out his arm to show Delbert the splint and inflated cast that encased his arm in transparent blue plastic from elbow to thumb.

"The fuck is that?"

"They said I gotta wear it. Bone's cracked in there. Just part way through, but it hurts like a sonofabitch."

"So they put a balloon on it?"

"No, it's a cast. It's blowed up real tight. Hold everything in place."

Delbert frowned, then winced when his busted face moved beneath the plastic mask.

"Shouldn't it be against your skin? You've got it over your fuckin' sleeve."

"No, see, I was thinking there. They wanted me to take off my uniform, but I wouldn't do it. Made 'em put it on over my jacket. That way, I can still work. They put it on my bare arm, I can't get my uniform on."

Delbert reached up, patted the top of his pompadour. The elastic straps that held the mask to his face made his hair stick out every which way. Mookie knew Delbert wouldn't like that, so he didn't mention it.

"So what you gonna do when you want to take your coat off? How you gonna take a shower?"

Mookie smiled. For once, he was way ahead of Delbert.

"I'll just deflate this fucker and take it off and clean up and then put it on again."

"And blow it up?"

"Right."

"With what?"

"I can just blow it up, like a balloon."

"You can reach that little nozzle there, blow it up yourself?"

"Think so."

"Well, you'd better figure it out. I sure as hell ain't blowing it up for you."

"Don't we got a bicycle pump at the house?"

"Let's just go, okay? I'm tired of standing around this fucking hospital. I'm gonna get a germ. That's what I need, start sneezing all the time. How do you sneeze when your nose is smashed flat? Can't even breathe."

"Better not sneeze then. You might blow out your eardrums. One time, my uncle—"

"Just get in the limo. You want me to drive?"

"I'll drive. You ain't on the insurance."

"I drove us over here."

"That was an emergency. Company don't allow anyone else to drive the limo, 'cept in cases of emergency."

"You can drive all right with that thing on your arm?"

Mookie smiled at him. "Guess we about to find out."

He got behind the wheel and cranked up the smooth engine and buckled his seat belt. Checked his mirror to make sure Delbert was settled way back there in the rear seat. Delbert still wore that red suit of his. Had some black stuff, looked like tar, on one of the knees. Mookie didn't mention it. No need to get Delbert started again on that guy Joe Riley.

Turned out he didn't need any prompting. Mookie asked where to, and Delbert said, "The Pink Elephant."

"Aw, Delbert. That guy's long gone by now."

"Let's go make sure."

"I'm starving. Let's get something to eat. We could stop at the Bourbon Street, get that prime rib special. It's right on the way."

"No."

"Burger King?"

"Fuck that. I want to go to that motel, see if we can get a line on Riley. I'm gonna kill that motherfucker."

"How you gonna do that? He took our guns."

"I can get more guns. This is Vegas, for Christ's sake. Give me an hour, I could locate a fuckin' bazooka."

"Can't kill him 'til you get a gun. Might as well eat first."

"I see that guy, I'll kill him with my bare hands."

"That ain't worked out so well so far. Sonabitch keeps

kicking me in the balls. I never have children, it'll be his fault."

Delbert sighed in the back seat. "Maybe that's for the best, Mookie. World don't need you swimming in the gene pool."

Mookie wasn't sure what that meant, but before he could ask, Delbert said, "Aw, Christ, you're not taking the Strip, are you?"

"Yeah. It's a straight shot."

"Traffic'll be elbow to eyeball the whole way."

"It'll be all right, this time of day."

"Why didn't you take the I-15?"

"It's all screwed up. Construction."

Delbert huffed and shifted on the seat. "That's the problem with this fuckin' town. Everything's under construction."

Mookie glanced at Delbert in the rear-view. Little man's knee was bouncing. His head swiveled from side to side as he looked out the tinted windows. Mookie smiled to himself. Here we go.

"How many times," Delbert began, his voice rising, "have you replaced the tires since you been driving this limo?"

"Three times."

"That makes twelve tires. And how many of those tires gave up the ghost because of a nail?"

"Nine. Fuckin' nails all over the road around these construction sites."

"This is what I'm sayin'. I moved to this town twenty years ago, just a kid, right? One day after I graduate from high school in St. Louis, I haul ass to Vegas in search of the good life. You know how many people were living here then?"

Mookie shrugged and glanced at the mirror. Delbert had his hands up, counting off on his fingers, looked like he was ready to count every resident of Las Vegas.

"Two-hundred-fifty-thousand. Nice-sized town. Just right. Never too much traffic. The Strip wasn't a fuckin' parking lot. Now, we got one-and-a-half million people. Fastest-growing city in the country. Fifty thousand a year moving here. Another thirty million a year coming here to gamble. Crowds everywhere you turn. Everybody running around like crazy. It's like living in a fuckin' anthill."

Mookie gunned the limo's engine as a light changed to green at Sahara Avenue. Circus Circus loomed on the right and the Hilton and the Riviera made their own bulky skyline to the left. Mookie changed lanes, trying to gain a little ground before the next red light.

"And you know why?"

Mookie had heard this speech a thousand times, but he said nothing. Delbert didn't need any encouragement.

"These fuckers right here, these so-called 'mega-resorts.' Thousands of hotel rooms fulla frat boys and tourists and snowbirds. All comin' here to lose their money, get drunk, party. And the people who live here? We don't count for shit. So what if we can't drive across town in less than half an hour? Or that construction trucks are ripping around everywhere, dumping nails and shit on the roads?"

Mookie got lucky at the curve at Sands Avenue and hit the green light, speeding through. Treasure Island's giant pirate and lagoon full of fake ships passed on the right.

"Look at this shit here," Delbert said. "Exactly what I'm talking about. The whole town's decked out like a fuckin' carnival. Everything's fake. The gondolas and the Eiffel Tower and the roller coasters. The whole Strip's got a layer of frosting, but underneath the cake's all the same. A shit cake."

Mookie made a face. That was a new twist in Delbert's diatribe. Kinda took the edge off Mookie's appetite.

Delbert didn't even slow for air. "Right up here now, we have the Bellagio, with its artwork and fancy restaurants and all that shit. And what have you got, really? A shopping mall, that's what, wrapped around a casino. Jesus Christ."

As they reached the man-made lake in front of Bellagio, its rows of hidden fountains sprang to life, shooting streams a hundred feet into the air. People crowded the sculpted railings along the edge of the lake, pointing and smiling.

"Look at those idiots. Standing out there in the hot sun, watching the 'famed dancing waters.' What horseshit. They could do the same thing at home. Set the sprinklers out in the yard, sit in a lawn chair, stare at the goddamn water."

Mookie smiled. He'd always liked the dancing waters himself, but Delbert was in rare form today. Mookie pushed the limo faster. Sooner they got this tour finished, got to that motel and checked things out, sooner he'd get to eat.

Delbert fell silent and Mookie checked his mirror. Delbert was leaning back in the seat, his hands on his thighs, his mouth open, gasping for air. Mookie guessed it was hard for Delbert to keep up his usual string of bullshit when he couldn't breathe through his nose.

He felt like laughing. Might be better if Delbert had to give his mouth a rest for a change.

Delbert's steady patter was one reason they'd become partners six years earlier. He amused the hell out of Mookie. Always so full of piss and vinegar, always *starting* something. Delbert had a million ideas, and he jumped from one to the other so fast, it didn't even matter that few ever came to anything. He was learning how to count cards so he could beat the blackjack tables. Or, he had a new plan that involved smuggling fake vitamins from Korea. Or, some VCRs fell off a truck and Delbert bought them up for resale, just as every movie nut in the country switched to DVD. These get-rich-quick schemes often blew up in their faces, but they kept life interesting for Mookie. Beat sitting in the limo all day, with nothing on his mind but Big Macs and Deputy Dawg.

"You want to pass this fucker?" Delbert snapped. "We haven't got all day."

Mookie steered the limo into the other lane. The Monte Carlo and New York, New York and Paris glided past the windows, the Strip's world tour of fakery. Just past the sphinx in front of the black pyramid at Luxor, he got into a left turn lane for the Pink Elephant Motor Lodge.

"All right," Delbert said. "Here we go."

Mookie got the long car across the oncoming lanes and into the motel's little parking lot. He stopped near the kidney-shaped pool.

"You want me to knock on his door?"

"Talk to that clerk. I'll bet our boy already checked out."

Mookie left the engine running so Delbert would have air-conditioning. He stepped out into chlorine-scented air and marched across the parking lot, the asphalt still sticky underfoot from the day's heat.

The same clerk stood behind the counter. Tall, skinny sister, about Mookie's age, mid-thirties. Looking fine, too, but fear came into her eyes when she saw him. Mookie could see bruises on her arms where he'd roughed her up before.

She took a step backward, her eyes darting from side to side.

"Easy, now," he said. "I ain't here to hurt you."

Her eyes met his and settled in a level stare.

"You did last time you were here."

Mookie felt embarrassed. He tried to put his hands in his pockets, but the inflated cast got in the way.

"Yeah, sorry about that," he said. "My buddy got a little carried away. He makes me do things like that sometimes."

"He can't *make* you do shit," she said coolly. "You *choose* what you do."

Jesus Christ. She sounded like Mookie's mother.

"Forget about it," he said. "Just tell me what I need to know and I'll get out of here, leave you alone. That guy Joe Riley, room 102, he check out?"

She watched him for a while, deciding, and Mookie thought he'd be forced to go behind the counter again, give her a persuasion.

"He's gone," she said. "Checked out while you two were rolling around on the sidewalk."

Mookie winced. "You saw that?"

She nodded, looked like she was trying not to smile. "He break your arm?"

Mookie hid the cast behind his back. "You know where he went?"

"He didn't say."

"Damn."

Mookie started to leave, but she called out to him: "You want my guess?"

He turned back. "About where he went?"

She nodded.

"What's your guess?"

"I'd guess that guy was going wherever you two *ain't*."

Mookie snorted and went out the door. Delbert wasn't going to like that answer. He'd want to race around town, trying to track this guy down, buy some guns, whatever.

Mookie wouldn't ever get any dinner.

27

Sal Venturi wrestled around in the airliner seat until he could free his handkerchief from his hip pocket. He wiped the sweat from his forehead, blew his nose and checked the handkerchief for results before putting it back in his pocket. The woman in the window seat huffed, bothered by all his squirming.

The aisle seat was empty, and normally he would've moved to it, given them both more room. But this bitch kept sighing and harrumphing at him, so no way would he give her the satisfaction of moving over. She'd given him a disgusted look earlier, when he was wolfing a cupcake he'd bought at the airport. Skinny witch. Probably never enjoyed a meal in her life.

Sal closed his eyes, tried to focus. He needed to find a way to reach Lily. She wasn't answering her cell phone and he wasn't sure how to track her down once he reached Albuquerque. And what would he do when he did find her? Sweet-talk her into returning to Vegas so the Vernons could kill her?

One thing for sure, the Vernon brothers meant business. Sal had seen the look in that Norm's eyes. If Sal showed up back in Vegas empty-handed, he was a dead man.

Might be a dead man anyhow. No guarantee the Vernon brothers wouldn't knock him off, even if he delivered Lily. And no guarantee they could actually take Lily out; he wasn't sure any killer anywhere was better than her. Sal could get caught in the crossfire. And if Lily found out he'd ratted on her, she wouldn't just kill him. She'd do it slowly, and it would hurt.

He wiped his forehead with his bandaged hand and pushed up his glasses. Jesus, the sweat. He had a bad case of nerves, and it seemed to have done something to his already overly-productive sweat glands.

Sal remembered something that made him groan. Ken Staley's goon, Loomis, probably was in Albuquerque by now. If Loomis caught Sal screwing around there, he'd assume Sal was trying to warn Lily about *him*. In which case, the race would be on to see who'd kill Sal first.

The woman by the window cleared her throat and sniffed the air. Sal couldn't help himself, he sniffed, too. Sure enough, someone had farted. Recycled air in the cabin meant he'd get to smell it again and again. He looked around in time to see the bitch shoot him a glare. She thought it was him! Sal frowned at her and looked away. He could feel his face flushing, which would only make him look guilty. Nothing he could do about it. One reason he'd gotten out of courtroom work was that his face tended to give him away. He needed to stay cool and collected in a trial, but he tended to bluster. His face would flush and the jury would assume he was lying. Which was usually the case, but what the fuck.

No, the courtroom wasn't for him. But it sounded better than his present situation. What's that they say? Kill the messenger? He was bringing Lily Marsden bad news. And of all the players in this fucking little soap opera—the Vernons, Loomis and Staley, the cops, and Christ-knows-who-else— Lily was the one who scared him most.

He sighed and belched, which drew another cold stare

from his seatmate. He ignored her, busy remembering the handful of killers and the dozens of marks that had marched through his life the past twelve years.

His sideline had come by accident. A client, Jimmy Rocchio, behind bars and awaiting trial, had been facing racketeering charges in Vegas, The prosecution's case rested mostly on the testimony of one man, George Barrett, a little weasel who'd worked for Rocchio and who knew way too much about Rocchio's numbers-running and loan-sharking and drug-wholesaling operations. As the trial neared, it became clear that Rocchio didn't stand a chance if Barrett made it to the witness stand.

Rocchio planted the idea in Sal's head: Get rid of Barrett. Rocchio knew the right people, and Sal helped set up the hit. He hired a pro Rocchio recommended, a rooftop sniper who caught Barrett entering the courthouse, surrounded by cops. One shot and Barrett went down, leaving baffled cops standing around, guns drawn, nobody to shoot. Within two weeks, Jimmy Rocchio was a free man.

Sal sometimes wished that first hit *hadn't* gone so smoothly. Because the sniper's success had made the next step easy. Somebody else called with a problem for Sal to solve, and Sal set up a hit to make the problem go away. Before he knew it, brokering contracts was his main occupation, one that made him rich.

He'd tried to work it smart over the years, as his business came to rely more and more on sending assassins to do their work. He had all the paperwork, could prove to the IRS that his billable hours covered his reported income. Trusty Velma handled the office, kept the real legal work from getting in the way of the moneymaking. And he kept his stable of killers away from Vegas and away from each other. Contact only by telephone and wire transfer. All very business-like, all very careful.

But word got around, especially in a town like Vegas. Pretty soon, Sal was getting approached by people he'd never fucking heard of, calling on him at the office out of the blue, as if arranging a killing was just another business appointment. Only a matter of time before the wrong people connected him to a hit. The cops or, worse, some aggrieved vigilantes like the Vernons.

Christ, he hadn't seen that one coming. He'd known Max Vernon was a big wheel around town, but he wasn't Mob or anything. Sal had figured it would be safe, just this once, to have someone removed in his own back yard. He hadn't counted on two old coot cowboys—twins, for shit's sake—hunting him down and waving pistols in his face.

A speaker squawked above Sal's head, making him flinch. The captain came over the intercom saying they were preparing to land in Albuquerque.

Sal gulped. The plane, for all its recirculated air and tight-fitting seats and bitchy passengers, suddenly seemed like a safe place. Once he reached the ground, he'd have to race around, make decisions, fucking *do* something. And there was a very good chance he'd end up dead.

Maybe he should get off this plane and get right on another. Run for it. He had cash stashed back in Vegas. He could disappear for a while, take a long vacation. Sal couldn't remember the last time he'd taken a trip. Hell, you live in Vegas, you can have a vacation anytime you want it. Just walk out the fucking door.

Running wouldn't necessarily save him from Lily Marsden. Once she learned what he'd done, she'd track him down; that's what she did best. But maybe Lily would be too busy fending off Loomis or the Vernons to waste time hunting Sal. Maybe they'd all kill each other. Once the dust settled, Sal could go home, set up shop again.

Might be best for now to just keep moving. He could keep in touch with Velma, work the phones. Hell, he might even be able to keep the money flowing.

A loud thump came from under the plane and Sal jumped. Oh, the landing gear. Almost there. He turned to the window, looking out past the witch's razor of a nose, and saw a night landscape dotted with lights.

Someone fell into the aisle seat and Sal, startled, turned to find a big guy sitting there where there had been no one. He had short, gray-flecked hair and a broad forehead and a jaw like a shovel. His lightweight gray suit was wrinkled, and he hadn't shaved in a day or two. Thick through the middle, but big in the shoulders, too. Dark, wary eyes. Something about him made Sal think: "Cop."

The guy gave him a big shit-eating grin, and Sal felt a chill run through him.

"Sal Venturi, right?"

"Who the hell are you?"

"Name's Joe Riley. I was at your office earlier?"

Sal squinted at the guy. Had he ever seen him before?

"You might not remember," Riley said. "You seemed a little out of it at the time. Right after those two old cowboys came to see you?"

Sal felt perspiration pop out on his forehead. Oh, shit.

The big guy looked around the plane. Sal sensed the hag beside him watching and Riley's eyes lit on her and held until she turned away to the window.

"Here's the deal," he said, smiling, his voice low and calm. "You and me just became best friends."

"What do you mean?"

"You know, Sal, friends. You've had friends before, haven't you, you fat little fuck?"

Sal flinched. Riley was still smiling. It gave Sal the creeps.

"You know what friends do?" Riley said. "They go everywhere together."

Sal shook his head, but Riley paid no attention.

"That's right, we're what you call *inseparable*. Starting now."

Sal felt hot inside, the bluster building. "You can't just sit down here and—"

Ouch. Riley clamped his fingers down on Sal's bandaged hand. Looked like it was just resting there, friendly. But his fingers dug into the sore hand, felt like he was ripping the bones right out of the skin.

"Not a sound, Sal. You can get in trouble, making disturbances on airplanes. They'd call the cops. I'd have to tell them everything I know about you."

Guy smiling the whole time. Fucking eerie. Sal nodded so briskly, he could feel his jowls bouncing around his chin.

"Good boy," Riley said, and eased the pressure on Sal's aching hand. He left his paw resting there, though, a little reminder.

"What—" Sal began, but he had to swallow hard and start over. "What do you want me to do?"

Riley patted Sal's hand. Gave him a wink. Bastard.

"Sit tight. We're about to land. Then we'll do what friends do when they're on vacation. We'll rent a car, go out and see the sights. Look up other old friends."

Sal's glasses had slipped to the end of his nose and he slowly reached up—he didn't want to spook this bruiser—and pushed them into place. He said, "Anybody in particular?"

"One."

The smile slipped from Riley's face. Now that it was gone, Sal missed it.

"A mutual friend of ours. Lily Marsden."

28

As she rode the elevator up to the executive suite at Tropical Bay, Detective Susan Pine gnawed the cuticle on her index finger, felt the sweet pain as a morsel of flesh pulled loose. She took her hand away from her mouth, looked over the finger, watched blood fill the ragged little tear.

Damn. Just what she needed Ken Staley to see. She dug in her purse, hunting a Kleenex.

The elevator doors slid open and she realized she must look like a nitwit, standing there with both hands in her big purse, her hair hanging down in her face. She straightened up and let the purse swing free on its shoulder strap and strode into the office.

Staley stood behind his desk, looked like he was a mile away, waiting for her. Susan steamed across the cushy carpeting and docked at his desk. The windows behind him were black with night, and she could see herself reflected there. She looked like hell: no sleep, clothes rumpled, hair tangled.

"Detective Pine," Staley said warmly. "Please have a seat."

"No, thanks. I don't plan to be here long. I want those other security videos I requested. I've got lab techs sitting around, twiddling their thumbs, waiting to process those videos."

Staley smiled, his teeth bright against his George Hamilton tan. He wore a blue blazer with brass buttons over a white shirt and white pants—captain of "The Love Boat," except with a mop of silvery hair. Susan wondered whether the hair was real. Those teeth sure as hell weren't.

"Is that what this is all about?" he said. "When they called me from downstairs, said you were demanding to see me right away, I was afraid something terrible had happened."

Susan tucked her bleeding finger inside her fist. She very badly wanted to put it in her mouth, give it another little nibble, get rid of that rough spot, but she didn't want Staley to see how nervous she was.

"There's plenty happening around here that's terrible," she said. "I'm way too busy. I suppose you've heard about the other murders?"

Staley let the smile slide from his face and replaced it with a look of concern. It was some of the worst acting Susan had ever seen.

"A tragedy," he said somberly. "But I don't see—"

"Your people are stonewalling me," she said. "I was supposed to have those tapes yesterday."

The still waters left Staley's face, replaced by his oily smile.

"I'm sorry. Mel Loomis was supposed to take care of that, and he was suddenly called out of town."

"Where to?"

"Don't see how it matters, but he had to go to Phoenix. A little business emergency."

"Something more important than Max Vernon's murder?"

Staley's face hardened, ever so slightly.

"No, of course not, but it *was* urgent. We've turned Max

Vernon over to your capable hands. Not much more Loomis could do here."

"Except get me my videos."

"Right. I'm sure it's just an oversight. I'll call down to Security. They'll have them ready for you downstairs."

The phone on Staley's desk emitted a little murmur. He glanced at the phone, then back to her, clearly wanting her to take the hint and leave. Susan talked over the ringing phone.

"What about those other murders? Marla Vernon and Teddy Valentine. Think they're connected to the hit on Max?"

Staley frowned, pretended to think it over.

"I wouldn't have any idea. That's your bailiwick, Detective."

Susan slipped her fist into her open purse, started feeling around again for a tissue. She didn't take her eyes off Staley. She felt she was a good judge of people, could read things on their faces, could tell when they were lying. Problem with Staley was that he was *always* lying. Everything was a big put-on, an act, a sales pitch.

"I was thinking," she said, "that if somebody wanted to hush up Max Vernon's death, to make it all go away, capping Marla and Teddy might be one way to do it."

Staley's hands twitched and he clasped them behind his back. Susan thinking: Ah, it's the hands. He's got his handsome face under control at all times, but the hands give him away. Now his hands were behind him, and Susan wouldn't get any help from them.

"Forgive me for saying so, Detective, but that seems far-fetched. Keep a murder quiet by committing two more? That would just generate more noise."

"It's plenty noisy already," she said. "The reporters are driving me crazy."

Staley blanched a little under that bronze tan.

"That's too bad," he said. "I was hoping the press wouldn't go nuts with it. That sort of news is bad for tourism. And, anything that's bad for tourism is bad for Las Vegas."

Susan shrugged. "Not necessarily. Tourists like to think Vegas is a little dangerous. It's part of the image. But it might make them stay in a different hotel."

Staley's hands came out from behind him, danced around a little until they found his pants pockets and landed there. She'd hit a nerve.

"We've already had cancellations. I've been fielding calls all day from our board of directors."

"That's too bad," she said. "Thing like that, bad publicity, can make cancellations snowball, right?"

Staley's smile turned brittle.

"Is there some point to this, Detective? Is there some reason you're torturing me with the realities of my own business?"

"I was just talking theoretically. Seems to me you'd have lots of reasons for wanting these murders to go away quietly."

The smile vanished altogether.

"You think I had something to do with these killings?"

She took her time answering.

"A case like this, three murders, all connected somehow, makes everybody a suspect. I don't know yet how it fits together, but I'll find out. You can count on that."

Staley took a deep breath, then forced his killer smile back onto his face.

"Perhaps everyone *is* a suspect at this point, but you can take me off your list. I've got nothing to do with any of this. I just want it all to go away. I hope you're smart enough not to toss my name around. I wouldn't stand for that. Let's not get a bunch of lawyers involved."

Susan finally located a ragged Kleenex and managed to wrap it around her finger. She took her hand out of her purse and hid it behind her hip.

"Don't threaten me, Mr. Staley. I'm not afraid of lawyers. I don't intend to draw attention to Tropical Bay unnecessarily, but I can't do anything to stop it, either. Truth is, I don't really care how it affects your business. That's your problem, not mine."

Staley tossed a little laugh up at the ceiling, then looked back at her.

"Forgive me for saying so, Detective, but your naivetéé is showing. Business is all anyone cares about in Las Vegas. You harm business and you're ruined in this town. Why do you think they assigned you to this case? Because nobody else wanted to touch it, that's why. Cops who've been around a while know to avoid problems with the casinos. It's too easy to make a costly error. You're brand-new to Homicide, right? That's what I was told. And your partner, where's he?"

"Probably at home, dreaming about his retirement."

"So he's got nothing to lose. You've got your whole career ahead of you, Detective. You can't afford to make a mistake. You need to keep this low profile. And keep Tropical Bay out of it as much as possible."

They stared at each other for a long moment, then Staley turned on the high beams again, and said, "Please?"

She couldn't help herself. She smiled back. Charming devil.

"Don't you worry about me," she said. "My career will be fine. I'm going to nail the killers to the wall, along with anybody who gets in the way."

She turned on her heel and stalked off toward the elevator. A good exit, only slightly marred when the heel of her shoe caught in the thick carpeting and caused her to stumble.

The elevator doors slid open as soon as she pushed the button. She stepped inside, turned to face Staley. He still stood behind his desk. He gave her a little wave, but he wasn't smiling, and that made her feel better about the exchange somehow.

As soon as the door whispered closed, she unwrapped her bloody finger and began to nibble.

29

Lily followed Martin Holguin to his girlfriend's condo, where he picked up his date, who was predictably young, blond and curvy. Then it was downtown to the symphony orchestra benefit. The KiMo Theater was a strange old building, decorated with terra cotta Indian designs and cow skulls and colorful tiles. A fancy-dress crowd milled around the entrance, and Marty and his girlfriend melted into it.

Lily was surprised to find that downtown Albuquerque was a happening place. A dozen bars and restaurants crowded along a neon-lit stretch of Central Avenue, people spilling out to dine in the open air. She set up half a block from the theater at a sidewalk café. She ordered coffee and a sandwich and waited.

Scores of people strolled past, out on the town on a warm Saturday night. Lily didn't like being this exposed, but she didn't have much choice. She wanted to be on Holguin's tail when he drove home.

Naturally, Mr. Social Butterfly couldn't go straight home after the benefit ended. He and the girlfriend sauntered up the street and went into a bar called the Liquid Lounge. Lily waited some more. The sidewalk café closed and she moved across the street, sat on a bench, tried to ignore the ogling drunks who passed by. She was dressed in jeans, a T-shirt, and a black denim jacket, her work clothes, as inconspicuous as possible, but drunks rarely overlook a woman alone.

Around eleven, Holguin and the girlfriend tottered out of the bar and down the sidewalk to his Mercedes. Lily was behind the wheel of her car before Holguin could even get his unlocked. She was right behind him as he cruised out of downtown, headed north toward the girlfriend's place.

If Holguin decided to spend the night with the girlfriend, Lily would have to wait another day. She was tired of waiting. She wanted to go home.

Luckily, Holguin didn't go inside the girlfriend's condo. He followed her to the door, but she gave him a big kiss and sent him on his way, closing the door in his face.

"Love's hard, isn't it, Marty?" Lily said behind the wheel.

She watched as Holguin got back into the Mercedes. Then she followed him to the freeway and east toward the foothills.

She felt a rush inside, a little thrill at what was coming. She leaned across the car, popped open the glove compartment and took out the gun. Stuck it inside her jacket.

Mel Loomis felt his pulse quicken. She was going for the hit.

He burped into his fist. Goddamned street-vendor hot dog. All he'd had time for, he'd been so busy chasing Lily Marsden all over town. Waiting for her to drop the hammer on the carpet guy.

Now he felt sure she was about to do it. It was nearly midnight, the city quiet, perfect time to knock off Holguin. Loomis followed as the Miata turned off Tramway onto the winding road that led up to Holguin's fancy house. He let some distance build between them. He didn't want to get too close, spook the killer before she had a chance to do her job. He wanted to time it just right to see her pull the trigger. Before she could get away, he'd pull a trigger of his own.

As they neared Holguin's house, Loomis flicked off his headlights. He slowed while his eyes adjusted. Not much ambient light out here, but Loomis' night vision was good. He could follow the road snaking up toward Holguin's house.

The gray car leaped forward through the darkness. He didn't want to be late.

Joe Riley gunned the engine on the Ford Escort as he turned off Tramway Boulevard onto a winding road that, according to the Budget Rent-a-Car map, should take him to Martin Holguin's house.

Joe yawned broadly. God, he was tired of no sleep and little food and being on airplanes all the time. Tired of driving around freaking Albuquerque, cooped up in the tiny car with Sal Venturi and the ooze of his flop sweat. He needed to get some rest. But first, he needed to warn Martin Holguin that Lily Marsden was gunning for him.

He'd thought about calling Holguin, giving him a heads-up over the phone, but had decided this sort of news should be delivered face-to-face. Even then, Holguin probably wouldn't believe him, and who could blame him? It was a crazy goddamned story. That was one reason Joe wanted Sal Venturi along. The lawyer might help persuade Holguin that the threat was real, that he should call the local cops, get some protection.

Joe had another, more selfish reason for going to Holguin's place. There was a chance Lily Marsden might be there, staking out the target. Might be his best chance of nabbing her before she disappeared again. If he could catch her before she got to Holguin, the carpet salesman need never know his life was in danger.

Venturi rode in silence, the map spread across his fat knees, pinned into place by his bandaged hand. He talked plenty earlier, telling Joe much of what he wanted to know. Venturi hadn't exactly volunteered anything, but he'd agree in the right places if hurt slightly. Joe hadn't sprung the big question on him yet, but now might be the time.

"Sal," he said as he steered over a hill, "I'm going ask you a question. One more question. And you're going to answer me truthfully."

"Or what?" Sal snapped.

"Or you're never leaving this car alive."

Sal choked on something, but finally said, "What's the question?"

"Did Lily hit a guy in Chicago, a loan shark named Bennie Burrows?"

"Hell, you can't expect me to remember every—"

"Think before you answer, Sal. You don't want to make a mistake."

Sal blinked at him, his mouth hanging open, his jowls jiggling.

"Bennie Burrows," Joe said. "Little guy, looked like Danny Devito. Killed exactly the same way as Max Vernon. This sounding familiar yet?"

Sal opened and closed his mouth a couple of times, but Joe could see the answer in his eyes.

"Nearly two years ago, Sal. Caused a shitstorm up there. Local cop got blamed for the murder. You remembering this?"

Joe noticed headlights up ahead, about where Holguin's

house should be. He let the rental car slow, wondering what could be going on up there, this time of night.

"Fuck, all right, I remember," Sal admitted. "Bennie Burrows. Yeah, that was Lily. Let me guess. You were the cop who got blamed."

"Very good, Sal. You're not as stupid as you look."

Sal snapped his mouth shut and glared at him.

"Who ordered the hit, Sal?"

"I don't remember." Looking away, pissed.

"You must have records—"

"They're in Vegas. Get me home in one piece, maybe we can find out."

"I think you're holding out on me."

Sal kept his mouth shut, staring straight out the windshield. Something up ahead caught his attention, and he said, "What the hell?"

30

It was the wink that did it.

Lily had misgivings about the hit, wasn't sure the timing was right. She'd noticed a car behind her on the serpentine road, but the headlights disappeared, and she assumed the car had turned into a driveway. Still, it made her nervous.

Up ahead, Holguin's Mercedes purred into his semi-circular driveway and stopped outside his home's front door. Now or never. Lily wheeled the Miata through the gateway into the drive, pulled up beside his car and stopped.

Holguin was already halfway out of the Mercedes. He hesitated, not recognizing her car. She wasn't sure he could see her inside the low Miata, so she turned on the interior light and leaned across the passenger seat toward him. He climbed the rest of the way out of the Mercedes and slammed the door. Then he bent over to peer in the Miata's open window.

"Hi," Lily said brightly, "can you help me? I'm trying to find a house up here. The Johnsons? Do you know them?"

Holguin snaked a hand into his pants pocket and jingled his change. Lily paused, not sure she wanted to hit this handsome guy. Holguin was still in his tuxedo, and he was a little drunk, but he was smiling, trying to help a stranger.

"No, I don't know any Johnsons in this part of town," he said. "Sorry."

"Okay, thanks anyway."

And then he winked at her. A slow, lascivious wink that, together with the smile, felt like a come-on rather than a friendly gesture. Lily felt heat crawl up her neck.

She pulled the little pistol from inside her jacket, brought her arm up so it was only inches from Holguin's face. She shot him through the eye.

The little gun's sudden pop sounded loud inside the car. The noise echoed away through the foothills.

Holguin's head snapped back and he stumbled backward. Already dead, Lily figured, and too dumb to lie down. She shot him in the chest and he fell, bounced off the Mercedes and crumpled to the pavement.

She hit the accelerator and the Miata leaped forward, then she slammed on her brakes. A gray Buick, lights out, had parked across the exit. A bulky guy was getting out from behind the wheel.

Lily threw the Miata into reverse, hit the gas and her car squealed backward. The big guy came racing around the Buick, carrying a pistol. Her sports car bumped out into the street, and she whipped it through a three-quarter turn, out into the dark road, shifting for the dash down the hill.

What the hell? Another car was coming up the hill, right at her. Lily gunned her engine and dodged around it, her hand up to shield her eyes from the headlights.

She glimpsed two men in the car as she flew past. Big, square-jawed guy scrunched in behind the wheel. And, in the passenger seat, looking frightened as hell, Sal Venturi.

What the fuck was he doing in Albuquerque?

For fat Sal to even come out from behind his desk, something must be bad wrong. She downshifted through a curve and checked her rear-view. The small car had turned around and was chasing her. Another set of headlights were back there, too. Must be the gray Buick, the guy with the pistol.

She gunned the Miata as she reached Tramway and screeched through a turn just as the traffic light turned amber. Then she headed south, pushing fifty, toward the interstate.

The last thing Lily needed was to get stopped by a cop, but the two cars chasing her didn't seem to care about the speed limit. She watched in her mirrors as they closed fast. Before she could reach the freeway, the little car—an Escort—was on her tail, with the gray sedan right behind.

Shit. Not the inconspicuous getaway she had planned. She was tempted to stop, face Sal down, find out what the hell was going on. But she didn't like that gray car back there. If the guy with Sal and the big man in the Buick were working together, they could hem her in, get her in a crossfire.

A freeway overpass loomed ahead, but Lily, on impulse, bypassed the ramp. She didn't want to be on the freeway with two pursuit cars, especially when one was that big Buick. Guy bumped the Miata with that tank, Lily wouldn't stand a chance.

She turned right through a wide intersection, onto an eight-lane avenue that was nearly empty of cars this time of night, then saw what she was looking for. An all-night coffee shop, big doughnut on its sign. And, predictably, three police cars parked outside.

Lily knew she was taking a chance. But she didn't figure the guys in the pursuit cars for cops. Odds were they wanted to kill her, not arrest her. Cops might be just what she needed.

An L-shaped parking lot wrapped around the coffee

shop, the long side facing the street. The diner's entrance was at the corner of the building, near the angle of the "L," and Lily parked as close as she could to the door. She stuck the still-warm pistol into her waistband at the back of her jeans and hurried into the coffee shop.

As the door swung shut behind her, she saw the maroon Escort and the gray Buick bounce into the parking lot. The front of the diner was wall-to-wall windows, and she watched as the Escort parked near the Miata. The Buick prowled past the café, then backed into a spot near the street.

Lily turned toward the crowded tables. Four cops sat in a booth near the door, and they were sneaking peeks at her and nudging each other. She smiled as a plump hostess greeted her.

"Table for one, please."

31

Joe Riley watched from behind the wheel of the Escort as Lily Marsden was seated at a table right in the window. Bold as you please.

His jaw muscles throbbed from clenching his teeth. He could've saved Holguin. He should've called ahead, alerted the local cops, something. But he'd been too hot to capture Lily Marsden on his own, playing hero, and now the poor bastard was dead. And Lily was taunting him, sitting in that coffee shop.

No way he could take her now. Good-looking woman like that, those cops would immediately take her side. By the time he could get it sorted out, she might kill them all.

She must figure that neither Joe nor the guy in the gray car would just shoot through the window, not with three squad cars right there, the place full of cops.

Who was that guy anyway? The gray Buick was parked at the opposite end of the parking lot, but Joe couldn't make out the driver because bright halogen lights glared on the windshield.

He turned to Sal, who looked pale, sweat glistening on his forehead. Sal was not a brave passenger. Joe thought he'd stomp a hole through the floorboard, trying for an invisible brake, on the chase over here. Now he just seemed grateful to be sitting still.

"Who's the guy in the gray car, Sal? You get a look at him?"

"Mel Loomis." Sal held up his bandaged hand. "He's the one who did this to me."

"What's he doing here?"

"Same thing you are. Hunting Lily."

"Why?"

"He works for Ken Staley. Guy who owns Tropical Bay? They're pissed because Lily bumped Max Vernon there. Bad for business."

"So he comes all the way here—"

"This guy took it personal."

"Jesus. You told him where to find her?"

Sal nodded again, looked away. His glasses slipped down his nose and he gave them an impatient shove.

"You know, Sal, you could've mentioned this before."

Joe thought it over. The first order of business was to make sure Sal stayed put. He wished he had some handcuffs, but his cuffs were back at the Vegas airport in his Chevy, along with his gun and the two pistols he took off those idiot gamblers. He was playing this one bare-assed. Time to improvise.

"So this Loomis," he said. "He sees you here? That would be bad, huh?"

Sal didn't look at him, but he swallowed heavily.

"You better stay here in the car," Joe said. "You get out, wander off, Loomis might shoot you."

Sal looked over at him through smudged glasses. "Where are you going?"

"Inside. Talk to Lily."

"You can't do that. The place is fulla cops."

"So what?"

"So, fuck me, that's what. If Lily sees you coming, she'll gun down everybody in the place."

"All those cops?"

Sal nodded.

"I don't think so. She went in that place to be safe. I think it's safe for me, too, for the same reason. But you need to stay here in the car. Don't let Loomis see you. I'll keep an eye out. If I see him heading this way, I'll run outside and cut him off."

Sal shook his head. His waggling jowls made Joe think of a bassett hound.

"This is a bad idea," Sal said.

"Just keep your ass in this car."

Joe got out and hurried across the pavement, watching the gray car out of the corner of his eye. He still couldn't make out the driver, but the guy had a silhouette like a boulder.

Frigid air-conditioning greeted Joe as he entered the noisy coffee shop. He strolled past a table of four cops, exchanging nods with one who looked up as he passed. Another pair of cops sat at a table at the far end of the room. A few civilians perched at the counter that stretched the length of the room. Lot of potential victims.

Lily Marsden was at a table for two, midway between the two sets of cops, facing him, sitting very straight in the wooden chair. Her hands were in her lap, and a black cell phone sat on the table next to a cup of coffee. She looked athletic, very trim, a little broad in the shoulders. A swimmer, he guessed, or maybe a rower. Her dark hair was short, cut so it came to little points around her face, focusing attention on her large brown eyes. There was intelligence in those eyes, along with the expected wariness. She watched without blinking as he approached.

"Hi there," he said as he plopped into the chair across from her and put his hands flat on the table. "I've been looking all over for you."

She forced up a smile, like she'd been expecting him. Joe noted she was wearing maroon lipstick, and he wondered about that. Woman makes up her face before she goes out to kill someone?

A waitress paused at the table, asked Joe what he wanted.

"Just coffee. For now."

As soon as the waitress was out of earshot, Lily leaned across the table. The smile was gone, and she whispered to him, biting the words off with her teeth.

"I don't know who you are, buddy, but you'd better get up and walk out of here right now."

He leaned toward her, until their faces were only inches apart.

"Joe Riley," he whispered. "From Chicago."

"Listen up, Joe Riley from Chicago. You don't want any coffee. You just remembered something and you need to hop up and run right out of here."

"Or what?"

"I'll pull the trigger on this pistol that I've got pointed under the table."

Joe hesitated a second, then said, "Under the table?"

"Guess where it's aimed."

He tried smiling at her. It took an effort. "You don't want to do that."

"*You* don't want me to do that. But it wouldn't bother me at all. In fact, I would greatly enjoy shooting your dick off. "

"Lotta cops in here," he said. "Going to be messy."

She lifted a shoulder. Casual. "I've seen messy before."

He straightened up, looked around. No one seemed interested in their conversation. The pair of cops down the way were arguing about baseball. He leaned in again, resumed the whispering.

"It's no good. There's six cops, plus me. You might get most of us, but somebody's going to take you down."

"Don't bet on it. I'm pretty good at this sort of thing."

"So I hear, but I can't take that chance. I need you alive."

"Yeah? Why?"

"It's a long story. I don't think we have time now."

"That's right. I'm still thinking about shooting you."

Joe sat back in the chair, but he kept his hands still.

"Don't you want to know how I found you?" he asked. "Aren't you curious, how we ended up sitting together in a coffee shop in Albuquerque?"

She opened her mouth to say something, but the waitress slipped up to the table and set a steaming mug in front of Joe. When she left, Lily said, "I saw Sal Venturi in your car. That explains most of it right there. Little bastard probably talked his head off."

"Sal's been talking to everybody. That gray Buick out there? Guy named Loomis from Vegas. His boss wants you dead. And there are others after you. That guy who died Thursday night at Tropical Bay?"

Lily glanced around the room, but no one was listening. Joe waited until her eyes came back to him.

"He's got two brothers. Couple of crazy old cowboys, look like Yosemite Sam."

"Who?"

"Never mind. These brothers, they're hunting you, too. And Sal told them you're here."

Some color came to Lily's cheeks. "Sal's got a big mouth."

"He's scared shitless. I could go out to the car and get him, if you want. Bring him in here, let him start talking to these cops."

"You wouldn't make it to the door. Not with your dick, anyway."

Joe smiled again. It was easier this time.

"You're not going to shoot me. You're too smart for that. You don't want to shoot all these cops. Why don't you just give up? We'll talk to the police, get it over with. Then you won't have to go out there and face Loomis."

She snorted. "He's the least of my worries."

Joe took a deep breath. He was running out of arguments. And, very likely, out of time.

"Lily, you're on the run, whether you like it or not. Sal's talked to the whole world. You've got guys coming after you from all over. Plus the Vegas cops. Plus me. Here's the difference: I'm not going to shoot you down in cold blood. I need you alive. Really. The cops? They've got rules. They're not going to shoot you unless you force the issue. But this guy Loomis? The Vernon brothers? God knows who else? Those guys are playing for keeps. You can't beat 'em all."

She leaned back, straightened her shoulders.

"I'll take my chances. First I've got to deal with you. How do you want to play it? Dick or no dick?"

Joe shrugged. "Guess I would prefer not to go around dickless."

"Then get up—right now—and go to the men's room. I'll be gone when you get back."

He scooted his chair back from the table.

"Do it slow," she said. "We don't want innocent people to get hurt."

Joe stood, slowly. Something caught his eye. The cell phone.

A number read out on its little window. It was upside-down, but Joe was good with numbers; it was why he was a good poker player. He memorized it at a glance, then looked back to her.

"I'll be in touch."

She faked a smile. "Don't trouble yourself."

He walked past her, not looking back, but he could feel her watching him over her shoulder. The men's room door was near the two cops who sat by the far wall, and Joe was tempted to alert them in some way. But that wouldn't accomplish anything except to get people killed. And it wouldn't solve his problem. What he told Lily was true: He needed her alive. Take her back to Chicago. Get her in court. Nail her for killing that little fuck Bennie Burrows.

He pushed through the men's room door, waited for a beat, then pulled the door open just enough to peek out. Lily was rising from the table. Her hands were empty. She strode out of the restaurant without a look back.

Joe came out of the men's room and watched out the windows, but he didn't see her in the parking lot. No shots. No revving engines. No squealing tires.

He went back over to the table, but he didn't sit down. Through the windows, he saw the gray Buick wheel out of its parking spot and creep toward the diner's front door. Still no Lily anywhere. He could see the Miata where she'd left it, empty. Where the hell had she gone?

He went to the exit, taking his time. He opened the door and leaned out, looking around. The Buick came back from the rear of the parking lot, then bumped out into the street. Looked like Loomis' silhouette was alone in there.

Joe cautiously stepped outside, searching for Lily, and his gaze settled on the Escort, still parked where he'd left it. Sal Venturi was gone.

"Shit!"

He felt a tug on his shirtsleeve, turned to find the waitress frowning at him. She handed him a piece of paper.

The check.

32

Mel Loomis sat in the Buick, watching the windows of the coffee shop, seeing the scene play out before him like a silent movie. The guy from the Escort goes in and sits down and he and Lily Marsden are smiling and talking and leaning across the table, practically brushing noses.

Loomis was thinking the whole time: Who the fuck is this guy? Friend of hers? How did he figure into this situation? Loomis didn't necessarily have a problem with shooting this guy, too, if that's what it took, but mostly he wanted one crack at Lily Marsden, away from these coffee-slurping cops.

Then her pal got up, headed to the crapper. Soon as the door closed behind him, Lily got to her feet, headed for the exit. Loomis was so ready for her. Car in gear, pistol on the seat beside him.

Then she pulled some sort of trick. He could see the door of the café at the far corner of the building, and he could see the Miata where she'd left it parked. Loomis was in the perfect position. No way she could evade him.

But she went out the door and turned left, instead of right, as he'd been expecting. He waited a minute, expecting her to make a break for one of the cars, but she was nowhere. Loomis cranked up the Buick and swung it around behind the building, but found nothing back there but a few cars and a trash bin and landscaped chain-link fences that separated the lot from the cheap motels that sat on either side of the coffee shop.

She could be hiding in the trash bin, he figured, or in some employee's car parked out back, wouldn't be noticed until the end of the shift. Or, she might've scaled a fence, gone to one of the motels to check in. No way to tell without doing a lot of obvious poking around in the parking lot that might draw the attention of the cops.

He turned around and drove past the coffee shop entrance, saw Lily Marsden's friend waiting at the door, watching the Buick. Loomis steered the car out into the street, went a couple of blocks west, then turned around in the parking lot of a place that sold mobile homes. He prowled back past the coffee shop, but Lily wasn't in the parking lot. And her friend had vanished, too. The Miata was still there, though, so Loomis found a place to park across the street.

He watched her car for an hour, but she never came back to it. Other cars came and went, but the little Miata sat right where she'd left it. Loomis drove around the area for another hour, looking for her, putting off the inevitable. He finally gave up and dialed his cell phone. Ken Staley answered.

"Hey, boss. Got a problem."

"Must be a big problem, you're calling me at two o'clock in the morning."

"Were you asleep?"

"Well, no—"

"Then what difference does it make?"

"All right, you're pissed. What happened?"

"The woman pulled that job in Albuquerque. Then she got away."

Loomis braced himself. Staley was not a man who took disappointment well.

"She got away?" Staley's voice had gone cold.

"I was right on her car, but I think she ditched it. She's nowhere."

"For fuck's sake. I thought I could count on you to do a job."

Loomis paused. One of the problems with corporate life: Sometimes you must eat abuse from lesser men, just to keep the sailing smooth.

"I can still do it," he said. "I'll go back to Scottsdale. Catch her when she comes home."

"No, screw it," Staley said. "I need you back here. Max Vernon's wife turned up dead, along with some guy who worked at The Cactus Ranch. Guy was screwing her, apparently, and somebody shot them both."

Loomis cleared his throat. He hadn't done much talking the past day or two. Sometimes, it felt like his voice forgot what it was supposed to do.

"Max Vernon's revenge, huh?" he said. "His brothers?"

"That's the prevailing theory, but the cops don't seem to have anything on them yet. Same squirrelly little woman is investigating that one, too."

"They'll get off scot-free."

"Probably. But I don't like all the gunplay around here. Those crazy Vernons might get it into their heads to come after us."

Gunplay. Staley was so full of shit.

"Why would they do that?"

"Hell, I don't know. I talked to Patti about them, and it turns out she's known Norm for years. She says the Vernons are meaner than alley cats and there's no telling what they'll do. I'd feel more comfortable if you were back here, keeping an eye on things. This other job can wait."

Loomis didn't like it. He felt Lily was still somewhere nearby. But Staley was the boss, and a fact of corporate life is that the bosses get to make the mistakes.

"I'll go to the plane right now."

"All right." Staley sounded suddenly far away, like he was thinking about something else.

"Too bad you didn't nail that woman," he said.

Time to eat more crow. Loomis said, "Sorry."

"I'm sure it couldn't be helped. I'm just wondering what I'll tell Patti."

Some suggestions came to mind, but all Loomis said was, "I'll see you in the morning."

35

Sal Venturi crouched under evergreen shrubs, hot and sweaty and prickly. He couldn't get comfortable. A metal sprinkler head poked up in the center of his hiding place, jabbing him in the ass. The shrubs had some kinda pollen or something, made him want to sneeze. He pinched his nose closed, and breathed through his mouth. Sounded like a freight train inside his head, but better than sneezing. Joe Riley might still be nearby. One of Sal's cannon-like sneezes would give him away for sure.

Sal thought of the way his secretary reacted whenever he got one of his sneezing fits. Four, five, six sneezes in a row. Velma counted them off out loud, egging him on, like she represented the fucking Guinness Book of World Records or something.

He wouldn't mind feasting his eyes on Velma about now. Get back to the familiar environs of Las Vegas, where he at least had money and contacts, an apartment and a car. Right now, he was like a fucking hobo, a homeless ragman hiding under the bushes.

Better this, though, than spend another minute with that spooky Joe Riley. Sal felt like Riley's eyes could cut right through him, peel away the fat and the lies and uncover the core truth. It wasn't a truth Sal could face.

He rubbed his nose, felt the sneeze impulse pass. He wiped the sweat off his forehead, then realized his bandaged hand was covered with dirt. Mud now. Which meant his face was covered with mud, too. Goddammit. He wiped his face with his sleeve.

Sal had seen Riley's little rent-a-car pull out of the parking lot earlier. He wasn't sure what had happened to Lily or Loomis. They might still be around somewhere, which would be bad for him. But so far, nothing had happened. People came and went at the coffee shop and one shift of cops eating doughnuts was gradually replaced by another.

Probably safe to come out from under these bushes now. No one around, nearly three o'clock in the morning. But still Sal waited.

He was at the far corner of the parking lot, as far as he'd been able to run after Riley had gone into the coffee shop. Riley thought he'd talked Sal into staying in the car, putting Loomis up as the bogeyman. But Sal was more afraid of Riley than he was of Loomis. At least on the run, Sal had a chance. He'd slipped out the car and waddled away, keeping as low as his round belly would allow. As soon as the coffee shop was between him and Loomis' car, Sal had straightened up and puffed his way to the rear of the parking lot.

The lot was surrounded by chain-link fences. No way could Sal climb a fence. Shit, most days, he was lucky he could get up out of his chair. He couldn't flee toward the street, past Loomis and Riley, so Sal had chosen to go rabbit. He crawled under the thickest landscaping he could find and hid there.

Now he felt certain he could come out. The others surely were gone. Riley was too busy chasing Lily to waste much time looking for Sal.

I should get up, he thought, go into that restaurant, clean up, call a cab. Go to the airport. Get a plane home as soon as possible. Get into some fresh clothes, get some sleep, see what the situation's like in Vegas. Maybe it would all work out. Or maybe I'll round up all the cash I can find and take off forever.

The evergreen bristles raked his bald head as he crouched lower to crawl back out to the pavement.

Sal heard a fizzle, a hiss. He tried to crawl faster.

The sprinklers erupted in a freezing spray.

34

Lily hung her arm out the window of a stolen Oldsmobile, feeling the soft desert air caress her skin. The ten-year-old car ran like a dream, but its air-conditioning was shot. Every time she turned on the cooler, the engine made a loud whine, like a cat trapped under the hood.

The night air was cool enough, though, once Lily shucked her denim jacket. It lay beside her on the seat, covering the little pistol that waited there. She'd like to ditch the pistol, but it was the only gun she had until she could get a new one in Vegas. Not much chance those assholes in Albuquerque would track her down, but she didn't want to be unarmed.

She got a flutter in her stomach, thinking about that business at the coffee shop. Of the dozens of contracts she'd served in the past decade, none had ever come so close to getting her caught. Witnesses to the hit, not one but *three*. A car chase. A café full of cops. Jesus, she must be slipping.

And that guy, Joe Riley from Chicago, coming right into the coffee shop, chatting her up like they were old friends. If he'd called her bluff, Lily would be in handcuffs by now, at best. More likely, she'd be dead, standing in line at the Pearly Gates behind Martin Holguin. Not much question about which way that verdict would go.

Riley smelled like a cop, but he sure as hell didn't act like one. He didn't look like one, either, with his rumpled suit, polo shirt, and scuffed loafers. And he needed a shave. She imagined he'd look pretty good cleaned up—that dash of gray in his hair, the spark of mischief in his dark eyes—but he was clearly unbalanced. Only a crazy man would've followed Lily into that den of doughnut-eating cops.

And he had Sal in his car. Had Riley forced Sal to lead him to Albuquerque? She didn't doubt Sal had blabbed about her to Loomis and to Max Vernon's brothers. Sal was weak. She supposed it was only a matter of time before he collapsed and got her in trouble. But what hold did Riley have over him? What did Riley *want*? He said he needed her alive, but for what?

The Olds slowed while she was lost in her thoughts. The highway was climbing higher, nearing the Continental Divide. She couldn't see much of the landscape in the dark. Just the occasional, random sprinkling of lights at ranches and hogans, a glow up ahead that signaled a town.

Gallup, New Mexico, lay on the other side of the divide, and Lily thought about stopping there, getting a Coke and something to eat. But she shook off the notion. Better to get more distance between her and Albuquerque first. The Olds still had half a tank of gas.

Nice of the owner to keep the tank topped off, Lily mused, save me some trouble.

Taking the car had been no trouble at all. She'd rounded the corner of the coffee shop and there it sat: An old Cutlass Ciera, a family car famous for being easy to steal. The doors were unlocked and Lily was inside, lying down, in an instant. She waited, figuring Loomis would come looking for her, but he didn't search car to car. His mistake. And, most likely, his good fortune. Lily had kept the pistol braced for the hour she'd lain in the seat. If anybody's head had popped up in the car's windows, she would've fired.

Once she felt safe, she decided to take the Olds. She hated to leave her Miata in Albuquerque, but maybe she could come back and get it eventually. Nothing in the car she couldn't live without. She had the pistol and her cell phone. There were two slim wallets in her hip pockets, each full of cash. One had her real ID and other was set up with a driver's license and credit cards in the name of Karen Marquette.

All she needed to jump the ignition was a screwdriver, and the owner thoughtfully kept a big one in the glove compartment. Lily sat up, popped the cover off the ignition switch and stabbed the screwdriver into the hole. Fiddle, fiddle, turn, and the engine cranked right up.

She'd been driving ever since. She was tired and her eyes felt scratchy, but she didn't want to stop. Better to drive through the night, get back to Vegas. With any luck, she'd be there waiting when that rat Sal Venturi got home.

The sudden chirping of her cell phone startled her. She hesitated before answering. Only Sal had this number. He no doubt was calling to make peace. Maybe she'd talk to him, assure him everything was fine. Make it easier to find him and kill him.

"Hello?"

"This is Joe Riley. Guy from the coffee shop?"

I'll be damned. Lily paused before saying anything, discarding the first reactions that came to mind: How'd he get this number? (Sal.) Why was he calling? (For Sal, probably.) Where was he calling from? (Who gives a shit?)

She said, "You tip the waitress?"

"You stuck me with the check."

"You got off easy. I'm not usually a cheap date."

"I'll bet. What do you like to do? Expensive dinners? Drinks and dancing? That sort of thing?"

"That sounds pretty good about now."

"Go to a casino, play the slots a while? Work off a little tension?"

"Maybe so." Hmm. He knew more about her than she'd guessed. Probably Sal again. Yakking his head off. She'd been thinking about slot machines earlier, after she passed the Acoma Sky City Casino right by the highway. Parking lot was full of cross-country semis, which had persuaded her to not even pause. She needed to keep moving, and she sure didn't want to sit in some joint, getting hit on by beer-bellied truckers. Too much like being back home in Dixie.

Again, it was as if he'd read her mind: "You've got an accent. You from down South somewhere?"

"I'm from down South, everywhere. We moved around a lot, looking for work."

"I like Southern accents, especially on women. They're soft."

Lily thinking: Great, I pass up romantic truckers so this Romeo can call me up, middle of fucking nowhere, and talk sweet. I've got to get rid of this phone.

"I knew you were from Chicago before you could get the word out of your mouth," she said. "South Side, right?"

"Hey, that's pretty good."

"Flat vowels, talk through your nose. I've heard it before."

"You spent time in Chicago?"

Lily wondered if she was being tape-recorded.

"I know all about you Southsiders. Let me guess: your whole family's cops. Dad, granddad, three or four brothers—"

"Five. All cops."

"Big Catholic family. All your uncles, they're cops, too. Or firemen."

"Uncle Alfred went with the Fire Department. The rest of the family won't speak to him."

"Lucky guy. So, your entire life, you were gonna be a cop."

"That's pretty much it."

"Get married, have eight kids, live down the block from your folks. Go to Mass. Get drunk. Get old."

"Gee, you make it sound like so much fun."

"So what happened, Mr. Chicago PD? What are you doing, chasing me around New Mexico?"

"My life took a wrong turn."

"Divorce?"

"I'm available, if that's what you're asking."

"Funny. Why'd she dump you?"

"How do you know it wasn't the other way around? Maybe I dumped her."

"Not likely, bubba. Cops and marriage don't mix."

"That's what my ex says. Too many temptations when you're on the job. She divorced me, then I went out and tried to prove her right. Drinking, gambling. Rolling around in temptations."

"Temptations get you in trouble."

"That's what happened. It's why I need to talk to you. Straighten out some things."

"What kind of things?"

"It's complicated."

An uncomfortable pause, then she said, "You still on the force?"

"No. I quit."

"So you're not even a cop. Why should I talk to you at all?"

"We've been talking. It's been pleasant enough."

It has, Lily thought, though I've done most of the talking. How did she know he wasn't still a cop? The phone call could be a way to track her down. Was it possible to trace a cell phone? At the least, the police could tell the signal came from a particular area, which could tell them where she was headed.

"I think it's time to hang up now," she said.

"Don't do that. I haven't had my turn yet."

"Your *turn*?"

"You got to analyze me, where I'm from, all that. Don't I get a turn?"

She smiled. "Make it quick."

"You're from the South, moved around a lot."

"I told you that two minutes ago."

"I'm just getting warmed up. You're single, no man in your life. You travel a lot. Don't have a lot of close friends."

"Easy enough to guess. Line of work I'm in."

"That's something I don't get. How did you—"

"How did a nice girl like me get into a job like this?"

"Yeah."

"It's like you said: A long story. We don't have that kind of time. I've gotta go now."

"Okay," he said brightly. "I'll call you later."

What was *wrong* with this guy?

"Don't bother," she said. "Soon as I hang up, I'm throwing this phone out the window."

"Don't do that. We need to talk some more."

She punched a button with her thumb and cut him off. She weighed the little phone in her hand, considering whether to toss it.

She might need it. Sal might call. She could get stranded

somewhere, run into trouble. She talked herself out of it and set the phone on the seat beside her.

But it worried her as she drove on through the desert night.

35

At 7 a.m. Sunday, Joe Riley turned in his rental car and caught a shuttle to Albuquerque International Sunport. He leaned his head back against the window of the van as it rumbled toward the "Departing Flights" ramp.

God, he was beat. He'd run all around Albuquerque looking for Sal, for Loomis, for Lily. He checked the motels near the coffee shop, but nobody had seen them. He prowled the streets, looking for Sal puffing down the sidewalk somewhere. Nothing. He'd even gone back to Martin Holguin's house, where patrol cars flashed and detectives scurried around, investigating the rug merchant's mysterious slaying. But Lily hadn't returned to the scene of the crime.

Finally, he stopped at a pay phone and called the cell number he'd memorized. She surprised him by answering. He'd done his best to keep her talking, trying to get some clue to where she was headed next, but she was too cool for that. And what had Joe done? Played cute with her, like a hardened assassin would melt under a little flirting.

He couldn't help himself. That killer drawl made him itch. Made it easy to picture her. Long legs and full lips. Wise brown eyes.

She had a quick mind, this Lily Marsden. She outsmarted him in the café, then outclassed him on the phone. Hadn't given up a thing about her location or her plans. She hadn't seemed too impressed by how cute he was, either.

He thought about calling her again from the airport, but figured it was no good. She said she was getting rid of the phone. He imagined it lying in the sand in the middle of some desolate desert, ringing its ass off, nobody around to hear. It seemed a pretty good summation of Joe's situation.

The van lurched to a stop and he opened his eyes. He was outside the America West entrance. He tipped the driver and stumbled out onto the sidewalk, so tired he could barely put one foot in front of the other.

The airport was relatively empty at this hour, and its wide tiled halls felt familiar. Joe thinking: I'm spending way too much time in airports. A good indication of how my life has gone to shit.

He stood in line behind a dozen others at the America West ticket counter, corralled by velvet ropes, the only passenger without any bags, probably the only one paying cash. Joe wondered whether he'd be mistaken for a terrorist, if he fit some profile the security people used. He hadn't shaved in a couple of days, and his lightweight suit was rumpled and soiled. He didn't smell too great, either.

Probably made a terrific impression on Lily Marsden. Looked like a raving wino. No wonder he couldn't get her to cooperate.

He had a hunch about where she'd go next, though. Lily seemed the kind of person who'd go straight at a problem. All that moving around she'd done as a child, all her traveling as a hired killer, none of it was running away. It was always running *toward* something. She wouldn't run from a fight. She'd run right at it. Which meant she was headed back to Vegas.

When it came his turn, Joe stepped up to the counter to be greeted by a round-faced brunette whose doughy cheeks rose when she smiled, turned her eyes into little crescents.

"I need to catch the next flight to Las Vegas."

"Do you have a reservation?" Her voice was high and bright. Perky. He tried not to wince.

He shook his head and her fingers danced over her computer keys. Joe leaned his elbows on the counter, taking some of the weight off his aching feet.

"You're in luck," she said. "We've got a few empty seats on the next flight. Leaves in less than an hour. You can just make it."

Joe pulled out his wallet and showed her his driver's license and she started punching up the ticket. She eyed him suspiciously when he pulled out three hundred-dollar bills to pay for it, and Joe thought, here we go, time for the airport strip-search. He still had a few of his Chicago PD business cards in his wallet and seeing them there, peeking out of the top slot, gave him an idea.

"Maybe you could help me with something."

He handed a card to the brunette. Her eyes lit up when she read he was a homicide detective. Joe pushed away thoughts of how he once again was impersonating an officer.

"Listen," he said, "I'm supposed to meet a friend in Vegas. Another cop. Could you tell me if he's on this flight?"

The clerk looked around, checking whether her co-workers were listening. Joe smiled, tried his best to look dashing. Tired as he was, it wasn't easy.

"What's the name?"

"Sal Venturi."

She clicked the computer some more. Joe had a good feeling about this. The timing was right. After Sal made his getaway, he might try to get a plane back home. First flight of the morning. . .

The brunette beamed at him. "This must be your lucky day."

Joe managed a weary smile.

"Officer Venturi is on this very flight," she said. "And there's an empty seat next to him, on the aisle. Would you like me to put you in that seat?"

"That would be great."

She punched some more keys, then gave Joe the crescent-eyes again.

"Won't he be surprised?"

"You have no idea."

36

First thing Lily did when she reached Vegas was phone a guy she knew, a hairy biker everyone called Happy Jack. Woke his ass up, which didn't seem to make him happy at all. She went by Jack's ratty apartment in North Las Vegas and paid him eight hundred dollars, cash, for a brand-new Glock 9-mm, still in its shipping box. Jack, half-asleep and eager to get back to bed, threw in a box of shells for free.

Lily left the motor running on the stolen Olds while she dealt with him, then drove to the Strip. She abandoned the car in a multi-story parking garage behind the Aladdin, after first wiping down the steering wheel and the dash. She dumped the .25 into a storm drain when she reached the curb downstairs. The new pistol went into her waistband and the extra bullets into her pockets. Then she went for a walk among the early birds on the Strip.

Bally's was a short hike away. It was one of the older casinos on this section of the Strip, the original MGM Grand before they built the new one with the big lion down the street. Lily picked it at random, entered the lobby and stepped up to the front desk, praying they had a room available. She needed to lie down for a few hours, get her wits about her.

Big mega-resort like Bally's would be the last place Sal and the others would look for her. Assuming Sal was still talking to everyone who'd listen, he'd tell them she liked out-of-the-way places—neon motels and roadside casinos. Or he'd send them to Scottsdale to wait for her to come home.

She pulled a wallet out of her hip pocket and gave it a glance. It was the correct one, with the documents that identified her as Karen Marquette. She handed the Visa card to a clerk behind the counter and asked for a room. The clerk was in her sixties, with the deep wrinkles of a lifelong smoker. She had high, thin arching eyebrows and red lipstick painted daintily at the end of her long upper lip. The makeup and the orange tint of her elaborate hairdo made her look like the Grinch done up as a circus clown—the perfect face for Las Vegas.

The front desk faced the huge, sunken-floor extravaganza of the casino. Even early on a Sunday, people sat at video poker and slot machines, some so bleary they had clearly been there all night. The bleeps, bloops, and clangs of the slot machines played a noisy melody. Lily didn't let it tempt her. She needed sleep.

"You're all set, Miss Marquette," the Grinch said, her voice like gravel on sandpaper. "Do you need help with your luggage?"

The clerk leaned forward, as if she could see over the tall counter to the floor.

"I don't have any luggage," Lily said. "The airline lost it."

"That's too bad. Anything the hotel can do to help?"

"They're tracking it down. Supposed to deliver it later."

"You need anything before it gets here, just ring the front desk. The elevators are right down there."

Lily took her card key and headed in the direction the Grinch had indicated. She couldn't wait to get to her room. Get her shoes off. Wash her face. Crawl into bed.

Her room was on the twentieth floor at the end of a winding hallway, felt like she'd walked miles. She let herself in the door, closed it behind her, then leaned back against it, blocking out the world. The room was large, with a king-sized bed, couple of armchairs, a built-in desk topped with Bally's trademark copper-colored marble.

Lily sat on the bed and kicked off her sneakers. Stripped off her jacket. Before she could toss the jacket aside, its pocket chirped at her.

She dug out the cell phone and held it up while it chirped again. Wondering what the hell she was doing, she pushed a button and answered.

"Hiya, Lily. Joe Riley here."

37

Joe grinned and shifted in his seat. "Guess where I'm calling from."

"The moon."

"Almost. I'm thirty thousand feet up in the air, using one of those phones they have in the back of airplane seats. Never used one before."

"Hurray for you."

Joe didn't like her flat tone. None of the flirtation he'd sensed there earlier. She sounded weary. Or maybe she simply was tired of his stupid phone games.

"Listen, the reason I'm calling," he said quickly, "I've got something you want."

"I doubt that."

"Don't be hasty. You haven't heard what it is yet."

"I can hardly wait."

"Hang on. Somebody here wants to talk to you."

The retractable cord on the phone wasn't long enough, so Joe had to sit forward to talk. He sat back now and handed the phone to Sal Venturi.

Sal looked like Joe was handing him a serpent. He dried his hand on his chest before taking the phone. Sal had found new clothes somewhere during his time on the lam—a cheap nylon running suit, dark green, made him look like a fucking watermelon. Since Joe joined him on the plane, Sal had sweated the clothes through.

"Hello, Lily. It's me."

Joe leaned toward Sal, but he couldn't hear Lily's end of the conversation. He could only imagine what she was saying to her talkative broker. Sal said nothing, but his face reddened.

After a minute passed, Sal handed the phone back. "She wants to talk to you."

Joe put the phone to his ear and said, "Yeah?"

"You've still got him."

"I lost him for a while, actually. But I got lucky. We were scheduled on the same flight."

It was all Joe could do to keep from hooting. The look on Sal's face when Joe sat next to him was something he'd never forget.

"So," she said, "what do you want for him?"

"You think Sal's for sale?"

"Everything has a price. I need Sal to disappear. He knows too much and he talks too much. I'll pay you to hand him over to me."

Joe hesitated. No way he could go along with such a transaction, send the little weasel to his doom. But maybe he could pretend to go along. He could agree to hand Sal over, but only in person. Could give him a last crack at Lily face-to-face.

"Maybe we need to sit down and talk about it," he said, stalling.

"What's to talk about? Name a price. We do a hand-off and you're through. Sal goes with me. You go back to Chicago with a pile of cash."

"How do I know you won't just shoot me as soon as you see me coming?"

"I'll give you my word."

"I don't think we know each other that well yet."

"This is as good as it gets," she said. "We're not gonna get to know each other any better."

"I'd like to know more about you, understand what makes you tick."

"You're never gonna get the chance."

"Stranger things have happened."

"Not to me."

They both fell silent, and the thought flashed through Joe's mind: This call's probably costing me five dollars a minute. Worth it, though, if I can get a new line on Lily.

"Where are you flying to?" she asked. "Vegas?"

"Good guess. I thought you might be going back there yourself."

"Maybe. If you've got Sal, Vegas is the place to be. Sell him to the highest bidder."

"I tell you, it's not like that. I'm not in this for money."

She breathed into the phone, sounded like a sigh.

"Look, Joe Riley, it's always about the money. We can dress it up in fancy clothes and paint its face and make it mind its manners, but underneath it's all about money. You don't believe me, look at Las Vegas. Underneath all the glitz, what have you got? Nothing but greed. They should have signs at the city limits: 'Welcome to Vegas. Leave your money and go home.'"

Joe smiled.

"Sounds like you're in Vegas right now," he said. "I recognize it in your voice. People spend any time there, they start talking like jaded gamblers."

"That's how I sound to you?"

"You sound tired. If you're in Vegas, that means you traveled all night. You must be beat."

"Don't worry about me."

"But I do, Lily. Your welfare is important to me. Eventually, I'll take you back to Chicago with me. I need you to talk to people there, help me get my life straightened out."

"That's what it'll take to make your life all better?"

"Maybe."

"Must not be much of a life."

Joe's cheeks warmed. She was right, of course. It hadn't been much of a life. His marriage had ended, and he was living in a shabby apartment over a reeking pizza joint. He gambled all night in backrooms and saloons. And maintained a perpetual hangover and money troubles. The only thing that went right was the job. Working with Sam, solving murders, putting in long days to see that justice was done. And Lily Marsden had robbed him of that.

"It wasn't much," he said. "But it was all I had."

She said nothing. Joe wondered whether she was thinking over what he'd said, whether she felt any empathy. Hell, like it mattered. No way she'd feel so sorry for him she'd turn herself in. He needed to find a way to trap her.

"We need to talk," he said. "You, me and Sal. We'll sit down, hash this thing out face-to-face."

"A meeting? So you can have a bunch of your cop friends waiting for me?"

"Wouldn't be like that. I give you my word."

"You said a little while ago, my word wasn't good enough for you. Now you want to turn it around, tell me I should trust you."

Joe's mind raced as he tried to figure a way to make it work. They'd be on the ground in Vegas in just over an hour. Plenty of time for her to hit the road again. If she was even there. This time, she could be gone forever.

"I've got it," he said. "We'll meet at McCarran."

"What?"

"The airport. No way anybody can show up with weapons. All of us will have gone through security."

Joe felt a bubble of excitement inside, sure she'd go for it.

"Only ticketed passengers get through security," she said.

"So buy a ticket. We're arriving in an hour, America West, flight seven hundred. Take the money you've been trying to throw at me, buy a ticket to anywhere. Go through security and meet us at our gate."

"You're assuming I'm already in Vegas, that I can make it to the airport in an hour."

Joe smiled. He glanced at Sal, who looked ill.

"I sure hope you are," he said. "Because it'll be your last chance to see our friend Sal. If you're not there, I'm taking him straight to the Vegas cops. I think they'll be interested in what he has to say."

"Wait—"

"Bye, Lily."

38

Sal Venturi's brain gnawed on his problem as the flight set down in Vegas. He kept at it through the interminable delay while the passengers wrestled down their carry-on luggage and inched toward the jetway. Sal and Joe Riley, neither with any luggage in the first place, stood in the crowded aisle. Riley's hand casually clasped Sal's elbow. If Sal made the wrong move, the former cop would squeeze that nerve, the one they call the "funny bone," and Sal would dance in place from the pain.

He tried to ignore his physical discomforts—Riley's big hand on his arm, the bruises and stinging scratches on his scalp, his bandaged hand, his sopping clothes. He needed to keep his mind on the problem, set priorities, try to figure a way out of this mess.

It all came down to two issues:

1) Stay alive.

2) Stay out of jail.

Everything else, up to and including physical pain, Sal would find a way to withstand. He'd proved that over the past two days. He'd been kidnapped and threatened and roughed up. Seen a man shot to death. Been in a car chase with people with guns. Made his escape, at great personal risk and suffering. Only dumb fucking luck had resulted in him falling back into Riley's clutches.

Sal would need to talk fast and think faster to get out of this jam, but one thing was certain: He wasn't leaving the airport with Riley or Lily. If Riley hung onto him, he'd eventually kill him or turn him over to the cops. Lily would kill Sal for sure, first chance she got. If he somehow escaped them both, made his way out into the city, there were the Vernon brothers and Loomis and the octopus arms of Ken Staley. He'd end up dead, one way or the other.

The only safe place, he thought as he and Riley ducked into the jetway, is here in the airport. No weapons. No way for Lily to kill him in front of witnesses, and with security guards all over the place. She'd sounded on the phone like she was ready to punch his ticket, no matter the cost, but Sal knew her sense of self-preservation was too strong. She wouldn't risk a scene in the airport.

But Riley was a cop. He didn't care about scenes. If Sal refused to leave the airport with him, Riley could hand him over to the airport police. They could jail him until the local cops could assemble charges.

Better jail than a coffin, though. Sal could get out of jail. He could cajole and demand and obfuscate. He could accuse Riley of kidnapping, so the star witness against him would be in the clink himself.

Sal would take his chances with the courts. There, at least, he was in his murky element. Out here in the world, where people ran around shooting each other, he didn't stand a chance.

Sal puffed up the ramp, Riley on his arm, and stepped into the cool air-conditioning of the airport. Slot machines down the way jangled and clanged. People scurried to and fro. Sal felt a genuine human warmth toward these people, these potential witnesses. They could be all that stood between him and a sudden death.

Hell, he could just live here at McCarran. It was like a little city, containing everything he needed. He could spend all day going from one fast-food stand to another, playing the slots, hanging out in waiting areas, chatting with travelers, having his shoes shined. He'd never leave the safety of metal detectors and security guards until this blows over.

Yes, Sal decided, and he actually nodded to himself, I'm not leaving this airport. Not with Riley. Sure as shit, not with Lily. If they try to force me, I'll slump to the floor and start screaming. Cops will come running. Then we'll see which one of us is quickest on the draw with a *habeas corpus.*

Riley pulled Sal to one side after they were inside the airport, let the other deplaning passengers pass by. Creating, Sal noted, a nice protective screen while they got his bearings.

Sal looked around, blinking against sweat, but he saw no sign of Lily.

"Over here," Riley said. He dragged Sal to a row of chairs near the windows. Tinted glass gave the sunny brown landscape a twilight cast. They sat down, facing indoors, both searching the crowd for Lily.

And then she was in front of them. Just like that. Sal hadn't seen her coming, might not have recognized her if he had. She wore black sunglasses and a crisp new baseball cap. A red bandana was tied carelessly around her throat. It hid her long neck and seemed to change the shape of her face. She wore black denim head-to-toe and high-topped black sneakers. Ready for action.

She stood over them, her feet slightly apart, straight under her shoulders. Balanced and poised, and Sal recognized she could kill him in an instant with her bare hands, and there wasn't a damned thing he could do about it.

What had he been thinking? No place was safe from Lily. She knew so many ways to kill a man, he'd never be safe, even in a crowded airport.

"Hello, boys."

Another row of chairs was behind her and she took a step backward and settled onto one of the chairs without taking her eyes off them. The way she moved made Sal think of a black cat.

"Well," Riley said, too loud, "here we all are."

"I looked around," she said. "I figured you would've called ahead, had the cops staking the place out."

"I told you I wouldn't."

"Looks all right so far, but I wouldn't make any wrong moves if I were you. You want to stay right there in those chairs. Keep very still. Otherwise, things get ugly."

"Nothing's going to happen," Riley said. "We're all safe here. Let's keep it that way."

Sal couldn't see her eyes for the dark sunglasses. Riley seemed transfixed, like a bird hypnotized by a snake.

Christ, the fucker's smitten with her! Here we are, might die any second, and Joe Riley's trying to come up with a way to make his move. Sal mopped his forehead with his sleeve, trying to think of a way to use this new insight.

He looked up, realized Lily had turned her gaze on him.

"Nice outfit, Sal," she said. "You taking up running?"

"Look, Lily." Sal's stomach rumbled and he wondered if he'd soil himself right here in the airport. That would change the tenor of this tense meeting. "I know you're mad at me, but I've been in a lot of danger. People are threatening to kill me."

The sunglasses turned Riley's way for a second, then back to Sal.

"Not this guy," Sal said impatiently. "He just drags me

around airplanes, poking holes in me with his thumb. But the Vernons and Ken Staley's man, Loomis, those guys came within an inch of dropping the hammer on me."

"So to save your pissant life," she said, "you told them where to find me."

Sal gulped. He had a bad taste in his mouth, tasted like death.

"I didn't have any choice." He cleared his throat and coughed into his fist. Gave him something to do other than look at Lily. The cold threat in her posture, those black sunglasses and dark clothes, made her seem like an automaton, a killing machine. She was trying to scare him, and she was doing one helluva job.

"It's like I told you, Lily," Riley piped up. "You came back to Vegas spoiling for a fight, but you're outnumbered. Staley will have the whole town after you."

Sal braved looking up, saw Lily staring at Riley now. She casually crossed her legs, but Sal could see the muscles coiled tightly under her clothes. He looked around the airport in search of security guards. None nearby. No one overhearing this conversation.

"No place to hide, Lily," Riley said. "You stay in this town, you haven't got a chance."

"How do you know I'm staying here? Here I am, at the airport, already bought a ticket. Maybe I'm moving on."

"They'll track you down."

"I don't think so. The only reason anyone found me is because of this fat fuck right here."

Sal ducked his head, took a sudden interest in his lap. Was the dampness there just sweat, or had he had a little accident? He waited until Lily started talking again before daring to look at her.

"If Sal had shown a little guts, kept his mouth shut, none of this would've happened. But he was too busy saving his own ass. Well, he's not saving it from me. Your ass is mine, Sal. Might not be today, but it'll be soon."

Sal belched into his fist. His nerves were playing havoc with his digestive tract.

"You don't have to kill him," Riley said, his voice low. "Make your disappearing act. I'll hand him over to the cops. They'll have a field day going through his files."

Sal felt a little hope blossom within him, but it wilted quickly when Lily shook her head.

"Too much there that might point to me. I'd spend the rest of my life looking over my shoulder."

Riley leaned forward and rested his elbows on his knees. Sal wondered whether this would be a good time to scream. Riley's distracted, busy making goo-goo eyes at Lily. Sal could get a good scream out before Lily could get to him. Of course, she might snap his neck before anybody even turned to look. He took a deep, shuddering breath, but let it out noiselessly.

"Word will get out either way," Riley said. "Pretty soon every cop in the country will be watching for your face."

"Maybe I need another country," she said coolly. "Maybe my airplane ticket says South America."

"I don't think so. I think you've got it into your head that you're going out in a blaze of glory. Take out Sal and the Vernons and Loomis and whoever else you can hit before they get to you. But it's not going to work, Lily. The odds are too great."

"I like to gamble."

Riley shook his head. "Hey, nobody likes to gamble more than me. But you know what? Long shots bring nothing but trouble. You need to bet on the short odds, the sure thing. Only way to beat the house."

She uncrossed her legs and mirrored Riley's posture, leaning toward him.

"The sure thing," she said, "takes all the fun out of it."

"Is it fun, Lily? Seems creepy to me. Erasing people from the planet. How do you live with yourself?"

Her face hardened.

"Let me ask you something, Joe Riley," she said. "You're a good Catholic boy, right?"

He grinned at her. "I think of myself as a practicing hedonist."

"Practicing?"

"Until I get it right."

She smiled a little. Jesus Christ, Sal thought, why don't you two get a motel room and let me go about my business?

"I grew up going to Baptist churches," she said. "Every Wednesday night, twice on Sunday. It was the one constant in my life."

Sal tried to picture that. Little ramshackle churches in the middle of nowhere, full of hillbillies praying their asses off, passing around snakes. It gave him a shiver.

"You know what they teach in those churches? Heaven and hell. That's it. Nobody cares about getting through this life. They're all worried about dying, as if dying wouldn't come as a relief to all their misery."

"That's religion everywhere," Riley said.

"But most religions, you can talk your way out of trouble. Confess your sins. Get a pardon. Not in these churches. They believe, you do something bad enough, you're bound for hell, no matter what else you do."

"Like killing a man?"

"That's right. You kill somebody, you're pretty much done for in afterlife."

Riley looked thoughtful, sorting it out. "You kill one person, you might as well kill a whole bunch more? Make a living at it?"

"At one time, that was the way it seemed to me. Now, I'm not so sure."

"How old were you? The first time?"

Sal thinking: The fuck is this? "This Is Your Life?" But he said nothing.

"Fourteen. My uncle tried to . . . touch me."

She paused, shook her head slightly.

"We were in the kitchen. There was a butcher knife on the table."

Joe frowned. "So you started out as a victim—"

"Bullshit. I don't buy that 'victim' nonsense. That just got me started, that's all. I chose this life for myself."

"Then why not choose something else? Why not go with me to Chicago?"

"No way."

"At least get the hell out of Las Vegas."

Sal watched a geezer with pants hitched up to his armpits, loaded down with two carry-ons, start to walk down the aisle that separated Riley and Lily. The old man stopped when he saw the trio sitting there, deep in conversation. He decided to go the long way around.

Sal turned back to the other two, found them both looking at him.

"What?"

"We've got to figure out what to do with you," she said.

Sal shook his head. "You're doing nothing with me. I've thought it over. I'm staying here at the airport. You try to make me leave, I'll start yelling. Cops will come running."

"This is your plan?" Riley said. "Get the cops here so I can turn you over to them?"

"Better than letting Lily take a crack at me."

"I already told you," she said. "It may not be today, but your time's coming."

Sal pushed up his glasses. "What about all that shit you were just saying? About going to hell. You kill me, you'll go to hell for sure."

Lily gave him a chilly smile. "You'll get there first."

"Easy now," Riley said. "This little talk has worked out fine so far. Let's not go crazy."

Sal kept trying to swallow. Felt like he had a hairball in his throat.

"Okay, here it is," she said finally. "I'll walk away from here. So will you. And so will Sal. We'll see what happens next."

Riley shook his head. "I didn't say I'd turn him loose. That wasn't part of the deal."

"We've got no deal," she said. "I said we all walk out of here alive. If Sal starts screaming, it won't turn out that way. Somebody dies. Sal for sure. Maybe all of us."

Sal's gut gurgled.

"All right," Riley said. "We all leave separately. Quietly. I can live with that. Besides, if I want to find Sal again, all I've got to do is get on an airplane."

Riley laughed at his own stupid fucking joke.

"I'll leave first," Lily said. "But I'll watch to make sure you let Sal go."

"I'll stick to it. Promise."

"So long," she said, and got smoothly to her feet.

They watched her melt into the airport crowd. Sal braced

for another argument with Riley, but the cop stood up, ready to walk away.

"See ya, Sal. Good luck."

Sal stammered out a thanks.

"You need a lot of luck," Riley said, "with that woman after you."

Sal waited until Riley disappeared from sight. Then he got up from his chair and hurried, taking quick little steps, to the nearest men's room.

39

Mel Loomis had feelers out everywhere for Sal Venturi and Lily Marsden, and it wasn't long until a friendly travel agent came up with the information that Venturi was on his way back to Las Vegas.

The tip came in only thirty minutes before the plane's scheduled arrival. Loomis raced into the stifling heat to one of the company Fords parked out back of Tropical Bay. It was a short hop over to McCarran, and Loomis parked the car and locked his gun in the glove compartment and trotted into the cool interior of the airport.

No time to get to Venturi's gate. Not these days, when long lines crept along at the security checkpoints. But there was only one way out of the concourse. Loomis leaned against a wall near the exit, waiting for Venturi to show.

He watched the passing throngs carefully, ignoring those who looked his way, their gazes snagged by the face that plagued him. Loomis sometimes thought about growing out his hair, growing a beard, *something* to detract from his resemblance to Curly Howard. But that would be surrendering to the gawkers. Fuck 'em. Better to give them the cold stare back, daring them to make a remark. Occasionally, it gave him reason to exact punishment on some loudmouth, which almost made it worthwhile.

If he hadn't been leaning against the wall, brooding, Loomis might've fallen over in surprise when he glimpsed the man weaving his way through the slow-moving crowd. It was the guy from Albuquerque, the one Lily met at the cop-filled coffee shop. Loomis squinted at him, but it was no mistake. Same guy. The man needed a shave and he looked rumpled, like he'd gone straight from the coffee shop to the airport, maybe slept in his clothes along the way.

Loomis looked around the crowd again, but found no Venturi. Shit.

Ken Staley wanted him to bring in Venturi, but here was this guy, who clearly knew Lily at least as well as Venturi did. Time for Loomis to show some initiative, to make a corporate-style snap decision, one he could justify later to his boss. He stepped away from the wall and, with one last look around for Venturi, set out after Lily Marsden's friend.

He followed him into a parking garage, then ran like hell to get to his own car and catch up with the man's twenty-year-old Chevy. Fortunately, there was a line of cars at the pay booth. Loomis found the Chevy there, trailed it out of the airport and over to the Strip, where the guy checked into an old motel.

He parked on the far side of the motel's asphalt lot and hunkered down behind the wheel while the man went into the motel office. Loomis worried what Staley would think about him abandoning his search for Venturi. It was important (and profitable) to stay on Staley's good side, and it wasn't always easy.

He thought about calling Staley, or maybe sending one of his security guys to look for Venturi. But he didn't dial his cell phone. Better if he waited. When he told Staley he'd disregarded orders, he'd need something better to offer.

Like Lily Marsden herself.

40

Joe Riley hesitated as he pulled into the driveway of the Pink Elephant Motor Lodge. Those two idiot gamblers found him here last time. Would they still be hunting him? Surely they'd learned their lesson.

He parked and went into the office. Mona was behind the counter, hanging up the phone. She seemed to always be on duty in this dump. Joe wondered whether she lived here, had a room in the back or something, and stood a round-the-clock vigil at the front desk.

She looked skittish as she offered him a room. Probably remembered what he'd done to those two morons who came to call on him. He wondered if she'd called the cops. He started to ask, but decided it was better to pretend nothing had happened. Just get his room and get into a shower. Wash off some of the road grit and airplane staleness. If Delbert and Mookie showed up here again, he'd deal with them. This time, he'd be the one with the guns.

Joe signed the register and took his key and shuffled back out to the Chevy. God, he was tired. He drove the car across the small parking lot, plucked his duffel bag out of the back seat and went into the cool room.

He dumped his duffel on the bed and stripped off his clothes and went directly to the shower. He stayed under the needling spray for twenty minutes, then stood naked before the mirror and shaved off three days' worth of beard. He dressed in jeans and sneakers and his last clean shirt—a Hawaiian number with palm trees on it. When he was done, he looked like a well-groomed tourist.

Joe sat on the bed and pulled the phone over into his lap. He lit a Camel, dialed a Chicago number, and asked for Sam Kilian. It took a while, but Sam finally came on the line.

"Hi, Sam. Got anything for me?"

"Where are you?"

"Back in Vegas. Lily Marsden came back here, but she slipped through my fingers. I thought maybe you turned up a lead on the computers."

"I ran her through NCIC and the rest and there's nothing. No record, no arrests, nothing. Sure you got her name right?"

"Might be another alias, I don't know. She told me today she killed her uncle when she was fourteen, her first. They lived somewhere in the South. There's got to be a record of it."

"Hell, she was a juvenile. All those records would be sealed. You know that."

"I'm getting desperate. Maybe she's never been caught since, never been printed or questioned. How good would that make her?"

"We knew she was good from the start," Sam said. "We wouldn't have had anything on her if it hadn't been for Bennie's camera."

"And she thought she'd broken that."

"There you go."

"She's in Vegas. There's this guy here, her broker. She wants to kill him because he ratted her out. Maybe I'll find him again, stake him out, catch her when she makes her move."

Sam was silent for a moment, then said, "You could end

up dead, Joe. Come back to Chicago."

"Can't do it, buddy. Not yet anyway. Thanks for checking the computers. I know it could get you in trouble."

"It's not *my* troubles I'm worried about."

"I'll be in touch."

He hung up before Sam could raise more objections. His friend's heart was in the right place and, hell, he might be correct. Maybe Joe *should* go back to Chicago, wait this thing out. But he'd come so close, he couldn't give up now.

He wondered where Lily was, whether she'd found Sal. Despite her cool confidence at the airport, despite the sunglasses, she'd looked road-weary. Maybe she holed up somewhere to get some sleep.

Crawling into bed sounded pretty inviting, but Joe's stomach rumbled, reminding him he hadn't eaten in twenty-four hours. First, food. Then he'd come back to the motel room, stretch out on the bed, and see if he could think through it all before sleep overtook him.

He checked to make sure he had the keys to the Chevy, then remembered something with a jolt. He'd left the guns in the car.

Hell, I must be tired, he thought. Maybe I'll just cruise a drive-thru, get some burgers, bring them back here. Bring the guns in the *room* with me this time.

Joe threw open the door and winced against the sudden blast from the scorching sun.

A long black car roared up in front of him, and its tires squealed as the driver hit the brakes. The limo's back door was even with Joe, and it flew open. There sat Delbert, his bruised face so many colors, it looked like something out of "Fantasia." He pointed a pistol at Joe.

"Get in the fuckin' limo."

41

Sal Venturi hauled himself out of the taxi and paid the driver. The cab was stopped at an angle in the parking lot outside Sal's office, leaving thirty feet of open space to the front door. The converted house looked shut up tight. Sal felt very alone after the taxi pulled away.

He hurried to the building, but saw no one in the empty parking lots surrounding his office. Panting, he got inside and locked the door behind him.

So far, so good. Sal had abandoned his plan to stay at the airport for the rest of his life. If he stayed at McCarran, Lily would come for him there eventually; she'd figure out a way around all the security. Better to keep moving. Make a few phone calls, gather up cash and clothes, and disappear. Maybe forever, certainly until somebody finished off Lily. As long as she was loose in the world, he would be on the run.

The door to Sal's inner office was half-open and a light burned in there. Goddamned Velma, he thought, I've told her a million times to turn out the lights when she locks up. She think I'm made out of money? Sal caught himself and snickered. As if the electric bill was the worst of his worries. He'd never even see the bill; he'd be gone. He wondered how long Velma would keep showing up to work before she figured out she was unemployed.

He pulled his office door open, and his breath caught in his throat. The Vernon brothers were inside. Hi sat at Sal's desk, facing the door, the light glinting off his glasses, his hand on the phone, as if he'd just hung up. Norm lounged in the guest chair, looking over his shoulder at Sal.

"Mornin', scumbag," Norm said. "We been waiting for you."

"Got a call from a friend of ours," Hi said. "Guy who saw you at the airport. We figured you'd head back here."

Sal stammered, trying to soak it all in. "At the airport?"

"It's still a small town," Hi said. "Lots of folks want to do us favors. You keep thinking you can outmaneuver us, but our friends are watching you."

"I wasn't trying to—"

Norm came out of his chair and got up in Sal's face.

"You little fucker," he said, his face flushing. "I told you before, you don't hand over that woman, you're gonna take her place at the graveyard."

"I was *trying* to hand her over. Where do you think I've been? I almost got killed tracking her down."

"Then where is she?"

"She was at the airport when I got here. Didn't your *friends* tell you that?"

Norm whacked him across the cheek with a quick backhand that turned Sal's head halfway around.

"Don't get smart with me, boy. Just tell us where to find her."

Sal's hand went to his cheek, felt the heat there.

"I don't know. She said she had an airplane ticket, that she might be leaving town, but I think she's still here. Hell, she might be outside right now for all I know."

Hi and Norm exchanged a look.

"She came back to Vegas on her own?" Hi asked.

"I told you. She was at the airport. There's this guy, this cop, or at least he used to be a cop. He set up a meet for the three of us at the airport, figuring it would be safe there."

"This cop, what's his name?" Hi asked.

"Joe Riley. He's got some beef with a job Lily pulled in Chicago. He wants to take her back there, turn her in."

"Where is this Riley now?"

"I don't know. We all left the airport separately. I was just stopping by here to get some things, then I'm gone. Lily knows I talked about her. I don't want her to find me."

Norm shook his head. "You're not going anywhere, boy. We might need you. You still owe us one killer."

"But—"

"Shut up, Sal," Hi said mildly. "I'm trying to think."

Sal wrung his hands, waiting. It was just as he feared. The Vernons wouldn't let him go this time. And Lily could walk through that door any minute.

"You don't know where she is?" Hi asked.

Sal shook his head. "Believe me, I'd tell you if I knew. Nothing I'd like better than for you to take her out."

The brothers looked at each other and Norm's eyebrow raised in question. Oh, shit, Sal thought, here it comes, more violence. But Hi shook his head and got wearily to his feet. Sal edged away from Norm.

"Let's go, Norm," Hi said. "She's here in town, it shouldn't take us long to turn her up."

The twins headed for the door. Sal said, "What about me?"

"You stay right here," Hi said. "We could take you with us, but I frankly can't stand to look at your sweaty puss all day. We'll have our friends watching. You try to run, we'll know before you clear the city limits."

Then they were gone. Sal stumbled to his desk, sat in his leather chair, which was still warm from Hi's scrawny old butt. Sal removed his glasses and cradled his face in his hands.

"Jesus Christ," he moaned, "what next?"

42

Joe Riley should've been scared with Delbert's gun pointed at his chest, but it was all he could do to keep from laughing. After surviving Lily Marsden, menacing Sal Venturi, chasing all over the countryside, he ends up here, facing down these two dopes.

"Wish you'd point that gun somewhere else," he said. "You look nervous. You might have an accident."

Delbert, his face mashed and Technicolor behind the clear plastic mask, said: "Shut the fuck up. Only reason I haven't shot you already is I don't want to get blood all over the limo."

Joe gave him a slow smile. The guy's voice sounded funny, with his nose smashed flat. Made Joe think of Elmer Fudd. Plus the pompadour and the purple velour suit. Elmer done up like a pimp, circa 1972. How was Joe supposed to take him seriously?

"This your car? This chauffeured limo? Got your friend up there behind the wheel. Nice bar here in the back, cut-glass decanters fulla booze. What's in that little cabinet? A TV?"

"The fuck do you care? What you wanna do? Watch a soap opera? Be the last thing you ever see."

The big black guy behind the wheel snorted. Joe took in

once again the inflated blue splint on his arm. Mookie had it all wrong. The splint was on the *outside* of his uniform sleeve. That couldn't be right. Moron.

"Way I got it figured," Joe said, "your buddy up there works for a limo company. You guys borrow it anytime you need a ride."

"What, you think I can't afford my own limo?"

"Not the way you play poker."

Delbert's face turned some new colors behind the mask, and his lips curled back from his teeth. He raised his revolver to point at Joe's face and thumbed the hammer back.

"You motherfu—"

"Careful," Joe said. "You don't want to get blood on the car."

Delbert's hand shook, looked like it took one hell of an effort not to pull the trigger.

"Hey, Delbert," rumbled the driver. "I think somebody's following us."

Delbert Nash pulled the gun down close to his body, but kept it pointed at Riley. He swiveled around in the seat.

"That white Ford?"

"Been behind us since we left the motel."

"Aw, shit." Delbert squinted through the rear window. The driver was a shadowy shape; all Delbert could tell was that he was a big man. "Who the fuck could that be?"

Delbert turned back to Riley, nudged him with the pistol. "That a friend of yours?"

Riley didn't even bother to look. "Nobody I know."

"Yeah, right."

They were clear of the city limits and the suburbs that

crowd Vegas to the south. Empty desert as far as the eye could see.

"Pull off onto that dirt road up there, Mookie. See if that car follows."

Delbert poked Riley in the side with the pistol again. "You better not be lyin' to me."

Riley frowned. "You stick that gun in my ribs again, I'm gonna shove it up your ass."

Delbert felt the heat rise within him, but he didn't jab Riley with the gun. Instead, he said, "Big talk, coming from a dead man."

Mookie swung the long car wide to turn into the narrow dirt road. The limo bumped off the pavement and was instantly swallowed up by a cloud of fine brown dust.

Mookie thinking: Shit, I'll have to wash the car again. Already did that once today, and it wasn't easy to handle the pressure hose with a broken arm. The splint got in the way, made it hard to grip anything with that hand. He used his other hand to tend the steering wheel as the limo roared up the straight dirt road to nowhere.

The Ford swung in behind, the driver not even pretending he wasn't trailing them.

"He's still back there, Delbert. What do you want me to do?"

"Drive another mile or two, get away from the highway. Then we'll see what's what."

Mookie didn't like this. It was one thing hunting Joe Riley, getting even with him for all the pain he'd caused—Mookie's nuts still felt big as cantaloupes. But it was another thing to have Delbert waving that gun around, ready to shoot Riley and whoever was in that other car, too. The whole thing was getting out of hand, but Mookie said nothing. This was Delbert's show, and Delbert knew best. Mookie would play along the way he always did.

"Okay," Delbert said from the back seat, "this oughta be far enough. Pull over here anywhere."

Mookie turned on his blinker, easing his foot onto the brake. He wanted to give the Ford plenty of warning. Didn't want it zooming out of the dust and creaming the back end of the limo. Mookie didn't need that kind of heartache. He'd be explaining that one away forever, trying to convince his boss he had a good reason to take the limo out in the middle of the desert and wreck it.

The limo bumped to a stop. Mookie watched in the mirror as the Ford stopped, too, about twenty yards away. The dust settled around them.

"What now, Delbert?"

"Go see what that guy wants."

"Say *what*?"

Loomis left the engine running while he sat behind the wheel. He might need to haul ass.

The limo sat there for a minute, its dark windows revealing nothing. The car's taillights stared at Loomis, waiting for him to do something. He stayed behind the wheel. They weren't going anywhere with him parked between them and the highway.

The driver's door opened and a beefy black chauffeur got out from behind the wheel. Had some kind of blue thing on one arm. He kept his other hand behind his hip. Loomis had a pretty good idea what he was holding.

Well, he thought, two can play that game. He popped open his door and got out, keeping his pistol near his thigh. He could drop behind the open door if the chauffeur started shooting. Fucker wants a shootout in the desert, Loomis could accommodate him.

The chauffeur took a hesitant couple of steps toward Loomis. The back door of the limo on passenger side opened and another guy got out, skinny little white guy with too much hair and some kind of mask on his face. He wore a shiny purple suit. The hell is this, Halloween?

Loomis' gaze shifted from one to the other, trying to decide who'd get brave first. He didn't want to shoot either of these guys. He wanted the one still in the limo, Lily Marsden's pal.

Then the chauffeur's face split into a big grin.

"Hey, Delbert," he said, "look at this guy. Who's he look like?"

Loomis' lips pressed together tightly. Here it comes.

"The hell you talking about?" Delbert said.

"He looks just like Curly. You know, on The Three Stooges."

Delbert looked confused. Loomis took a deep breath, feeling anger building within him.

"Hey, buddy," the chauffeur shouted. "Say something like Curly. Go *woop-woop-woop.*"

Loomis raised his pistol in a smooth motion and shot the chauffeur through the shoulder. The impact of the .45-caliber slug spun him around and he hit the ground face-first.

Pop! The white guy got off a shot, but it zinged harmlessly off into the desert. Loomis opened up on him. Five holes thunked into the limo's skin, and the rear windshield shattered.

The guy with the pompadour ducked behind the limo, but his hand appeared over the trunk and fired his pistol blindly. One shot ricocheted off the grille of the Ford, another spider-webbed the windshield. Loomis squatted behind the car door and fired again, but hit only the limo.

Then the window in the door shattered, spraying Loomis with glass. He threw up a hand to protect his face, then wondered why he bothered. Some scars, and perhaps he'd no longer resemble Curly.

He peeked through the shattered window and saw the chauffeur lying in the road, his gun in his splinted hand. The blue balloon didn't keep him from pulling the trigger.

Fuck, Loomis thought, they've got the angles. And this clip's about empty. He jumped behind the wheel, threw his car into reverse and gunned the engine. The Ford lurched backward up the dirt road.

Delbert fired one last shot, which pinged off the hood. Loomis kept his foot to the floor, dust roiling into the car through the broken windows.

He got a last glimpse of the skinny man in the purple suit before dust obscured the view. Delbert shook his fist, his mouth going to beat sixty.

Talk all you want, Loomis thought. I'll be seeing you again. And I'll have the last word.

43

After the shooting stopped, Joe Riley carefully raised up from the floorboard of the limousine. He peered through the shattered rear windshield, saw the Ford backing away through a cloud of dust.

"Motherfucker!" Delbert shouted at the retreating car. "Come back here! I'll *murder* you."

The Ford didn't slow. Soon, Joe couldn't hear its engine anymore. The desert seemed extra silent now that the gunfire had finished echoing about.

"Look at this fuckin' limo," Delbert said. "It's shot to shit."

Mookie groaned from the far side of the car, and the sound caught Delbert's attention. He leaned into the back seat, waved his pistol at Joe and said, "Don't move a muscle."

Delbert trotted around the rear of the limo to check on his friend. Joe watched out the window as Delbert helped Mookie to his feet. The chauffeur's shoulder was covered in blood, but it didn't look like a life-threatening wound.

Joe reached for one of the cut-glass decanters set into a shelf. He picked it up, uncorked it, took a sniff. Bourbon. He turned up the heavy square bottle and took a healthy slug. He put the glass stopper back in tight and waited.

The back door of the limo was yanked open and Delbert

leaned inside, Mookie's big blue arm draped over his shoulder.

Joe swung the decanter as hard as he could, caught Delbert square in the face.

The decanter didn't shatter. It was like hitting Delbert in the head with a brick. Blood spurted behind his plastic mask, his head snapped sideways and he tumbled backward. Mookie toppled over with him.

Joe set the decanter on the floorboard and climbed out the other side of the limo. He walked around to where both men writhed in the dirt. Delbert had his hands to his face, whimpering. Mookie wept and rolled on the ground, trying to get to his feet, blood and dust covering his uniform.

Mookie's pistol lay in the powdery sand at Joe's feet. He bent over and picked it up. Cheap revolver, a piece of shit, but it would do the job. He pointed it at Mookie.

"Okay," he said, loud enough to be heard over all the caterwauling. "Get in the car. I'll drop you at the nearest hospital."

"You ... can't ... drive ... the ... limo." Mookie gasped between each word. "You ... ain't ... on ... the ... insurance."

44

Ken Staley stood at his office's tall windows on Sunday afternoon, looking out over the phantasmagoric skyline of the Strip. Loomis sat in an armchair behind him, on the far side of the desk. He recounted how he'd pursued the wrong man, gotten into a gunfight, and escaped to come back here and give his pitiful report. Ken thought it was better to face the windows so Loomis couldn't see the anger in his eyes.

This situation was bad, and getting worse. Now there were new men involved, shooting it up with Loomis in the middle of the flat desert. It was a wonder somebody hadn't seen it, even way out there, and called the cops. Think how that would look, casino tycoon Ken Staley's chief of security arrested at the scene of a shootout. Christ.

Loomis finished his terse report and silence fell over the large room. Ken sighed. He needed to tell Loomis off, get him back on track. The man could be valuable, but he'd certainly blown it this time.

Then the elevator doors hissed open. Ken didn't turn to look. He knew what was coming: Patti's acerbic whine. "Ke-e-en!"

Oh, for Christ's sake, not now.

"Ken!" Sharper now, angry. He took a deep breath and turned to face her.

Patti stood in the middle of the room, her hands on her hips. She wore an icy pink dress with a short, flared skirt and a plunging neckline, probably by some fancy designer. Her silicone tits were pushed up to her chin by a redundant Miracle Bra and her blonde hair was arranged into a tight French twist. Your average man would give his left nut for a woman who looked so good, but all Ken could think was how much it cost.

"Yes, dear?"

"The public relations department just a got a call from one of the networks. They've heard about the murders. They're tying them together, want to do a story. I thought you were going to take care of that?"

God, her voice grated. If only Ken could get her an operation there, too. He'd heard about surgery that veterinarians do, trimming the vocal cords of dogs who couldn't learn to stop barking all the time. He wondered if such a procedure existed for humans—

"KEN!"

He snapped out of his reverie, met her frosty eyes.

"Am I talking to myself here or what?" she said. "We've got a problem and you're standing there like you're in a coma."

Ken thinking: A coma sounds pretty good about now. Can comatose people hear? Wouldn't do him much good if he still had to listen to Patti.

"I heard you," he said. "What were you doing talking to PR?"

She narrowed her eyes. "Checking on things. Somebody's got to do it. We've got a *situation* here."

"Yes, I know. And more players are popping up all the time. Mel just had a shootout with three men out in the desert."

"Oh, my God! Were there police? Reporters?"

"No, nothing like that. Everything's fine. But we're still having a little trouble tracking down the woman who committed the murder here." Ken shot Loomis a glare. "We need to get to her before the cops do, before this thing gets out of hand."

Loomis stared back at him levelly, unfazed. Patti strode to Ken's desk on her high heels, her face flushed. Ken noted the way the light shone flatly off her surgically tightened skin. Maybe the next time she went for a facelift, Ken could pay off the doctor, make sure she got an overdose of anesthetic.

"It's already out of hand, you idiot," she said, her voice murderously low. "We've got reporters coming in here, snooping around. They'll try to make it look like a Mob thing. Then we get to go to the capitol and explain it all away, pay off a bunch of hick legislators. We can't afford that right now."

Ken thought the usual bribes in Carson City were small change compared to the losses that could be generated by bad publicity, but he said nothing. Let her rave. Better not to remind her about canceled tours and empty hotel rooms.

"And you!" As Patti turned to Loomis, Ken felt a little murmur of relief. "I thought you were going to make this go away *quietly*."

Loomis didn't even look at her. Ken thought once again that the man had excellent self-control, even if he couldn't always be trusted to follow orders.

"He's working on it," Ken said. "But this Lily Marsden seems to attract a lot of followers. They keep getting in the way."

He thought about mentioning the way Loomis had gone off on his own to pursue the limousine when he was supposed to be after Sal Venturi. Keep Patti's wrath focused on the hired help. Might be worth it, even if it meant consoling Loomis with a pay raise later.

Patti turned back to Ken, though, and put her fists on her hips. "So what's the plan now? You were going to handle this, remember? 'The Vegas way.' If this is the way Vegas fixes things, it's no wonder this town is such a hellhole."

Ken put his hands behind his back and clasped them together. He'd like to clasp them around Patti's throat, but better to appease her. For now.

"It'll still work," he said. "It's a bigger job, sure, with these other people involved, but Mel can solve the problem. Can't you, Mel?"

Loomis kept silent, probably recognizing that the slightest peep would send Patti into another frenzy.

"Go do it, Mel," Ken said. "No more shootouts. I want Lily Marsden and all these others to simply disappear. No headlines. Just vanish them."

Loomis' eyebrows raised. "All of them?"

"Every single one. Lily Marsden, Venturi, the men in the limo. I want this cleaned up. If any of them are left standing, they could go to the cops and we'll never hear the end of it."

Loomis got to his feet. "Consider it done."

Patti snorted, but Loomis ignored her and went to the elevator.

Ken put his hands on his desk and leaned toward Patti.

"There," he said. "Satisfied now?"

Patti glowered at him. "You've never satisfied me before. Why should now be any different?"

45

Lily awoke to a chirping sound in her room at Bally's. Once again, she thought she should lose that damned phone, get one annoyance out of her life. But not only had she kept it, she'd plugged it in to recharge.

She rolled over in the bed, located the phone and answered it.

"Hi, Lily. It's me again."

Joe Riley. The man couldn't leave her alone. She'd seen the eagerness in his eyes at the airport, the way he leaned toward her, as if drawn by magnetism. Now they were back on the phone. "It's me again," like they were old friends, lovers, something. Like Lily should be pleased to hear from him.

"Too bad," she said. "I was hoping it was Sal."

"Don't sound disappointed. You'll hurt my feelings."

She smiled at that, the ex-cop coming on like a spurned beau.

"I imagine it takes more than that to hurt your feelings, Joe Riley."

"I'm a very sensitive guy."

"Yeah, right."

"Ask anybody. They'll tell you: That Joe Riley, he's a regular puppy dog."

Lily sat up in bed. The bedside clock said 3:12. She'd been

asleep a long time. Only way she could tell it was p.m. instead of a.m. was that sunlight leaked in around the edges of the drapes.

"A puppy isn't the animal that comes to mind."

"Yeah? What animal am I?"

"Maybe a jackass?"

"Ouch. I don't know why I keep calling you and taking such abuse."

"I don't know, either. I keep thinking I should get rid of this phone, and maybe I'd get rid of you in the process."

"But you haven't. I think you enjoy these conversations."

Lily wasn't sure what to say. She *did* enjoy talking to him, even though he was bad news in every possible way. Maybe I'm just lonely, she thought. It's an occupational hazard.

"I can't enjoy talking to you," she said. "I'm too busy wondering what the hell you *want.*"

"I've told you. I've got a problem back in Chicago."

"And I'm the solution."

"Part of it. Look, here's what happened: There was this guy there who got killed, a loan shark named Bennie Burrows. I owed him thirteen grand. Gambling debts. I got assigned to the case, but I didn't tell anybody about the loans. The investigation didn't go well. Evidence got lost, leads weren't followed. Somebody ratted me out to Internal Affairs, about my connection to Bennie. Then the press got wind of it. It looked bad. People thought I'd offed Bennie so I wouldn't have to pay him back."

"And then blew the investigation to cover it up."

"That's the way it appeared. But you and I both know it's not true."

Lily tucked the covers around her. Outside, it was probably like a blast furnace—Vegas in July—but this air-conditioned room was positively arctic.

"I don't know any such thing," she said.

"Yes, you do. You're the one who hit Bennie. Sal told me so."

Lily bit her lower lip. Fucking Sal. Was there anything he *hadn't* told Joe Riley?

"The question is," he said, "who ordered the hit? Bennie Burrows was a snake. He had lots of enemies. I need to know who was behind the murder before I can put this thing to rest."

Lily caught herself wanting to help him out. What was the matter with her?

"Too bad for you," she said. "I don't know. All the hits come through Sal. I just get a name, an address. I don't ask who's paying the tab."

Lily thought again that she should hang up, quit playing games. The longer she stayed on the line, the greater the odds the cops would come knocking on her door.

"You're sure?" he said. "Maybe in this case, you've got some idea?"

Lily felt a sudden sadness well up within her. He sounded so desperate, so hopeful.

"I don't have a clue," she said. "Sal's the only one who can tell you."

Her thumb eased up to the button that would disconnect the phone. This really had to stop.

"I asked him once," he said. "Guess I'll have to do it again."

"You'd better find him before I do. Once I'm done with the little bastard, he won't be talking anymore."

"No problem. I don't know where you are, but I know where Sal is. I'm parked outside his office right now."

"And he's there?"

"Not for long. I'm taking him with me."

Damn him. He'd gotten ahead of her while she slept.

"Bye, Lily."

46

Sal Venturi's fingers shook as he checked the magazine in the chrome-plated pistol. He'd never shot anyone in his life, had never even fired the little pistol before, but he was tired of people slapping him around. The Vernon brothers come through that door, or Loomis or Lily or Riley, and Sal would shoot. At least he'd go down fighting.

He heard a tapping at the outer door. Someone knocking tentatively, not really expecting to find anyone at the office on a Sunday. The hell could that be? Not Velma; she had her own key. The Vernons, back so soon? Or, sweet Jesus, *Lily*?

Sal grunted up from his desk and tiptoed into the reception area, pistol at the ready. He passed Velma's desk, then crowded against the wall, edging toward the front door. The door had a small, barred window set into it, and Sal could see no one out there. He whewed in relief, but then he heard the tapping again. Sounded like someone striking a quarter against the front window.

Sal held the little gun before him in his bandaged hand as he eased up to the door. Still couldn't see anyone out there. He grasped the doorknob and slowly turned it.

The door burst open and a big body barreled through, Joe Riley, coming in low. Sal's finger twitched and the little gun cracked, but Riley was all over him, slapping him upside the head, grabbing his wrist, twisting the pistol free. Before the gunshot finished echoing around the room, Sal was disarmed and stumbling backward.

He landed on his wide butt and slid a few feet, the damp polyester jogging suit slick against the hardwood floor. He blinked up at Riley, who stood over him, the shiny little pistol pointed at Sal's face.

"Jesus, Sal, you tried to shoot me."

Riley looked over his shoulder at the door frame, where the stray bullet had left a blaze of bare wood in the jamb.

"Look at that. That was close. Good thing I was ready for you."

Sal thinking, No, it's not a good thing at all, but he said nothing.

Riley grinned. "I was crouched down by the door, so you couldn't see me in the window. I knew you'd have to come take a look."

Sal took a shuddering breath. First the Vernons, now this guy again. Coming back to his office certainly had been a mistake.

"Better get up off your ass," Riley said. "We have unfinished business."

Sal rolled over onto all fours, clambered to his feet. This could be worse. Riley just wants to talk. He's maybe the only one who's got no reason to kill me. I tell him what he wants to know, maybe I can still skip town.

He tugged the jogging suit to cover his belly. Hard to hold onto one's dignity when the old blubber is hanging out. He went into his office and sat behind his desk. Riley followed him and stood in the middle of the room, keeping his distance, the little pistol still aimed Sal's way.

"I wasn't trying to shoot you." Sal tried to sound calm. "I

didn't know who was out there tapping. Could've been Lily, for all I knew."

"I don't think that's Lily's style," Riley said. "I think she wouldn't wait for you to come answer the door. She'd just bust in here, guns blazing."

Sal tried to shrug, but his shoulders felt tight. "Never can tell. That's her secret. She never kills the same way twice."

"Ah, but that's not true," Riley said. "She did do two the same way. Max Vernon at Tropical Bay and Bennie Burrows in Chicago. That's how I knew she was in Vegas."

Sal shifted in his chair. He was feeling more confident now. This guy wanted something from him, which meant there was room for negotiation. That was Sal's forte. He'd run circles around Riley.

"You're still stuck on that Chicago hit, even after what's happened out here? Why don't you drop it? You might live longer."

Riley frowned. "See, that's the problem. I might live longer, but it's not the life I want. If I can't have my old life back, maybe I don't want to live at all."

Sal placed his fat hands on the smooth edge of the desk, let them slide back and forth.

"What do I look like to you, frigging Suicide Hotline?"

Riley raised the pistol slightly so it pointed directly at Sal's nose.

"Don't get smart with me. You're in no position. I just told you, maybe I've got nothing to live for. That means I wouldn't have a problem killing you before I go."

Sal gulped, gave his forehead a swipe with his filthy bandage.

"Killing me wouldn't do you any good."

Riley shrugged his beefy shoulders. "You said the

information I wanted was in your files. I kill you, I can search the files in peace."

"Won't do you any good." Sal smirked. "They're in code."

Riley jabbed at the air with the pistol and said, "Get them. The files on Bennie Burrows. Right now."

"Okay, okay." Sal got up slowly. "Should be in this bottom drawer over here."

He squatted down and dug around in the drawer until he came up with the file on Burrows. The folder was slim, contained only a couple of sheets of paper, just enough to protect him down the road, something to trade to the cops in a plea bargain. Instead, this *former* cop, this renegade, would get the benefit of Sal's careful planning.

He carried the folder back to the desk. He'd used the same code for years, a simple substitution code, and it came naturally to him now. He could read it as easily as someone fluent in French could read *Le Monde*. It only took a glance to tell him he had further problems. He slumped into his chair.

"What?"

"I don't know who ordered the hit," Sal said. "The contract came from Chicago, but it was through a broker there. I don't know who wanted Burrows dead."

"Who's the broker in Chicago?"

"Mike Villetti. He's real low-profile."

Riley appeared to run Villetti's name through his mental catalogue of crooks. He focused on Sal again and said, "So Villetti called you up. The two of you worked out the details. You never talked to the guy who paid for the hit."

Sal nodded.

"Guess you've got a call to make." Riley gestured at the desk phone with the little pistol.

Sal's mind raced. He couldn't call Mike Villetti. Villetti

had Mob connections. He found out Sal was talking about him, even to an *ex*-cop, and it would be cement-shoes time.

"You pick up that phone and call Chicago right now," Riley said hotly. "Or I'm gonna shoot a hole in you."

"It won't do any good—"

"You've got until the count of three."

"Look, you don't know this guy—"

"One."

"He's not going to tell us anything—"

"Two."

"Okay, I'll call. But you're asking for a miracle. Villetti won't tell me."

"You'd better use your powers of persuasion. Otherwise, it's gonna go bad for you."

Sal dialed Villetti's number and waited while the goon who answered went off to find his boss. God, he hoped Villetti was there. Riley didn't look like he'd take no for an answer.

"Hello, Mike? Yeah, it's Sal Venturi. I've got a, um, situation here."

47

Joe sat in an armchair while he listened to Sal's end of the conversation. Villetti clearly didn't like giving out the information, but Sal wheedled and pleaded. He smiled broadly as he hung up the phone.

"Got it," he said brightly. "Guess what? It's a cop."

"You're shitting me."

"That's what Villetti said. Mike kept it quiet that a cop was behind it, and the cop managed to hush it up after the fact, too. This one's buried deep."

Joe adjusted his grip on the little gun. "Not anymore. Give me a name."

Sal sat back in his chair, looking relieved.

"The guy who ordered the hit is a homicide dick," he said. "Can you believe that? Perfect, really."

Joe went cold inside. "Just give me the name."

Sal's smile faltered, like he suddenly wasn't sure how Joe would react to the news. He stammered a little, then spit it out: "Sam Kilian."

"You lyin' sack of shit." But even as the words left Joe's lips, he knew it was true. It explained everything, the missing evidence, the bungled investigation. Joe had always discounted them, figuring he and Sam blew the murder investigation because neither of them really gave a shit. The murder of Bennie Burrows should've been a red-letter day for the world; one less Bennie made Chicago a better place. But Sam could've easily engineered a cover-up.

"You know the guy?" Sal babbled. "Look, I *don't*, okay? All I can tell you is what Mike told me. He said the cop owed this loan shark a lot of money. So much that it was cheaper to pay Mike for a hit than to pay back the loans."

Joe let the words wash over him. Before Sam got on the wagon, he gambled as much as Joe did, and often not as well. Acted like his losses weren't any big deal. Then Ellen got him into Gamblers Anonymous, and it was like he got religion. Always offering Joe advice, telling him to give up poker, pay off his debts, forget his divorce, get on with his life. But Sam, the family man, the good cop, must've still been into Bennie big. He was the one behind the scenes, getting rid of the debt.

Sal was still talking, so Joe said hoarsely, "Shut up."

"I got you what you wanted," Sal said. "That's the name. You don't like it, I'm sorry, but—"

"I said shut the fuck up."

"I heard you. But our business is done now. You got what you came for. Why don't you give me back my gun and get the hell out of here?"

Joe suddenly lunged toward Sal. "I'll give you the fuckin' gun."

He couldn't stop himself. The rage was too great; it needed an outlet. He slapped the little gun against the side of Venturi's head. Sal yelped and squinted his eyes shut. Joe brought the pistol back the other way, caught him across the face, sent his glasses flying across the room.

Not Sam. It couldn't be Sam.

He whacked the lawyer again, saw blood spritz from his eyebrow.

Fucking Sam. No wonder he kept trying to get me to come home. No wonder he wanted me to stop investigating Bennie's murder.

Joe got a fist full of Sal's slick shirt, straightened him up in the chair. His other arm was cocked to pistol-whip him some more.

A man's cool voice came from behind him, said, "Let him alone."

48

Mel Loomis kept his .45 trained on the big guy, Lily Marsden's boyfriend. No need to worry about Venturi. The lawyer's bloodied head lolled on his thick neck. But this other one looked like he'd gone insane. Red in the face, spittle on his chin, his eyes wild. Made Loomis think of a startled horse, ready to rear up and kill somebody.

"Drop the gun," Loomis said. "Or I'll drop you."

The guy had the gun up by his own ear, ready to swing at Venturi. No way he could bring it around before Loomis could fire. But did he know that? Was he so out of his head that he'd make the big mistake?

The man took a deep breath and released his grip on Venturi. He let the little peashooter dangle on his finger.

"Drop it," Loomis said. "Not that the little fucker will shoot anymore. I think you broke it on his head."

The man glanced at the gun, then let it fall. It landed with a clatter.

"That's fine," Loomis said. "Now come over here and sit down. I need some answers."

The big guy measured the space between them with his eyes, recognized it was too great and gave a little shrug. He stepped around the desk and turned the visitor's chair to face Loomis, who backed up a couple of steps, keeping his distance. The man seemed to be calming down, but Loomis wanted no room for error.

"Who the hell are you?"

"Joe Riley. And you would be?"

"I would be Mr. Fuck You. I'm asking the questions here."

"'Cause you know who you look like, right? I mean, I don't have to tell you."

Loomis bristled. "You want a bullet in the head?"

"Warren Beatty, right? You probably hear that all the time."

Riley grinned up at him.

"I get it," Loomis said. "You're a smartass."

"So I've been told."

"Get smart with me again. Give me a reason to shoot you. Where's Lily Marsden?"

"I don't know."

"You don't know, or you won't say?"

"Up yours."

"I'm gonna shoot you now."

"All right, all right. I think she's here in Vegas, but I can't prove it."

"You know how to reach her?"

"No."

"You're her friend, right?"

"Hardly."

"I saw you together. In Albuquerque. Then I saw you at the airport here."

"And you followed me here?"

"I followed you out to the desert. You were in that limo."

"That was you, in the Ford, nearly got your ass shot off by a couple of morons?"

"Who were those guys?"

"Nobody. Couple of gamblers, don't know how to lose like gentlemen."

"Where do they fit into this?"

"I'm telling you, they don't. And they're out of the picture anyway. I left them at the hospital."

Loomis considered this. "Both of 'em hurt?"

"You hurt one. I hurt the other."

Loomis grunted. Riley was a smartass, but he got to the fucking point.

"How did you find me here?" Riley asked.

"Got a call from a buddy of mine, told me Venturi was here."

"Let me guess. The guy called from Chicago. Mike Villetti."

That made Loomis pause. Riley clearly knew more than he was letting on.

Venturi moaned, began to stir. Loomis tilted his head toward him. "He know where Lily Marsden is?"

"Ask him."

Loomis couldn't figure this guy out.

"How do you fit in this? What's your connection?"

"I used to be a cop. Now I just run around getting into trouble."

"That's sure the way it looks."

Loomis kept his pistol pointed at Riley, but he turned his head to shout at Venturi.

"Wake up, fatass. I need to talk to you."

Venturi sat up a little, squinted in Loomis' direction, trying to make out who was standing there without his glasses. He blanched when he recognized Loomis.

Riley's eyes went shifty, searching for a way out. Loomis

kept the gun pointed at him. Nobody but Loomis was leaving this office.

"Venturi!" he yelled, and Sal's head snapped up. "Where's Lily Marsden?"

"I don't know," Sal whined. "I was telling this guy—"

Loomis swung the barrel of the .45 to his right and pulled the trigger. Sal's shoulder exploded, spattered his chair and the wall behind him with blood. He screamed and Riley flinched, but Loomis had the pistol pointed back at the cop before he could make a move.

He had to shout to be heard over Sal's howling. "Where's Lily, Sal? I'd better get an answer right now."

"I don't *know*! That's the truth."

He moved the pistol again, shot Sal in the other shoulder. He missed a little on this one, just creased the fat meat on the outside, but it set Sal to screaming again.

"Come on!" Riley shouted. "This isn't doing any good."

"Shut up," Loomis said. "You're next."

He pointed the pistol at Venturi again, aimed dead center on his chest. "Last chance, Sal. Where is she?"

He heard a noise behind him, in the outer office. As he turned, Lily Marsden flashed through the door, dressed in black, gloved hands around a square black Glock pointed his way.

"I'm right here," she said.

49

Joe Riley had never seen a person move so smoothly. Lily came into the room like a panther, her weight on the balls of her feet, the gun held in a perfect shooter's stance. Says, "I'm right here," cold and slick as black ice. Joe felt a thump in his chest at the sight of her.

Then all hell broke loose.

Loomis was startled by her voice and his gun jumped in his hand. Sounded like a cannon in the close room.

Joe dived forward out of his chair, hit the deck crawling on his elbows and knees. His head up, trying to see everything at once, as he squirmed across the hardwood floor toward Sal's desk.

Loomis did a quick pirouette, graceful for a fat man, pulling the trigger on the .45 before he got turned all the way around. Shots buzz-bombed the air, blasted a hole in a wall, shattered a window.

Lily didn't flinch. She pulled the trigger, aiming at Loomis' head. He jerked to his left, and Joe saw the big man's right ear vanish in a puff of red spray.

Joe reached the side of Sal's desk and sat up, trying to roll into a ball behind his tenuous shelter.

Loomis growled as he brought the pistol around, still firing. The plaster wall erupted in foot-wide craters everywhere a bullet struck. The air suddenly was thick with white dust and acrid smoke.

Lily dived to her right, hit the floor and rolled, coming back up onto her feet. Joe had never seen anything like it. She was a gymnast, a tumbler, a fucking comic book superhero.

Her pistol roared and the bullet hit Loomis in the chest, knocked him backward toward the chair where Joe had been sitting. Loomis hit the floor with a mighty whump, but he wasn't dead. And he still had his gun in his hand.

He reached across his thick body and fired wildly at Lily, who lunged forward onto her belly as bullets peppered the wall.

Joe was only six feet away from Loomis, and he had the sudden urge to jump him, wrest the gun away before Loomis could get lucky and kill her. But that would put him in Lily's line of fire. He pressed against the desk and covered his head with his hands and watched the gunfight.

Loomis had trouble aiming; his big stomach was in the way of his arm. His shot went high, missing Lily by inches.

She rapid-fired three times, and her brown eyes didn't even blink as the gun barked and spent shells spewed hotly into the air.

Three red holes stitched a line up Loomis' thick torso. His eyes squinched shut, then he went limp all over. His head hit the wood floor with a thump, sounded like somebody dropped a pumpkin.

Joe looked to Lily, and their eyes met. He looked deep into hers and found nothing there. Nothing. No spark of attraction. No lust for the kill. Her eyes were flat and opaque and unblinking. She started to get to her feet.

Joe spun around and crawled behind the desk, through the pool of blood that dripped from the wheezing Sal. Christ,

Sal. Joe had forgotten about him. Sal still sat in his desk chair, probably too petrified to move.

He found the lawyer's little .25-caliber desk gun where he'd dropped it when Loomis surprised him. The shiny gun was slick with blood, but Joe got it in his grip and swung his arm up over the top of the desk.

He was crouched next to Sal, hiding below the edge of the desk, and poked his head up just enough to see. Lily stood ten feet away, near the door, her black pistol trained on his face.

Joe was afraid to fire. The little pistol—if it even worked anymore— had no stopping power. His shot would have to be perfect, or she'd kill him for sure. Her Glock could drill bullets right through Sal's flimsy desk.

She hesitated, and he saw his opening.

"Hold up, Lily. You don't want to shoot me."

Her eyes narrowed, sighting down the barrel. "Why not?"

"I didn't do anything."

"You're holding a gun on me."

"I'll stop if you will."

She didn't even blink.

"Come on, Lily. This is crazy. I don't want to kill you. You know that."

"No, you want me alive. In prison."

"Not today," he said. "Maybe not ever. I think you just saved my life."

"So?"

"Be a shame to kill me now, wouldn't it?"

"A heartbreaker. Drop that gun."

"Forget Chicago. Forget me. Just walk away. Right now."

"So you can come after me again?"

"Maybe I will. Maybe not. Maybe I owe you one now. Hell, I'm all mixed up. I don't know what I want anymore. But I know one thing: I don't want it to end like this."

One eyebrow cocked up her forehead. Joe took it as an encouraging sign.

"Go. I'll handle the cops. You killed Curly there in self-defense. I'd testify to that. I'm your witness. You kill me, you'll just make it worse on yourself."

Her voice was low and calm. "I kill you, and nobody knows I was ever here."

"What about Sal?"

At the mention of his name, Sal Venturi unleashed a loud fart. He coughed wetly, twice, then expelled a shuddering breath. Joe looked him over, found a red blotch centered on his chest. Loomis' first startled shot had nailed the lawyer to his chair.

Joe looked back to Lily, found amusement in her eyes.

"Okay," he said, "I'm the only witness. But I won't talk. Just go before the cops get here."

The Glock still stared at him. The black hole in the end of the barrel looked like the mouth of a well.

Joe heard the first bleat of a siren approaching from far away. He turned his head to the sound, just for a second, said, "Uh-oh."

When he looked back, she was gone.

50

Ken Staley wouldn't ever be exactly relieved to see the fidgety police detective, but her arrival at least interrupted Patti. His wife had come at him full-bore when they got word that Mel Loomis was dead. Now they were in for it, she shrieked, the media would be all over these killings. Tropical Bay, everything they'd worked for, was in ruins. All because Ken insisted on acting like Bugsy fucking Siegel.

Patti clamped her mouth shut as the elevator doors hissed open and Susan Pine stepped into the room. She looked dour in her stern brown suit, a mudhen next to the pink flamingo that was Patti. She was trailed across the room by her partner, little gray fellow whose name Ken couldn't remember.

Ken gave them his patented smile. Patti stood with her hands on her hips, frowning, impatient to resume berating him.

"Detective Pine," Ken said. "We just heard the awful news."

The cop looked brittle, standing across the glass desk from him, her arms straight at her sides.

"Do you know what Mel Loomis was doing at that law office?"

"I have no idea," Ken said. "We only this minute—"

"The other victim, Sal Venturi, what's he mean to you?"

"I never heard of him until one of my security people phoned me about this terrible shootout. What happened?"

She chewed her lower lip, looked like she was deciding how much to tell him. Her partner hung back, watching.

"Only one gun at the scene, and it was in Loomis' hand. But someone shot each of them several times. There's evidence a lot more shots were fired in that room."

Ken brought his hand up to his chest. Nice dramatic effect. "Oh, my God."

He glanced at Patti to see whether she was looking appropriately alarmed, found her staring at him, venom in her eyes. He turned back to the detectives.

"I can't imagine what happened," he said. "I don't know why Mel would've gone to see this lawyer, or why they might've shot each other. Clearly, there were others involved. I mean, Mel didn't shoot himself—"

Susan Pine nodded impatiently. "There was a witness, a guy driving a truck nearby, heard the shots. He saw two people leave the office before the first squad cars arrived. A man with dark hair. And a woman."

Ken felt a little dizzy. "A woman?"

"Could be the same woman who killed Max Vernon," she said. "Maybe the others, too. She's leaving a trail of corpses behind her."

"And the man?"

"No positive ID, but I've got a pretty good idea who he is."

Ken raised his eyebrows, waiting, but she didn't cough up any more information.

"Well," he said, "this is indeed dreadful news. If there's anything I can do to help—"

"Stow it, Staley. I don't believe you for a second. Loomis was your man. He did what you told him. I don't think he'd get into a gunfight unless you put him up to it."

Ken felt his hands dancing around and stashed them in his pants pockets. The little bitch! He'd make her pay for those words. A few well-placed phone calls...

"Well? You got anything to say?"

"Talk to my lawyers, Detective. Believe me, you'll be hearing from them."

Pine turned on her heel. Her partner followed her to the elevator without looking back.

They boarded the elevator and Pine gave Ken a steady stare across the wide office until the doors slid closed.

Bracing himself, Ken turned to face Patti. She lit a long, thin cigarette. Squinted at him through the smoke, sizing him up, making him wait.

After a minute, he couldn't stand it anymore. "Now what?"

"Now you're fucked. You're on your own, Ken. You made this mess. You find a way to clean it up."

She stalked toward the elevator, smoke trailing behind her.

Her departure should've been a reprieve, but as Ken turned toward the windows and looked out at the bustle of Vegas, he felt very alone.

51

Hi Vernon hung up the phone, thinking: This damned thing gets weirder all the time.

He'd been at the desk in his den for a couple of hours, and his knees creaked as he got to his feet. He paused to clean his glasses, then padded in his sock feet to Norm's matching den next door. Norm sat at his desk, which was covered with an old leather harness, so weather-beaten it looked like rawhide, and tools and rags and a round tin of saddle soap.

"Norm, what the hell are you doin'?"

"Mending this harness," Norm said without looking up from his stitching. "Any damned fool could see that."

Hi stood there, staring at him, wiggling his toes inside his socks.

"All right," he said. "I'll give you that one. Now, you want to tell me *why* you're mending that harness?"

"Look at it! It's in bad shape. Things are going to hell around here."

Norm pushed a big needle through the dried-up holes in the harness edge and pulled waxed yellow cord through it. The dusty, cracked leather looked as if it could give way at any time.

Hi stood watching, shaking his head.

"Hell, Norm, we don't need no harness."

"Might."

"There ain't even *been* a horse on this spread in thirty years. What are you planning to harness with it?"

Norm stuck out his lower lip. His big eyebrow knitted.

"We might want to hang it up somewhere. Over the fireplace or something. Max would've like that. He decorated The Cactus Ranch in all that Western stuff."

Hi exhaled loudly.

"Let's do that," he said. "And I'll round up some cowpies and we can nail 'em on the walls. Tell people they're *art*."

Norm grunted, but his face relaxed a little.

"Shit, Hi, you know I think better when I've got something to do with my hands."

"You must be pretty desperate to hunt up that old harness."

"Kiss my ass."

Norm set the harness to one side and Hi sat in the chair across from him.

"You having any luck on the phone?" Norm asked.

"A little. You?"

"Some. You go first."

"You heard about Venturi and Loomis?"

Norm nodded. "Our girl is still in town."

"Damn, I was hoping I was ahead of you on that one. Looks to me like she came back to silence Venturi. Loomis just got in the way."

Norm leaned back in his chair and rested his well-polished boots up on his desk.

"That's not the way I heard it," Norm said. "I heard Ken Staley sent Loomis over there to pin the tail on that jackass Venturi, make him tell where the woman is. Things went wrong, and now Staley's trying to hush this all up."

"Hell," Hi said, "it's too late for that. This thing's done got messy."

"Staley likes to think he's smarter than he is."

"I got that impression. Where did you hear he sent Loomis after her?"

"From his wife. Patti. You remember her?"

"Can't say that I do."

"Me and her, we had a little fling long time ago."

"I can't remember the last time *I* was with a woman. How d'you expect me to remember which ones you used to run around with?"

"It wasn't no big romance or anything. She was working over at the Desert Inn, had legs up to her neck—"

"Will you get to the point?"

Norm frowned, then continued in the same tone, as if Hi had said nothing.

"Anyway, we stayed friendly. I'd see her around town now and then. We'd talk. Few years ago, I read in the paper that she was marrying Staley and I sent her a big bunch of flowers to congratulate her."

"Aren't you a romantic old buzzard?"

"That ain't it, ass-wipe. I figured that girl was going places. She's a cold-blooded bitch."

Hi was running out of patience..

"That's all good business," he said. "I would've thought of it myself, if you'd ever bothered to introduce me to her. But what difference does it make now?"

"I called her up. Just a few minutes ago. She's steaming mad. Told me her idiot husband was gonna sink their ship. That the police had been there, asking pointed questions."

"What did you say?"

"I played along. Told her I'd heard Staley was mixed up

in Max's death. Told her the police were after his ass, and she should be careful she didn't go down with him."

"You peckerwood," Hi said. "You're just stirring the pot."

"Didn't see how it would hurt. I never liked that asshole Staley. Too slick. Ole Patti's probably sinking her claws in him about now."

"That's just fine, but it's not doing us much good in finding that woman who killed Max."

Norm sat back, sobered.

"Patti and Staley turn on each other, it should keep the cops busy."

"Is that all you got?"

Norm shrugged. "Seemed like pretty good progress to me. You got anything else?"

"I found out about that cop Venturi mentioned. Joe Riley. Not just a cop, a *homicide* detective. Quit the force because people thought he'd killed some loan shark. Riley owed the man money. Never charged with anything, but it looked bad. After he quit, Riley left Chicago and hit the road. Guess who he's looking for?"

"The woman who really killed the loan shark."

"You got it, hoss. He's been tracking her all over the country. That's how he ended up here."

Norm considered this. "He's the wild card."

"That's the way I see it. But you ain't the heard the rest. The cop I talked to in Chicago said something funny. Said it's the third call he's gotten about Riley in the past two days. One was the Vegas cops. No surprise there. But the other call was from a guy here in town, Delbert Nash. Ever heard of him?"

Norm shook his head.

"I checked him out," Hi said. "Low-rent gambler. A nobody."

"Why's he interested in Joe Riley?"

"Don't know yet. But I reckon we ought to find out."

"We don't need two wild cards. We need to play this hand, get it done."

Hi studied his twin for a moment.

"We could just quit," he said. "Venturi's dead. The rest of 'em probably gonna kill each other. We might ought to fold our cards, wait it out."

Hi could tell before he'd finished that Norm was having none of it. His eyes glinted with resolve.

"Not until we get that woman who killed Max."

"I figured that's what you'd say."

Hi stood and moved toward the door, but Norm held him up by calling his name.

"This information from Chicago. You sure it's reliable?"

"Should be. It came from a man named Sam Kilian, used to be Riley's partner."

52

Joe stretched out on the bed at the Pink Elephant Motor Lodge, his hands clasped behind his head, and stared at the ceiling. The sun had dropped below the horizon an hour ago, and the last light was fading outside. He needed to get out of this room in case the local cops had gotten a line on him. He'd tell them everything eventually, but he wasn't ready yet. He wanted one more crack at nailing Lily himself. But first he just wanted to lie still for a few minutes.

He'd had no time to recover after the shootout at Sal Venturi's office, too busy getting rid of his blood-soaked clothes and ditching Sal's pistol, which he'd carried with him, just in case.

Only when he was safely back in his motel room, showering the blood from his skin and the dust and smoke out of his hair, had he gotten a moment to consider what Sal had told him.

Sam Kilian. Joe didn't want to believe it, but how else would Sal have turned up Sam's name during that phone call to Chicago? Sal didn't know Sam had been Joe's partner. He'd spoken the truth: It was Sam who ordered the hit on Bennie Burrows. It was Sam who set Joe up to take the fall.

Joe cleared his throat against the sand there. His eyes felt hot and he blinked rapidly.

Sam was like family. Hell, the big redhead was more than family. He was Joe's partner, his running buddy, his late-night poker pal. Joe hadn't bothered to keep in touch with his real family back in Chicago; they didn't even know where he was. But he called Sam regularly, seeking his help, bouncing ideas off him, getting information.

Damn it, Sam had tracked his every move, and Joe never suspected a thing. When Sam said he worried about his safety, Joe took it at face value. They'd spent years watching each other's backs.

All Sam's speeches about giving up the hunt, coming home, Joe had written off as his usual tendency to lecture. Like when Sam quit gambling, always making a big deal about how he'd turned his life around.

Sam must've been deep in the hole when he saw the light. Even after he reformed, still paying the vig to Bennie every week, no hope of ever catching up. Only one way to get a fresh start.

Hell, Joe thought, Sam *introduced* me to Bennie. It wasn't long before I was deep into Bennie, too. Had Sam known that would happen? Had he been setting me up from the start?

More likely, he became Sam's only out after the newspapers got hold of story. But how come the papers knew Joe was into Bennie, but never heard a peep about Sam owing him money?

Son of a bitch. Sam tipped the newspapers. He'd been the snitch to Internal Affairs.

Joe felt sick to his stomach. He got up from the bed, stumbled into the bathroom. He knelt on the cool tile for ten minutes, but never got the release of throwing up. The sick feeling stayed with him as he returned to bed.

Should he call Sam, give him a chance to tell his side of

the story? That wouldn't do much good, and it would alert Sam that Joe was onto him. Should he return to Chicago, prove Sam was the guilty one? He thought about Sam's wife, his redheaded kids. Could Joe send daddy to prison?

Could he prove it, even if he wanted to? Not without Lily. With Venturi dead, Lily was the only proof.

He sat up and turned on a lamp, dialed her cell phone number from memory. It rang four times before an anonymous recorded voice asked him to leave a message.

"Hi, um, this is Joe Riley. Time for us to have another talk. Hope you haven't skipped town. Uh. Bye."

He hung up, thinking: Nice going, jackass.

53

Delbert steered the bullet-riddled limousine up the long, straight dirt road, the Monday morning sun knifing him in the eyes. He pulled down the visor, but was too short for it to do him any good. Too bad. Squinting hurt his battered face.

The painkiller that let him sleep the night before had worn off and his broken nose and shattered cheekbone throbbed, steady and persistent as a toothache. He'd like another dose of codeine, but he was afraid to take any until this was over.

The limo pancaked over a low spot in the road as it wallowed toward the isolated house. Mookie whimpered in the passenger seat. Delbert knew Mookie was in a world of hurt, but he was withholding his painkillers, too. He needed Mookie alert during their meeting with the Vernon brothers.

Not that Mookie could do much. One arm still was in its inflated blue splint, and the other was in a plaster cast up over his shoulder, held out from his body by a metal rod that connected to a brace taped to Mookie's ribs. They'd cut his bloody jacket and shirt away the day before at the hospital, and Mookie remained half-naked. The car's every jolt made him wince with pain.

"How you doing, Mook?"

"Just thinkin' about my job. I'm gonna get fired. Can't drive anyway. And look at this limo, shot to hell. The boss is gonna be mad."

Brown dust unfurled into a cloud behind them, enough coming through the broken windows to coat the car's interior.

"Don't worry about it, Mookie. We'll ditch the limo soon. Take it out to the desert and set it on fire. Let the insurance jerks figure that one out."

Mookie moaned.

"It'll be all right. Maybe we'll burn it out here, if we can find another set of wheels to get back to town."

Delbert looked around the flat basin, not even a tree as far as you could see. Just the one lone ranch house in the middle of fucking nowhere, and one set of power lines marching in formation, following the long dirt drive to the house. Probably cost a fortune to run that juice all the way out here. From everything Delbert had heard, the Vernon brothers had several fortunes. They could afford eccentricity.

An old cowboy waited on the stoop when they reached the house. He wore a business suit with a string tie and a cowboy hat and he had a giant mustache that covered half his face. Thick eyeglasses glinted under a bushy brow.

"Look at this guy," Delbert muttered. "Fuckin' 'Hee-Haw.'"

He opened his door and got out, leaving Mookie to creak out of the limo on his own. Delbert extended his hand as he stepped up to the old man, gave him a painful smile, trying to pretend he didn't look like a fuckin' horror show.

"You must be Mr. Vernon."

"Hi."

"Hi. My name's Delbert Nash. You called us?"

"We need to talk a little business. Y'all come on in the kitchen."

Vernon walked away from the house, though, and Delbert followed, unsure where they were headed. The old man walked all the way around the limo, checking out the damage.

"Lot of car you boys got here," he said. "I always appreciate a big, heavy car. Drive a Lincoln myself. Not one of those new ones, either. An old one. Big."

He looked up, met Delbert's eye.

"Too bad somebody's been using yours for target practice."

Delbert had trouble keeping the smile on his face.

"We got into a little firefight yesterday. Mookie here caught a bullet in the shoulder. Broke the bone."

"You've seen better days yourself."

"I've got a broken nose, broken cheek. Doctor makes me wear this mask."

"You're kinda wheezing there, son."

Delbert coughed and cleared his throat.

"Just a little early for me, Mr. Vernon. Haven't had my coffee yet."

"Come on in. We've got some on the stove."

The old man walked across the dusty yard to a side door of the brick house. Delbert followed him inside, Mookie doing the Frankenstein shuffle behind them.

Another old man—identical to the first except without the glasses—sat at a scarred oak table. A big Colt revolver lay next to his coffee cup.

"Come in, boys," the man shouted. "I'm Norm Vernon. I see you've already met my brother Hi."

Hi? That's the man's *name*?

Norm shook Delbert's hand without rising from the table. Mookie didn't have a hand available to shake. He waved the blue arm. Delbert sat at the table, but Mookie stayed standing by the door.

"Don't mind my saying so," Norm said, "you boys look like you belong in a hospital."

"Had a run of bad luck," Delbert said.

Hi Vernon set a cup of oily-looking coffee in front of Delbert, then pulled a chair out from the table and twirled it around backward so he could sit with his elbows resting on the back. Nobody mentioned the pistol on the table. Delbert noted that Norm's hand never strayed far from it.

"Way we hear it," Hi began, "all your bad luck has to do with a man named Joe Riley."

Delbert nodded. "Word gets around."

"We've got a lot of friends in this town. They call us. That's how we stay on top of business living way out here."

Delbert wanted to ask why anyone would choose to live out here in the fucking desert when a thriving playground was thirty miles up the road, but he held back. The Vernons had called him. Let them do the talking.

"From what we hear, you're ready to kill this man Riley."

"You hear right," Delbert said. "I'm gonna cut that bastard down next time."

"No, you're not," Hi said calmly.

"Say what?" Mookie's voice was even more of a rumble than usual. Neither Vernon looked his way.

"You'll get your chance to snuff him," Norm said, smiling wickedly. "But not till after we're done with him."

Delbert leaned back in his chair. He didn't like the crazy look in Norm's eyes.

"Here's what we want," Hi said. "You boys go into town

and pick up Riley and bring him back to us. We need to talk to him. When we're done, we'll hand him over and you can do whatever you want with him."

Delbert didn't like this. The old man talked as if it were a done deal.

"Why would I do that?" he said. "What's in it for me?"

The brothers exchanged a look. Delbert had heard about twins who could read each other's thoughts, shit like that. He wondered if these two old men did all their communicating with their eyes.

"You get to kill Riley," Hi said. "You can even bury him out here on the ranch."

"Why don't I just shoot him where he stands, soon as I find him?"

Norm glowered at Delbert and said, "Because we just *told* you—"

"Hold on, Norm," Hi said. "That's a reasonable question. These boys haven't heard what we have to offer yet."

Delbert thinking: That's more like it.

"See, boys," Hi continued, "you could leave here and spend a lot of time hunting for Joe Riley. Might never find him. But we know where he is."

"You do?"

"Riley checked into a motel in town last night. Our friends knew we were looking for him, so they gave us a call."

Doubt crept up Delbert's spine.

"You know where he is, why don't you go get him yourselves?"

Hi smiled. Looked like somebody's uncle.

"We're keeping a low profile. Our brother got killed the other day, and we're supposed to be in mourning. His funeral's tomorrow."

"I heard about your brother," Delbert said. "Is that somehow connected to Riley?"

Norm grumbled, but Hi talked over him. "That's what we're trying to find out. Riley knows a woman. She's the one we really want. We need to talk to him, find out where she is. Then you can have Riley."

Delbert thought it over. Should be a way to make some money off this deal. He weighed whether he should risk trying to lift some cash off the Vernons. That was a big pistol on the table.

"One more thing," Hi said. "You do this for us, and we become fast friends. We could find ways to help you boys out, the way friends do. A little information here. A tip there. The occasional job. You interested?"

Delbert recognized such a friendship could be worth more in the long run than a quick shakedown now. He glanced at Mookie to see what he thought, but Mookie was trying to get his coffee mug to his lips. He held the cup's handle pinched between the thumb and forefinger of his right hand, barely able to touch them together because the inflated cast was in the way. Mookie took a big slurp. He winced and his lips puckered.

That cinches it, Delbert thought. I'm not drinking that coffee.

"We're in," he said. "Where's Riley?"

Norm sat forward in his chair. "If we've got a deal, let's shake on it. I prefer to do business that way."

They shook hands all around. The cowboys' hands were leathery and strong.

Hi said, "Riley's at a Motel 6 on Sahara, over by the Maryland Parkway. Room 110. He checked in late, probably still sleeping. You boys hustle, you could get him right now."

"We bring him back here, then just wait around until you're done with him?"

"You got something better to do this morning?" Norm said.

"No, no. Just making sure I understand, that's all. Let's go, Mookie."

Delbert stood up, then something occurred to him.

"One little problem," he said, and he could feel his face flush.

"What's that?"

"We got no guns. This guy Riley keeps taking our guns away. He must have a fuckin' arsenal by now."

Norm and Hi exchanged that look again.

"Hell, son," Hi said, "why didn't you say so? Norm'll loan you that pistol right there."

Norm used his thumb to push the big Colt across the table. "Just give it back when you're done. It's got sentimental value."

"Yes, sir." Delbert picked up the gun. Fucker weighed ten pounds. He started to stick it in his pants, ended up letting it dangle from his hand.

"We'd better get going then," he said.

He turned toward the door, but Hi reached out, clasped his arm.

"Hold on, son. You haven't even touched your coffee."

54

Detective Susan Pine settled behind her tidy desk and sipped the mocha decaf she'd picked up at Starbucks on her way to work. Susan never drank police station coffee. Stuff sat on a burner all day, developing the texture and taste of hot asphalt. Besides, caffeine made her jumpy.

Plenty to be jumpy about these days. Corpses turning up all over town, all linked somehow to the killing of Max Vernon. Reporters calling every few minutes, wanting updates she didn't have. The chief breathing down her neck, threatening to send the whole thing to a task force. She needed to solve it quick, and she wasn't getting any help from her partner.

Harold sat at his desk a few feet away, reeking of cigarettes and rot. He was looking through a pamphlet.

"What you got there, Harold?"

"Brochure about Guatemala. You know where that is? This says a retiree can live down there on ten dollars a day. Sandy beaches, warm oceans, fishing. Sounds pretty good."

"Don't they have revolutionaries down there, running around with guns?"

Harold smiled, showing his gray dentures. "How's that any different from here?"

Susan sighed. "When somebody gets shot here, we're supposed to arrest them."

Harold tossed the pamphlet onto his cluttered desk and swiveled to face her. She caught a whiff of his breath and fought the urge to roll her chair across the room.

"I been thinking about that," he said. "If we can figure out who killed Max Vernon, the rest will click into place."

"That's a big 'if.'"

"I'm betting Marla and Teddy hired that woman who killed Max," Harold said. "And the Vernon brothers got pissed off and took them out. Or had somebody do it."

"That doesn't explain Loomis and Venturi."

"Odds are good that woman killed them, too."

"I don't know, Harold. She used a garotte on Max. All the others were shot with various guns, different calibers. Forensics says Loomis' gun shot Venturi. So why was she there to shoot Loomis?" "Why did Loomis even go to Venturi's office? What's the connection between Venturi and these other killings?"

"I don't know," Harold said. "But this might help. I got a call from the traffic bureau, just before you got here. Said a body shop reported receiving a white Ford that was full of bullet holes. Company car. Registered to Tropical Bay."

Susan set her coffee on her desk. "Loomis' car?"

"Could be. But then how did it get from the shootout at Venturi's office to a body shop? No spent shells in the parking lot outside Venturi's. Did the car get shot up somewhere else?"

"Good questions for Ken Staley," she said. "I think that rich bastard's behind all this."

Harold's eyes wandered back toward the pamphlet on his desk. Susan thinking: He doesn't want to tangle with Staley. None of this matters to him anymore. In a few months, he'll be swatting mosquitoes in Guatemala and I'll still be sitting here with these case files piled on my desk.

Her phone rang. She sighed, figuring it was another reporter, and picked it up. "Homicide."

"Is this Detective Pine?" A woman's shrill voice.

"Yes, who's this?"

"Patti Staley. Over at Tropical Bay."

Just what she needed. Another pep talk from a civic booster.

"Yes, ma'am. What can I do for you?"

"I need to talk to you. My husband—Ken, you've met him—I think he's in trouble."

Susan tried to keep her voice calm as she said, "What kind of trouble?"

Patti sniffled, sounded like she'd been crying. Susan had trouble picturing that. Patti seemed the kind of woman who'd smile as she sank the knife between your ribs, not a weeper.

"These killings," Patti said. "He's somehow mixed up in them. He sent Mel Loomis—"

Susan cut in, her heart racing. "I think we need to talk in person, Mrs. Staley. Where are you right now?"

55

Lily didn't know where she was when she woke to her chirping phone—an unsettling feeling. Cheap motel room. Harsh Vegas sunlight peeking around the edges of thick curtains. It came back to her in a rush: the shootout at Sal's office, the standoff with Joe Riley, checking into this cheap motel rather than risking a return to Bally's.

She glanced around the room at the faded wallpaper and the cigarette-dotted furniture and the framed bullfight poster hanging crooked on the wall. Sure as hell ain't Bally's.

She rolled over and picked up the little cell phone. She didn't recognize the number on the readout, but she had a pretty good idea who it would be. She pushed a button and said, "Yeah?"

"Good morning, Lily. Sleep well?"

"Joe Riley. Thought I told you to lose this number."

"I can't help myself. It's stuck in my head."

"You're lucky that's all that's stuck in your head. You nearly got a bullet stuck there instead."

She sat up in bed and stretched.

"But you didn't shoot me," he said. "You could've. I know that. You're probably a much better shot than I am—"

"Count on it, bubba."

"I'll try not to be in a position to find out."

"Good idea."

"Anyway, I've been thinking a lot about that," he said. "I mean, you're standing there, got your gun pointed right at my face. You decided to take off instead."

"Cops were on the way."

"You don't worry about mere cops. I think you didn't shoot me because you know I'm right."

"About what?"

"About getting this thing finished."

"Don't start that again."

"I've got a plan, Lily."

"I know you do. I don't like your plan."

"You haven't even heard it."

"It always ends the same way. With me in jail."

"No, it's different now—"

"Because I didn't shoot you? We're suddenly friends now?"

When he spoke, his voice was softer. "Not shooting each other, that's a start."

"Not much of one. Ain't like we met in Sunday school."

"No," he admitted, "but I can't get you off my mind. I think you're headed for a bad end. You need to get out of Vegas—"

"How do you know I'm in Vegas at all?"

"Because you still think you're going to win this thing. That's crazy, Lily. You can just walk away."

"The Vernons won't follow? You think leaving town solves my problem?"

"In the short term. We could work out the next step."

Lily put her feet on the floor, rested her forehead on one hand.

"Listen, Joe Riley. There is no 'we.' We're not friends.

We're not even on the same side. I'm sure you mean all this good advice from the bottom of your little cop heart, but I know what the 'next step' is. I'll handle it. You need to butt out. I can't keep pulling your ass out of hot water. Next time, I might *have* to shoot you."

He paused, then his words came out in a rush.

"I've got a *new* plan. A way to get you out of this mess and solve my problems, too. I think it'll work."

"I just told you—"

"Listen to me. We need to talk face to face. I'll tell you my plan. You turn me down and I—" Another pause. "—I'll leave you alone. But you need to hear me out first. I'm at the Motel 6 over on Sahara, by the Maryland Parkway, room 110. Come over here and talk."

She hesitated. It could be a trap. It couldn't accomplish anything. Yet she was tempted. His motel was only a few blocks away.

Lily heard him yell, "Just a second!" away from the phone, then he was back, saying, "Hold on. Someone's at the door."

She should hang up. Stop kidding herself about this guy and his *plan*.

Then she heard voices over the phone. She couldn't make out the words, but they sounded angry and "motherfucker" came through loud and clear. She heard scuffling and grunting. Then someone hung up the phone.

Oh, hell.

56

Joe came to slowly, his head hanging, his eyelids fluttering. He could see his own knees, blurry and far away. His head throbbed, just above his left eye. He blinked, trying to focus, and became aware of people talking.

"I don't know about this," a deep, thick voice said. "We better do what those cowboys said."

"Stop worrying." This voice was high-pitched, whiny. Delbert. "The Vernons said bring him back alive, but they didn't say we couldn't have a little fun first. Besides, I want to ask him about the woman."

Joe came more alert, but he resisted the urge to raise his head and look around. Better that they think he was still out cold. It took only a few seconds for some things to come clear:

—His head ached because Delbert had smacked a giant pistol into his face as they were wrestling around his room.

—He was still in the motel room. He recognized the putrid green carpet.

—Delbert and Mookie were deciding how much to hurt him.

—He was tied to a chair.

He flexed his arms, felt rope tighten at his wrists behind him. The motel chair was made of shaped plywood and plastic cushions. The back of it came up as far as Joe's shoulder blades. Another loop of rope went around his waist, attached him to the chair.

He heard Delbert say, "I'll get some water. Wake him up."

Joe saw a way out. He could get his feet under him, swing the flimsy chair against a wall until he broke it to pieces. Only problem: Delbert could shoot him several times before he could get free.

Jesus Christ, his head hurt. Little Delbert must've swung that heavy gun with everything he had. His ribs ached, too, like maybe he'd been kicked a few times after he was out. An image swam in Joe's mind: Mookie standing behind Delbert, his bare chest glistening in the sun, both arms done up in casts. Shit, he'd *have* to kick. His arms were out of commission.

Splash! Cold water hit Joe's face and his head snapped up.

"There we go!" Delbert said. "Rise and shine, asshole."

Joe blinked the water out of his eyes and looked around. Mookie sat on a corner of the bed, his plastered arm sticking out straight, the blue one resting on his knee. Mookie was wearing black dress shoes, like a good chauffeur. The toes came to a rounded point, and Joe was certain he had bruises on his ribcage that matched them.

Delbert stood a few feet away. He was wearing his cherry-red suit over an open black shirt. The suit clashed with his swollen face, which was mutating toward yellow with green edges, like the yolk of a hard-boiled egg. He still wore that clear plastic mask, keeping everything smooshed into place.

He gestured at Joe with the big pistol and said, "Got a little headache?"

Delbert leered, which only made his face look more like a mildewed jack-o'-lantern.

"Doing better than you guys," Joe muttered.

That straightened Delbert up. He scowled. "So far, motherfucker, so far. But that's about to change."

"Hey, Delbert," Mookie rumbled. "Let's get him out of here, 'fore he starts yelling."

"He yells, I'll give him another one upside the head."

Delbert waggled the gun at Joe, who wished he'd point the damned thing somewhere else.

"Those guys," Mookie said, "said bring him right back."

"I'm gonna break his nose first."

"I don't know, Delbert—"

Someone knocked on the door.

Mookie stopped with his mouth hanging open. He and Delbert looked at each other and Delbert pointed at Joe. "Watch him."

As Delbert went to the door, Joe scooted his feet backward a few inches and flexed his knees. This might be his only chance.

The door had a cheap security chain, and Delbert slipped it into place. He held the pistol behind him as he opened the door a few inches.

Bang! The door kicked open and spun Delbert around. He was suddenly facing Joe again, his eyes wide amid the discolored flesh.

Joe lurched forward, got his feet under him.

Mookie jumped up from the bed and teetered because the plaster cast threw him off-balance. Joe charged, head down, the chair lashed to his back. He thudded into Mookie's chest and knocked him backward. Their legs tangled as Mookie bounced off the edge of the bed, and they both crashed to the floor.

Pain shot through Joe's ribs as he fell on top of Mookie. He yanked at the ropes, trying to get free of the chair before the big man could hurt him.

A gunshot cracked. Joe whipped his head around.

Lily stood in the open door, her Glock held in both hands, smoke curling from the barrel. Delbert was against the far wall, clutching his bloody forearm. Joe couldn't see the Colt anywhere.

Mookie struggled under Joe, striking up with his knees and batting at his head with his balloon-like splint. Nothing Joe could do about it.

Lily squatted beside them and whacked Mookie across the temple with the barrel of her pistol. Mookie's eyes rolled back in his head, and he stopped moving.

Joe looked up at her, but she was watching Delbert. She fumbled with one hand, got hold of the rope that went around Joe's waist, and stood up, rolling him off Mookie and onto his back. One of the chair legs cracked as it hit the floor.

"Hey, you want to untie me?"

"Wait a minute," she said, still watching Delbert. "I've got to shoot this guy again first."

Delbert made a sound like a contented sigh, and fainted dead away. He fell forward, his arms still clutched in front of him, and his face bounced off the carpeted floor.

"Nice bluff," Joe said.

"I wasn't bluffing."

Lily went through Mookie's pockets and came up with a knife. She flicked it open, slipped the blade under the rope at Joe's waist and sliced through it cleanly.

"Get up."

"Be easier if you cut my hands loose."

"Try it my way."

Joe rolled off the chair and managed to get to his knees. He found Lily pointing the pistol at his face.

"The hell is going on here?" she said. "Who are these guys?"

"Couple of morons I met playing poker. They've been after me. Turns out they work for the Vernons."

Lily's right eyebrow rose, and something glinted in her eyes. Joe thought it might be anger.

"I should just kill all three of you," she said.

"These guys are errand boys. They're harmless."

"You ought to see the lump on your forehead."

"He got shot for his trouble."

Sirens howled in the distance. Lily's jaw clenched.

"Cut me loose," he said. "We need to get out of here."

She took a step back, told him to stand up. Joe got to his feet slowly, thinking: Might be better if the cops got here, put an end to all this.

"Turn around."

He pivoted, feeling a cold spot on the back of his neck, a premonition of a bullet to come. The knife sawed through the ropes at his wrists.

"Let's go," she said.

57

They took Joe's Chevy. Lily sat in the passenger seat, turned toward him, her back against the door, the Glock pointed at his aching ribs.

Joe drove fast, west on Sahara. The front of his polo shirt and the legs of his jeans still were wet from the water Delbert had thrown on him, but they were drying fast in the Vegas heat. He rolled down his window, let the arid air pour inside. Lily put on her dark sunglasses. Her black denim matched the gun that pointed at him, unwavering.

When they stopped for a red light near the Strip, he said, "We going anywhere in particular?"

"You're doing fine," she said. "Get on I-15. The Vernon brothers live south of Vegas, middle of nowhere."

"We're going to see *them*?"

"I am. You're just along for the ride."

"What if I don't want to take you there?"

He looked over in time to see her smile. Goddamn, she was beautiful.

"I'll shoot you and take your car."

"All right, all right. I'm driving."

Once he was on the freeway, he said, "There's no guarantee the Vernons will be alone. They might've assembled an army out there. That doesn't worry you?"

"If I get in trouble, you'll bail me out. I keep saving your ass. Maybe it's your turn to save mine."

He had no answer for that. His head pounded, and he was running out of time. He needed to get back on track.

"Look, Lily, here's that plan I was talking about on the phone—"

"Another plan. I liked your last one, where you let two goons come into your motel room and tie you to a chair."

"That wasn't my plan. It was theirs."

"Didn't work out too well for them."

"If you're done congratulating yourself, I need to tell you something important."

"Shoot."

"I don't think much of your choice of words," he said. "Point that gun somewhere else."

"Just watch the road."

He slowed for a construction zone. Big yellow earth-moving machines sat around idle. Orange cones narrowed the lanes.

"I told you, they tried to blame me for that murder in Chicago."

"Don't start with that again."

"No, listen, damn it. This is hard to say, and I only want to say it once. The newspapers, the finks in Internal Affairs, were right. It *was* a cop who hired you to bump off Bennie Burrows. They just got the wrong cop."

"Meaning you."

"Right. But I got to Sal before he died. He told me another cop set up the whole thing."

"Why?"

"Same reason they all blamed me. The cop was into Bennie for a lot of money, thought getting rid of him would make the problem go away."

274   Steve Brewer

"Particularly if you took the fall."

"But that's not the worst of it."

"There's more?"

"Here's the capper: The cop who set it up is named Sam Kilian. He was my partner."

"Ouch."

"He's been keeping tabs on me the whole time since I quit the force. He knows I'm out here hunting you."

She was silent for a time, then said, "Any chance he's on his way out here?"

"I don't think so. He's still on the force. Homicide detective. Family man. He couldn't suddenly leave without some explanation."

"He could dream one up. He's good at covering his tracks."

"I'll never be able to prove Sam screwed me over unless I get you to come back to Chicago with me."

"Forget it."

"We could get you some kind of a deal. The D.A. could make political hay with the police department if he found out about this. They arrest Sam, put him on trial, and you could testify against him. You could get immunity."

"From murder charges? I don't think so."

"You might not walk away free and clear. But we cut a deal, get you a light sentence, a long probation. Maybe even Witness Protection."

He wished she weren't wearing the dark glasses. Her eyes might tell him something.

"You're a real dreamer," she said.

"Come on, this makes sense. Big case, lot of publicity. The prosecutors would make any kind of deal to get it."

"I'm not buying it."

"What are you going to do instead? Go after the Vernons, guns blazing?"

"Something like that."

"Then what?"

"Then I retire."

"Sounds like loads of fun. Sit on a beach somewhere the rest of your life, too busy looking over your shoulder to enjoy it."

A furrow appeared between her eyebrows. "I'll be fine. Don't worry about me."

"I can't stop myself," he said. It felt like a confession.

They said nothing for a while, the only sound the hot air rushing into the car. Finally, Lily said, "Maybe you'd feel better if you helped me out."

"I'm *trying* to help you."

"I mean with the Vernons."

"You need backup."

"Not really. I need a distraction."

"And that would be me."

"If you're willing."

"You kill 'em, that makes me your accomplice."

"Maybe I'll let them live. I've let *you* live, haven't I? So far."

Joe's mind flashed back to the motel room: Him on his knees, still tied up, looking up at her. She could've shot me. Slit my throat. Instead, she wiped out Delbert and Mookie, helped me get away.

And who sent Delbert and Mookie to do me? The fucking Vernon brothers.

"I'll do it," he said. "We'll set your trap. I'll be the bait."

Her face brightened, but she kept the Glock pointed his way.

"After this is over," he said, "we'll see if you come around. Play ball with me on Chicago."

"I wouldn't count on it. Once the Vernons are no longer a problem, all bets are off."

58

Hi Vernon moped at his desk, thumbing through a catalogue of gardening tools he'd never use, thinking about Max. He had his boots up on the desk and his hat tipped forward to shade his eyes from the sunlight pouring in the windows.

He looked up as his hatless brother appeared in the doorway. Norm's eyebrow bowed down in the middle, the mirror opposite of his droopy mustache, two perfect parabolas on his face.

"Shouldn't we have heard from those clowns by now?"

"Take it easy, Norm. They might've run into some difficulty."

"I can't believe we sent those two dipshits. Both of 'em all stove up already. Riley probably ate 'em alive."

Hi dropped his feet to the floor. "They had surprise on their side."

"Aw, horseshit. Surprise is only good for a second or two. What a man needs is balls, and those two seemed lacking in that department."

The phone on Hi's desk rang.

"See?" he said. "That's them now. You need to calm down."

As Hi reached for the phone, Norm muttered, "Should've handled this myself."

"Hello?"

"Uh, hi, uh, Mr. Vernon?" The deep voice sounded like distant thunder over the phone line.

"This is Hi Vernon. Who's this?"

"Mookie. Delbert's friend?"

"Mr. Mookie. We were just wondering where you boys got off to."

"We're at the hospital. And there's cops here and all."

Hi snarled into the phone, "Cops are there, so you call me?"

"They ain't around anywhere right now. They're seeing about Delbert. He got shot."

"He did?"

"In the arm. He'll live."

"Riley shoot him?"

"Naw, we had Riley all tied up and ready to go. Then this woman busted into the room and shot Delbert and knocked me upside the head."

"A woman." Hi looked at up Norm, whose face had gone crimson.

"It went bad," Mookie said. "Sorry, Mr. Vernon. I don't know—"

"Don't get your panties in a knot, son. This could work out fine. This woman, did you know her?"

"Never seen her before. Hell of a deal, though. Shot Delbert right through the arm, made him drop that gun of yours."

"Sounds like the woman we're looking for," Hi said. "Where is she?"

"When I woke up, her and Riley were gone."

"And the police were there."

"They brought us to the hospital, but me and Delbert aren't saying nothing."

"Good. Y'all just sit tight."

There was a pause. Hi wanted to hang up, but Mookie was holding something back.

"There's one more thing," Mookie said. "Delbert mentioned your name when we had Riley tied up. We thought we had him and everything, but this woman shows up—"

"Aw, hell," Hi interrupted. "So he knows who sent you."

"Maybe."

Hi chewed on that until Mookie said, "Guess we're not friends anymore."

"Sure we are!" Hi said. "Long as you don't mention Norm and me to the police, we're still friends. You look us up after things cool off. We'll find something for you."

"Thanks, Mr. Vernon. That's real nice of you. I sure am sorry—"

Hi hung up.

"'We'll find something for you?'" Norm said.

"Like a bullet. Those idiots told Riley we sent them."

"I gathered."

"A woman shot her way into the room and disabled them and left with Riley."

"Hell, Hi, I was standing right here. I done figured that out. The question is: What do we do now? How we gonna find her?"

Hi stared at Norm, not really seeing him.

"We're not gonna have to find her," he said "She's gonna come find us. I imagine she's on her way here now."

Norm's eyebrow rose.

"She seems like a person who goes head-on at a problem. That big-mouth Delbert just made us her new problem."

Norm pooched out his lower lip, making his mustache bristle.

"So she's on the warpath," he said.

Hi sighed and got to his feet, feeling creaky and tired. This sort of business jazzed Norm up, but Hi was aging by the second.

"Let's go, you old coot," Norm said. "Time to lock and load."

59

Joe smoked a Camel as he let the Chevy creep up the long, straight dirt road to the big house in the desert. Even going slowly, the car stirred up a telltale cloud of dust, visible for miles.

As the car bumped over the rutted road, Joe leaned across the empty seat and opened the glove compartment. Three pistols fell out into the floorboard with a clatter. He froze, then relaxed and exhaled loudly.

Dumbass.

He felt around on the floorboard and came up with his own service revolver and the two cap pistols he'd taken off Delbert and Mookie. He stuck his own trustworthy gun into the back of his belt, put the other two back in the glove compartment. Might need them later.

Lucky for him Lily hadn't thought to look in the glove box. She would've made off with all the guns, and Joe would be walking into a firefight empty-handed.

On the other hand, Lily had that Glock. One gun was all she'd need.

The Chevy reached the house and stopped. Joe stubbed out his cigarette and climbed out of the car.

The yard was bare dirt, well-tamped by cars and pickup trucks parked haphazardly around the place. Five vehicles that Joe could see. Could mean the Vernons have a whole gang here. Could mean nothing. Could mean the brothers like cars.

The two-story house had symmetrical windows that stared down at him. The windows were triple-glazed and tinted, and Joe couldn't tell if anyone was home. The house had no front porch to speak of, just two steps up to a door set squarely in the center.

Joe walked to the door, keeping his hands in plain sight. He thumbed the doorbell, waited only a few seconds before the door flung open. The brother with the glasses stood there, grinning under that mink stole of a mustache. He tipped his hat and said, "I reckon you must be Joe Riley."

"You expecting me?"

"Not exactly, but I'm mighty glad to see you. Come on in."

Not the welcome Joe had anticipated, but he followed the old man through the door and down a long hall to the kitchen.

He heard a loud click beside his left ear. *There's* what he'd been expecting. He cut his eyes toward the sound. The other brother stood against the wall, pointing a revolver at Joe's temple.

"Come on in," Brother No. 2 said. "Keep your hands where I can see 'em."

Joe did as he was told. The brother with the glasses patted him down and yanked his gun from his waistband. He backed away, pointing the pistol at Joe.

"Now that we got that over with," he said, "why don't you take a seat there at the table. Want some coffee?"

"No, thanks."

"Suit yourself." The brother with the glasses straddled a chair and rested his arms on the back. His suit coat bulged with a shoulder holster, and Joe's pistol dangled in his hand. His twin was behind Joe, breathing down his neck.

"I'm Hi Vernon. That there's my brother Norm. I don't believe we've had the pleasure of meeting you before."

"I've seen you around."

"Is that a fact?"

"Hard to miss those mustaches."

Hi smoothed his big mustache with a gnarled forefinger.

"They do seem to be out of fashion. But you didn't come all the way out here to insult our facial hair. What the hell you want, son?"

Good question. Joe didn't have much confidence in the story he'd cooked up, but he took a deep breath and trotted it out anyway.

"I came to warn you. There's this woman, here in Vegas, name of Lily Marsden. She's after you two."

Hi's eyes looked enormous behind the thick glasses. He blinked once.

"She's the one who killed your brother. She knows you're looking for her. She plans to get you first."

Hi blinked twice more, then looked over Joe's head.

"You got any idea what this boy's talking about, Norm?"

"Not a one. We're just a couple of respectable business-men."

"And we're in mourning for poor Max."

"Poor Max," Norm intoned. He nudged the back of Joe's head with the pistol.

"If you don't expect trouble, then what's with the guns?"

Norm poked Joe in the head again.

"One problem with your story, hoss," he said. "You were seen with this woman an hour ago. We hear there was some kind of a shootout at a motel, and you left with her."

"News travels fast around here."

"Bet your ass it does."

Exactly what I've done, Joe thought. And it looks like I'm about to lose.

Something banged in the far end of the house, like somebody slamming a window or dropping a heavy book.

Norm said, "The hell was that?"

60

Lily was breathing hard when she reached the back of the big house. The dash across the desert had taken longer than she'd expected. The thorny foliage and the loose sand made running difficult, and she had to follow a shallow arroyo that meandered in the general direction of the house so she wouldn't be spotted by the Vernons. She'd covered a couple of miles in twenty minutes, but she'd told Joe Riley to ring the doorbell in fifteen. She hoped she wasn't too late.

Her pulse pounded in her ears as she squatted against the wall of the house. She duck-walked to the nearest window. She raised up slightly, glanced inside, then ducked down again, closing her eyes for a second to hold the image of what she'd seen: an old-fashioned parlor with heavy furniture and oval photographs of eyebrowed ancestors on the wall. No one in the room.

The window slid up smoothly. She boosted herself up on the sill and slithered inside.

Lily crouched low and took off her sunglasses, looking around, trying to figure the best way to get things started. The rough-hewn furniture was coated with dust—hell, out here, everything, including Lily, was covered in dust. She slipped up to an open doorway and peeked around the door frame. There was a central hall, maybe twenty feet long, doors coming off either side, and an open kitchen door at the far end. She heard voices coming from there, but couldn't make out what they were saying.

Lily didn't want to go down that hall. If the Vernons spotted her, the narrow hallway could come alive with bullets and ricochets. Better to get them to come to her.

Next to a plump chair sat a wooden side table, a round, three-legged affair with a thick top, more of a stool than a table. Lily pushed it with her foot and it toppled over, crashing against the hardwood floor.

She pressed against the wall, the Glock held up near her face.

Silence came from the kitchen, then chair legs scraped on the floor and she heard the cautious footfalls of someone coming to investigate. Lily heard him opening doors, checking the other rooms before reaching hers. When the steps were close, she whirled into the doorway, the Glock held out before her.

A cowboy with a big mustache and glasses stood in the hall eight feet away. He had a shotgun pointed in her general direction, but no time to pull the trigger. Lily fired twice. The first shot hit him in the chest, high and off-center, spun him around. The second caught him in the back of the head, blowing off his hat and spewing blood as he was thrown face-first to the floor.

"Aaaah!"

The hoarse scream came from the far end of the hall. The other cowboy stood there, his mouth a ragged hole under his mustache as he howled in grief and surprise. He held his pistol in both hands and it erupted in flame and lead. Lily dived out of the doorway.

"You bitch!" Vernon shouted. "You done killed Hi!"

His boots thumped on the floor as he ran toward her. Lily didn't want him to get too close. Guy that crazy with grief might not even feel the first bullet.

Lily rolled into the open doorway, firing down the hall. Vernon lunged forward, throwing himself to the floor next to his brother's body. One shot skipped off the top of his shoulder, but he fired twice before she reached cover again.

He couldn't have many bullets left. But there was that shotgun on the floor.

Lily slid to her feet and risked a quick glance around the door jamb, yanked her head back as a bullet splintered the wood. She'd seen what she needed to see. Vernon had a semi-automatic Glock of his own now. He wouldn't run out of bullets anytime soon.

"Come on out of there," he shouted. "Let's get this finished."

Lily said nothing.

"I got your boyfriend in the kitchen. You don't come out of there, I'm gonna go shoot him."

"Go ahead. He's not my boyfriend."

She listened hard, heard the shuffle of Vernon getting to his feet.

Lily went low as she wheeled into the doorway. Vernon stood in the center of the hall, his gun pointed directly at her. She brought her Glock around, but a gun roared before she could fire.

Vernon pitched forward on top of his brother. A hole gushed blood from his back.

Joe Riley stood at the other end of the hallway, holding a smoking revolver. It was aimed right at her.

She kept the Glock pointed his way as she straightened up. She spread her legs slightly, got her feet planted.

"Here we are again," he said.

61

Joe's legs trembled as he faced Lily. Twenty feet apart, nothing between them but two corpses and a haze of gunsmoke.

He stood like a duelist, the gun heavy at the end of his reaching arm, his body turned sideways to make as narrow a target as possible. Not that it mattered much. If she started shooting down that narrow hall, every bullet would end up in him.

"Put it down, Lily. You're not gonna shoot."

"Try me."

"You had your chance before. You always let me walk away."

"My mistake."

Her brown eyes were flat and unblinking. Joe knew she could see everything—the slightest twitch, the hair standing up on his neck. If he pulled the trigger, she'd see the tightening of the muscles in his hand. In that instant, she'd fire. Even if he got lucky and hit her first, he'd be too dead to gloat.

"Drop the gun," she said. "Walk out that door and don't look back."

"I can't do that."

"This is over, Joe."

It was the first time she'd said his name that way, just his first name, familiar. Not "Joe Riley" or "buddy" or "bubba" or "jackass." Just "Joe," softly.

He hesitated. He'd come a long way, spent months in search of her. If he let her go now, he'd never find her again. He'd never settle accounts with Sam Kilian and those who'd accused and shunned him.

His pistol wavered. He couldn't pull the trigger. Not while looking into that hard, beautiful face. If he wasn't willing to shoot, then she had him. Nothing he could do but walk away.

He let his arm drop, the gun pointing at the floor. He squared up in the doorway, facing her dead-on. Lily sighted down the barrel of the Glock. Joe figured it might be time to summon up some last words.

A lump of fear rose in his throat, but he managed to say, "I want my old life back."

In answer, Lily adjusted her aim, fired.

Pain blossomed in Joe's hand as his pistol kicked out of his grip and skittered back into the kitchen. He clutched the injured hand to his chest.

"Jesus Christ!" he said through clenched teeth. "What'd you do that for?"

Lily had her pistol pointed squarely at him again. Otherwise, she hadn't moved an inch.

"I told you to *drop* that gun."

She came toward him, paused by the piled bodies of the Vernon brothers.

"Back up," she said. "Into the kitchen."

Joe obeyed, and she followed down the hall, keeping ten feet between them.

"Sit down."

Joe returned to the chair where he'd been sitting when

the Vernons held him. It was turned out from the table, facing her as she came closer.

"You can't get your old life back," she said. "With or without my help. Too much has happened. People have died. Your partner betrayed you. Your life has changed whether you like it or not. You need to move on."

Warm blood from his hand seeped through Joe's shirt, felt sticky against his chest.

"I can fix things," he said. "I can go back there—"

"Forget it, Joe." His name again, soft. "This ends here."

He looked her in the eye, tried to find that attraction he'd felt before. He wasn't sure how she felt about him—too much of what had passed between them had been bluff and banter. But he was the last witness. Would she finish him off?

"You can't kill me," he said. "You like me too much."

She smiled, and Joe felt a glimmer of hope.

"I don't want to kill you," she said. "But I don't want you following me anymore."

She pointed the gun toward the floor, and shot him cleanly through the left foot.

Joe howled and thrashed in the chair. Hot blood filled his shoe and overflowed.

He bent over, his face nearly to his knees, his hands clasped in his lap. Felt light-headed as the pain roared through his body. He recognized that the back of his head was right there, available, if she intended to kill him. Might as well have a sign saying, "Open this end." But he couldn't do anything about it. If he raised up, he'd pass out.

He opened his eyes, saw blood pooling around his foot. Her dusty black sneakers came into view. He tilted his head up, searched for any sign of mercy in her eyes.

She reached out with her free hand and pushed him upright.

"Jesus," he gasped. "How many times you planning to shoot me?"

The hot barrel of the Glock pressed against his chest, right over his heart, which skipped several beats at the contact.

Lily leaned closer and her free hand snaked into his pants pocket and came out with his car keys. She let them dangle from her index finger.

"I'll need your car."

"My *car*?" This came out loud and clear. Like he gave a shit about that pile of junk. But it was the final indignity. Sudden anger flooded him with heat, drowned out some of the pain.

"You won't need it," she said. "You'll leave here in an ambulance."

She surprised him again. She leaned closer. The Glock remained pressed to his chest, but her face came down to his and their lips met.

Lily kissed him long and hard, a savage kiss that took his breath away.

She stepped back and wiped her mouth with her hand. Gave him one last enigmatic smile. Then she went out the door without looking back.

62

Joe didn't tell the cops about the kiss. It seemed too *personal* to disclose. Hell, nobody would believe it anyway.

He told them everything else, every last detail, up to and including the fact that he shot Norm Vernon in the back. He knew ballistics tests would show the bullet came from his service revolver, the one Hi had tossed aside in favor of a shotgun. Joe's prints were all over that gun. Better to put his cards on the table.

He started talking in the ambulance that responded to his 911 call, telling the cops he had information about several deaths beyond the ones at the Vernon place. He talked all the way into the operating room.

He resumed talking Monday evening after he awoke from the anesthetic to find Detective Susan Pine chewing her fingernails in his white hospital room. Joe thought he might catch a break from her. He was a former cop, just out of surgery, two bullet holes patched up. He deserved a little consideration. But Pine was determined to hear every detail if it took all night.

He told her and her sickly-looking partner the whole story three times. He didn't give them Sam Kilian's name or say what he'd learned about the killing of Bennie Burrows. He hadn't decided yet how to handle that. And he'd said nothing about that kiss. But he told them everything else.

He admitted to all kinds of crimes—assault, battery, interfering with an investigation, impersonating an officer, aiding and abetting, to name a few. But it was the big one—shooting Norm Vernon—that counted to Pine. She sat through his wild tales about Delbert and Mookie and Loomis and Marty Holguin and she asked few questions, letting her tape recorder do the work. Her partner said nothing at all.

When it was her turn to do the talking, Pine kept coming back to the shootout at the Vernon place and the way Joe had shot a prominent businessman rather than Lily Marsden, a professional killer. She kept pressing, trying to get Joe to say he'd intended to kill the Vernons when he drove out to their house, but he wouldn't cave. He told her his life was in danger, that he was forced to shoot Norm.

Pine was saying again that the danger came from Lily, not Norm, when Joe gestured with his bandaged paw toward her silent partner.

"Doesn't he ever say anything?"

Pine looked over her shoulder like she'd forgotten the gray man was sitting there.

"I prefer to let her do the talking," the old detective said. "She needs the experience."

Pine winced.

"New to Homicide?" Joe asked.

"My first week."

Joe nearly smiled. Suddenly, some things made more sense. Pine was new, strictly by the book, and she wouldn't let him off the hook, former cop or no. She'd bring charges. He could hire an attorney, do some fancy footwork, and blame everything on Lily Marsden. Maybe he'd get off, but only if he fought the charges in open court, getting the newspapers involved. This young, anxious detective would collapse under the pressure. She'd make mistakes. A mistake here or there was all Joe needed to walk away.

A newsworthy court battle might get the cops to focus on tracking down Lily Marsden. Get the public watching for her, put her on "America's Most Wanted." They'd find her and take her back to Chicago.

Joe pictured himself in a courtroom, announcing to the world that his partner, Sam Kilian, was behind the killing of Bennie Burrows. It would be a "Perry Mason" moment, one of those sweet surprises that make the jurors gasp and the reporters sprint for the phones.

Pine snapped him out of his reverie, saying, "Hey! You kinda drifted off there. I was talking, but you weren't hearing me."

"I'm not feeling so hot. The anesthetic left me kinda groggy. You shouldn't even be questioning me now. I've got a diminished capacity."

Pine's face tightened into a frown.

"Yeah," Joe said. "Did you even ask me if I wanted a lawyer? I don't remember."

She snapped off the little tape recorder and got to her feet.

"Nice try," she said. "But nobody's gonna believe you were too doped up to talk."

"I don't know," he said. "Whole thing sorta sounds like a hallucination."

Pine put her hands on her hips and glared at him.

"I tell you what it sounds like," she snapped. "Something you dreamed up on the spot. But you can't bullshit me, buddy. I don't fall for every cockamamie story I hear. You don't believe it, ask Ken Staley."

Joe leaned his head back against his pillow. "What's Staley got to do with anything?"

"Ask him yourself," she said. "Once we move you from the hospital to the jail, you two can be cellmates."

"Staley's in jail?"

"I arrested him this morning for the murder of Sal Venturi. As you said before you got so 'groggy,' Staley's man, Loomis, was the one who shot Venturi. Staley ordered the hit."

Pine's voice got a little raspy, and her cheeks flushed. Yeah, Joe thought, she's hot on the case, charging after the evidence, wanting to round up everybody and throw them in jail. He would've been the same way in her shoes. But he wouldn't make the same mistakes.

"Staley's too big," he said. "You'll never convince a jury he ordered it. He'll say Loomis went off on his own, went crazy. He'll walk."

"I've got a witness who was there when he told Loomis to do it."

"Must be one helluva witness, if you're pinning your hopes on that."

"It's his wife."

"His *wife*?"

"She thinks Tropical Bay's gonna sink unless she gets Staley out of the way. She wants to run the place herself if she can get the board of directors to go along."

"So she'd say most anything to nail him."

Pine tossed her dark hair back from her face. "That's for the jury to decide."

"Good luck," Joe said. "But you'd be better off putting your effort into finding Lily Marsden."

"Leave that to me," she said as she turned toward the door. "We'll find her."

Then she and her partner were gone. Joe was finally alone in his room, thinking: No. You won't.

63

Lily rolled the windows down in the stolen minivan, letting in the hot Arizona air. She'd noticed an odor in the van while she was driving through the forested mountains around Flagstaff, something stale and acrid. Probably ancient spills or old dirty diapers. The minivan had an empty child safety seat in the back.

Too bad. Ruined some family's vacation. But they'd get their van back eventually. She'd leave it in Albuquerque, if she could find her Miata there. She'd much rather be ripping across the desert in her convertible.

The landscape had gone flat east of Flagstaff, dotted with mesas and rock outcrops that glowed red in the sunset. Looked like a cowboy movie.

Hot wind buffeted the minivan, riffled her hair. It felt cleansing. She liked the desert, the long-range views, the stark heat. But she wouldn't be here long. She was pushing east on I-40, back to Albuquerque, then north up the east face of the Rockies on Interstate 25. Up to Denver, then east again, across the broad prairies to Chicago.

Right where Joe Riley wanted me to go, she mused. Last place the cops will look for me. Once I get there, I'll find a cop myself. A homicide detective named Sam Kilian. One last piece of business. Kilian's death would be a gift to Joe Riley, compensation for the two bullets she put in him.

Then she was done. No more killing. No more stealing cars and dodging cops. No more gun battles in narrow hallways. Finished. Retired.

She wasn't sure what she'd do or where she'd go. Someplace warm. Someplace with a swimming pool and slot machines.

Lily steered the minivan around a tractor-trailer rig that was moving slowly, its hazard lights flashing. She got back into the right-hand lane, set the cruise control for five miles per hour over the speed limit.

Long way to Chicago, but she was in no hurry. From what Joe had said, Kilian wasn't going anywhere.

Her phone chirped in the seat beside her. She should've thrown the damned thing away. The fact that she'd kept it made her wonder whether she *wanted* Joe to call.

She answered on the third ring.

"Hiya, Lily."

"Calling from the hospital?"

"I was wondering whether you'd still answer this number."

"I keep meaning to do something about that."

A pause. She said, "You gonna live?"

"Doctor says I'll have a dandy scar on my foot. You plugged it dead-center. Looks like I've been crucified."

"I don't think anybody's going to mistake you for Jesus."

"I used to be an altar boy."

"I thought you were a hedonist."

His voice went fuzzy. "You never got the chance to find out. Just that one kiss . . ."

She looked in rear-view mirror, saw she was blushing. Christ.

"Don't flirt with me, Joe Riley. You're on drugs. You're a very sick man. You've got an obsession."

"I thought it was those bullets you put in me."

"What do you want me to say? 'Sorry?' It was the only way. I had to get out of there. I couldn't keep babysitting you."

Another long pause.

"I've told the cops everything," he said. "They'll be combing the country, looking for you."

"They won't find me."

"This cop here in Vegas is arresting everybody she can get her hands on. She's locked up Delbert and Mookie and she put Ken Staley behind bars. But she doesn't have a clue how to find you."

Interesting, thought Lily, but she didn't want to hear the rest. She'd learn the whole story eventually. Right now, she needed to get off the phone. But one more question first.

"She going to arrest you, too?"

"Probably. But I'll be all right."

"You seem to keep landing on your feet."

"Foot."

She smiled. "Bye, Joe."

"See you around."

Lily clicked off the phone, thinking: No, Joe Riley. You'll never see me again.

She realized she was holding the cell phone against her lips. She took it away from her face and smiled at it, as if Joe could see her there.

Then she hurled the phone out the window, out into the sand and stone of the empty desert.